MW00795537

THE HEART IS A STAR

MEGAN ROGERS

central
avenue
2025

Copyright © 2025 Megan Rogers
Cover design © 2025 Travis Bedel

Originally published 2023 in Australia by Fourth Estate an imprint of
HarperCollins*Publishers*

All rights reserved. No part of this book may be used or reproduced in any manner
whatsoever without written permission from the author except in the case of brief
quotations embodied in critical articles and reviews.

This is a work of fiction. Names, characters, places and incidents either are the
product of the author's imagination or are used fictitiously and any resemblance to
actual persons, living or dead, business establishments, events or locales is entirely
coincidental.

Published by Central Avenue Publishing, an imprint of Central Avenue Marketing Ltd.
www.centralavenuepublishing.com

Published in Canada
Printed in United States of America

1. FICTION/Family   2. FICTION/Women

THE HEART IS A STAR

Cloth: 978-1-77168-390-6
Ebook: 978-1-77168-391-3

1 3 5 7 9 10 8 6 4 2

For Joseph, Ava and Maia
My reasons for everything

We grow accustomed to the Dark—
When Light is put away—
As when the Neighbor holds the Lamp
To witness her Good bye—

A Moment—We uncertain step
For newness of the night—
Then fit our Vision to the Dark—
And meet the Road—erect—

And so of larger—Darknesses—
Those Evenings of the Brain—
When not a Moon disclose a sign—
Or Star—come out—within—

The Bravest—grope a little—
And sometimes hit a Tree
Directly in the Forehead—
But as they learn to see—

Either the Darkness alters—
Or something in the sight
Adjusts itself to Midnight—
And Life steps almost straight.

– Emily Dickinson

ONE

LIKE A SPLINTER IN MY FINGER, I ALWAYS THOUGHT IF I LEFT MY MOTHER ALONE, SHE WOULD WORK HERSELF OUT. AS MY phone rings and her rat-trap voice springs into action, I assume this time will be just like the others: that all I need to do is listen, withstand the burst of fire in my blood, say the words she needs to hear and then hang up.

For the past twenty-seven years, on the twentieth of December, I've heard the same declaration. "I'm tired, Layla," Mum would say. "Maybe it's the cold or the town or your father's shadow lurking." There would be a pause then, the silence magnifying her martyrdom. "Always," she would whisper, "lurking." And I would think of her in that husk of a house, curled up beneath the faded painting of Lazarus, the phone cord wrapped around four of her fingers. Her minus-sign eyes. I would imagine the threadbare carpet and dusty childhood photographs; outside, the soaked soil and the Huon pine trees, creating their own darkness under dense cloud. "The forecast is nothing but trouble," she'd declare. "The wind will blow salt into every nook and cranny." She'd stand and pace the kitchen linoleum, her feet making suction-cap sounds; grief as energy. "I need to know that you will come for Christmas. Say it," she would hiss. "Say it or you'll find me in the bathtub."

And every time I would sigh. Plane tickets already purchased never enough assurance. Her tone of voice turning over a heavy stone in my stomach, the weight that only children who've grown up with a bottomless-pit parent can understand. We learn to ignore the heaviness. Hell, we learn to blame it on ourselves, until the only way we believe the load will lighten is by making ourselves as small as their problems are big. Part of me wished I could just say no, to see if she'd go through with the threat. "Yes, yes," I would always concede, "of course we'll be there."

But this time is different. The conversation starts the same as before, but my mother doesn't ask me to come, doesn't demand reassurance, and adds a never-spoken-before sentence: "After I'm gone, look in my wardrobe, the locked drawer. I need you to know the truth about your father. I just can't be around when you do. I've left the key under the kettle." The finality of those words like a rope's knotted end, which I try to hold on to but which slips through my hands.

The phone tucked between my ear and shoulder, I finish wiping down the kitchen counter. Cup my hand beneath crumbs. Run the water to wash them free. I let the tap stream scald my hand and my skin winces from steam. She's never offered those details before. Since I was a teenager, I've lived with a constant feeling of something nameless and unknown. There were nights when I would lie awake, with the jangling wires inside me sparking and shorting. All I could do was walk around the house, sit in chairs and on benchtops and wait for the light of morning. Knowing that I need the truth about Dad but not knowing how to ask for it.

Mum has gone quiet. I sit down, place the phone on speaker and slump over the kitchen table, my long hair pouring over my forearm; the familiar smell of bergamot shampoo clashing with the sudden departure from our regular script. I try to bring her back to her part: "So, I'll bring the kids. Gabe's…" Now I'm off-script. My husband usually comes to Christmas at Mum's; usually gets frustrated at her wobbly dining table until he asks everyone to move aside while he turns the timber square over, finds a wrench from God knows where, and tightens the legs. Always one to make things, as he sees them, right. "Gabe can't make it this year, but he sends his love." Of course, he didn't say that; the Christmas trip is probably the last thing on his mind, but it's what we say. Covering his arse even now, even after everything. "I thought that kettle was broken?" is all I can think of saying. For the past two years Mum has been boiling water for tea in a saucepan on the stove, like she used to boil our hot milk when we were young. I wait for her to ask me to come.

"I rang Dawn," she says instead. "To tell her she's not getting your grandmother's leadlight lampshade in my will."

"C'mon, Mum…" I stand up from the table, take the phone off speaker and press it to my ear, tuck my left hand under my right elbow, an arm protecting my heart.

"She's at a music festival; who holds a festival on a Tuesday?" Mum continues. "Can you imagine her there? Though I shouldn't be surprised. Seventy-six and gallivanting around with teenagers. I'm going to end it all, while your aunt's starting a twilight-years crisis."

"Audrey won the local painting show, best under fourteen," I try. A mention of grandchildren usually brings her round. "She was in the local paper. She wants to show you the article. You were always the artist in the family." I stoop to false flattery. The kids will rush through the door from their school holiday's art program at any moment. Soon, there'll be bags, unzipped, perched on the hallway bench seat; shoes left strewn across the hallway, even though it's a pocket-money violation; bodies sweeping through the house. I've always protected them when Mum gets like this. Though she's never been quite like this. Silence stretches between us.

The air in the kitchen cools. I rub my legs, shaved last night until they gleamed like elephant tusks—a vanity I allowed myself in preparation for tonight's dinner. Gabe and I are supposed to be celebrating the second chance I've been given at work. The second chance after fucking up so badly they had to put me on unpaid leave while they "mounted an investigation." The more I speak to Mum, the more unlikely that dinner seems. I can't even tell her about it. That's the thing about martyrs like Mum: they take up so much room in a conversation that there's not a sliver of space for anyone else.

Silence, still, but I can hear breathing. And then she says, "I knew I'd made up my mind when I stopped reading clocks. As if there was suddenly no point."

"What's going on, Mum? Has something happened?"

"Everything you need to know, everything that happened, it's in the drawer."

For all these years Mum has used these threats to get something she wants. You do this or I'll do that. Like some deranged version of Newton's third law. I never thought she would actually kill herself. But now I don't know. *Fuck you*, I think. *Fuck you.*

Pulling a cigarette out of my pocket, I walk outside onto the veranda. The irony of a doctor smoking would not be lost on my children's seven- and twelve-year-old minds. Even if it is only when Mum calls. My cupped hand blocks the wind from blowing out the match flame. The crackle of lit paper and nicotine always reminds me of my nipple when breastfeeding, though one is so obviously giving life and the other, well, I prefer to think of it as more inoculation than carcinogen.

"We're flying down on Saturday, Mum, like we usually do. On the twenty-fourth," I say, playing with the back screen-door handle, always ajar to catch the breeze. Silence, but breath, still. You have to give it to Mum, her timing is impeccable. She's always known just how to pinpoint the exact moment you feel like life is improving, that second you think, Hey, you know what, maybe life isn't so batshit after all. Then bam, Mum reminds you that, Oh no, wait, it is. "Mum, please," a little-girl voice coming up to plead. "I'll bring the kids, and they'll bring their glass jars. You can fill them with eggshells and feathers like you did with me." I hope mentioning our one happy memory might change the conversation's direction.

"Poppy," she hasn't used that pet name since I was a girl, "after this no one will say I haven't taken action against shame."

"Wait, Mum, wait." My voice is panicked now, shrill with the realization I have to stop her from hanging up. "The trifle, Mum, I'll bring the trifle, the one with layers of custard and cream and jam scrolls from the supermarket, and thinly cut strawberries, but no peaches, Mum. No peaches. I'll do the version you like, not like last year."

4

"Everything you bring curdles, even in the cold."

It's always been so much easier for Mum to inflict pain rather than to feel it.

"I'll fly down earlier, Mum, please, we need to talk about this properly." I try to do the calculations in my head…plane, bus…how soon can I get from the mainland to the island? When are the next flights out? The distance between Queensland and Tasmania stretches, along with my growing annoyance over having to purchase a second ticket on top of the unchangeable one I already have.

"I never asked you to come," she says. "I won't be here." Her voice is someone else's, someone with resolve.

Keys hit the entrance table's glass top and the kids' voices echo along the hallway. I throw the cigarette onto the ground and toe-tap it before waving my hand around, slipping a piece of gum from my pocket into my mouth, chewing for a second, then spitting it out. I brace the phone hard against my ear.

"Mum," is all I can say, "Mum." I stride into the house. Usually, the kids bang around the kitchen looking for food, but today they stand in the lounge room laughing and wanting to chat.

A click. "Mum!" I shout.

The kids stop, eyes wide at my distress, their breathy giggles tossed up and out of the room like flotsam. I run to the front yard as if I might go straight to my mother now, to stop whatever it is she intends to do, but when I see the closed front gate and feel the afternoon sun, I stop and realize I am a world away.

The kids stand in the doorway. One of Jack's shoelaces is undone, lying limp next to the cast-iron kangaroo doorstop. A year ago I would have crouched down and tied it back up, but now I know he will pull his foot away, push me aside, tuck his hair behind one freckled ear. His salmon-colored shorts are speckled with mud and I can see that his fingernails need to be cut.

The waistband of his big sister's skirt is rolled over twice to make it shorter. The cotton, frayed from constant tucking fingernails, makes my insides contract.

I try to call Mum back, two, three times, but she won't pick up. With the phone hanging heavy by my side, my breath imbibed, I turn to look at the tall flame tree that Audrey and I planted before Jack was born. The scarlet bells have browned and fallen, replaced with boat-shaped pods containing masses of thin bristles that can stick in human skin.

I sense the reality of my life and all at once my imminent denial. As if there isn't a self-destructive mother or a disappeared father; as if there isn't a kettle hiding a key or an urgency to get on a plane today; as if there aren't babies who have grown up and away from me; and as if I'm not about to miss the one chance I will get to redeem my career. But as I see my sister's name appear on my phone, any chance of denial becomes a transient moment that lights like a flare, then disappears, unremembered.

TWO

"DON'T TELL ME THERE'S NOTHING TO WORRY ABOUT."
I CUT WILLOW OFF BEFORE SHE HAS A CHANCE TO SPEAK.

"You always turn our molehill mother into a mountain," she says slowly.

"This time it's different," I say. I live with a constant desire to shake my sister awake. Now more than ever.

"It's always the same, Layla." Willow only calls Mum around Christmas. She moved away from home when I was ten and she was sixteen. "I spoke to her last night." I sometimes forget Willow is hours behind.

"What did she say to you? Did she mention a key?" I ask.

"Being here, in these forests, it gives you a lot of time to think. I realized that not saying the things I need to say, well, it was a kind of crutch and I wanted to knock it out from under me. See what would happen."

"Sounds like a risky experiment."

"You're the only one who's ever been cautious."

"Someone had to be. Has to be. We can't all go traveling around the world doing whatever we want."

"That's hardly what I've been doing."

"I don't know what you've been doing—you never call."

"I'm calling you now," she says.

I pace back and forth around the front yard, and then remember what Mum said about Dawn. There's only one music festival in town. Gabe pulls his Wild Oceans seafood van into the driveway, and I point a finger into the air as if I'll just be a second. Walk out through the picket gate and onto the road, "Hang on a minute," I say to my sister, and stride up the hill, past glowing white houses on stilts, and clipped but lavish lawns. The weather is always the same, like a sunny uniform the land puts on every day. "So, what did you say to her?" I ask.

"We spoke about my childhood," she says. *My* childhood, not *our* childhood. "There are things I needed to say."

Jesus. I imagine Willow murmuring harsh words at Mum like she did when she was a teenager. Stuck at the age she left home. When talking to Willow, my job is, always, to remind her of reality. I point out that I was there too.

"Remember that time we found Mum in the chicken coop?" I ask.

"She was so drunk, chasing the chickens around, screaming our names and that it was time for bed," Willow replies. "At least you were the pretty brown one. She chose the featherless, mangy one for me."

We let out a thin laugh. Genetics has connected us with an invisible wire, and even though a messed-up childhood and Willow leaving has stretched it to its breaking point, the connection is kept through shared experience. Eventually, Mum passed out on the straw, thighs resting on half-eaten celery and carrot tops. We held a compact mirror up to her mouth. The foggy glass always a relief. And took ourselves to bed.

"She didn't ask me to come for Christmas, like she always does. I think this time it's bad. She means it." I've tried to tell Willow before about Mum's episodes, but she doesn't want to hear it. "Please don't tell me there's nothing to worry about. This time, it's different." An estate agent's sign boasts a specialization in "fully renovated heritage homes" for the "discerning owner 'moving up' in the world." It's only now that I'm four blocks away, standing in front of the Knick Knack Paddy Whack shop with its cluttered front window, that I realize I'm not wearing any shoes. A detail that would stand out in our neighborhood as much as this ramshackle shop.

"She was already like that when I called, Layla, so don't blame me. And anyway, I don't think anything I told her was news. Could be anything upsetting her; God knows what goes on inside that woman's mind."

"See, you do think she's upset," I catch her. "Willow, I'm worried. And you calling couldn't have helped."

"I wasn't trying to help," she fires back.

"Dad would want us to make sure," I say. And there it is, his name filed sharp against our history. "Don't you want to know the truth?"

"What are you talking about?"

"That's the other thing. Mum said she'd leave me a key, that she has something that will tell me the truth about what happened with Dad. She's finally going to tell me."

"There is no truth, Layla. It was his own fault. She's only saying that to manipulate you. Can't you see that?"

"You don't understand," I say. "It's not as if you were there anyway. For any of it."

"Oh God, don't start that again. I couldn't stay. I…" Willow trails off.

I roll my eyes and spin my finger in a "finish what you're saying" gesture I perfected in our childhood. Through the shop's window I watch a ceramic Maneki Neko lucky cat's golden arm wave up and down.

"I'm tired of being the one to always pick up the pieces," I say.

"Then don't. No one is asking you to. No one ever did. Even if I wanted to, flying home at Christmas is impossible. With the Sri Lankan election coming up. The trees need me."

"Christ, Willow. The trees?" It's now my turn to sigh. I watch the two of us communicate from afar. Notice, like an onlooker, how our childhood infected us with a virus; the way our relationship is neither living nor dead.

"Actually, that's why I'm calling," she says.

"I thought you were calling about Mum."

"When you go to Tassie, there's some Tarkine documentation I'd love for you to find, photograph and email back to me, and—"

I hang up the phone.

The internet takes a while to load on my phone. There are no available

9

seats on flights to Jericho Airport, so I have to fly to Hobart. I select my plane seat, no check-in luggage. I fall short of pushing pay when I see the price. I've already booked a flight and being on forced leave without pay makes the additional flight seem indulgent. The lowering sun hits a silver bowl in the shop window, and light flicks across my eyes.

On the door is a handwritten testimonial on yellowed paper:

It reminds me of my childhood, going to my grandmother's house, only in here I can touch everything! Michelle.

I squint into the shop. There is a yellow melamine bowl full of old war medals, a green velvet mid-century chair that seems pristine from the top but is torn at the bottom, and then, on the chair's armrest, an old Konica Hexar AF camera. Just like the one Dad used to lend me when I was little. Only me, nobody else. Willow resented me for it. Not because she wanted to use the bloody camera, but because it was his most prized possession; and to lend it to me made me prized as well.

Even though I haven't taken photos since school, it's still the only object that can suck the air out of my lungs. The matte-black rectangle small enough to fit into my school jacket pocket, the noiseless shutter for capturing moments without anyone noticing. All I had to do was point and shoot. I savored the ability to retreat from my family into the school's developing room, with Jesse, my first boyfriend. I'd love to buy that Konica, but the shop doesn't open till Monday.

A vision of Mum pacing the carpeted floor of my childhood home. I start to jog, feel my pulse race, the pace of my childhood. My bare feet storm up a steep slope, past the nursery that ignores water restrictions, but who nobody reports because it's the only place that sells plants that stay alive, and toward the racecourse until I stand staring into a sea of people. Music thumps the ground.

I look around and almost give up and go home but catch a glimpse of Dawn's wig through bobbing heads: a quiff of strawberry-blonde hair. Her eyes meet mine and I gesture at her to walk over before I clasp her elbow and maneuver us onto the pavement. She loses her balance, so I brace her to me by holding her upper arm as well; feel her hanging flesh, white hairs like a kiwifruit's skin. But when I look at her face it contradicts what I feel. Pink, purple and blue teardrop-shaped jewels adorn her eyes, and glitter streaks her cheeks. One image is old, the other trying so desperately to be young.

"What are you doing here?" I ask.

"I could ask you the same thing," she says. Her voice is tire on gravel.

"Mum told me you were here."

"And that she's giving our mother's leadlight lamp to the thrift shop, no doubt."

"Well, yes, but that's not the point." I look behind her at the racecourse that has been transformed into a music festival; a usually green space now a slurry of summer mud after several days of spilled drinks and the constant traffic of heavy vehicles. "Have you escaped from the nursing home? This isn't exactly a safe place for you."

Dawn throws her head back and laughs. You can tell she's been a smoker; the fits and shakes turn into shudders and coughs and then back again to a series of high-pitched, half-strangled guffaws.

"Safe? Don't patronize me," she says. "You're just like everyone else. You think old people are dim-witted and broken. If safety is waking up, waiting in a chair for three average meals a day, going to sleep, and doing the same thing all over again, I'd rather be in constant, imminent danger."

A lanky man walks up to Dawn and kisses her on the cheek, then strides away with an arm held triumphantly above his head. A tuft of his hair blows up and away from his neck in the wind. I look down at my short, aging aunt.

"I've known other countries, darling," she says, looking off at the young man, "foreign foods and the beating hearts of strangers on clay-tiled dance floors. I've seen rivers turn gold at sunset. Ancient as the world."

There's still the thrum of music; the smell of marijuana, sandalwood and sweat. When I went to festivals in the nineties, the most dangerous drug was relatively pure ecstasy. Now there are concoctions of God knows what. Every year, someone overdoses.

"I'll take you back." I make this a statement, not a suggestion.

"Don't start caring now, darling. You haven't visited in weeks." Every conversation with Dawn is barbed. I suppose that's what you get when you put people away.

An official-looking woman walks up to us with a lanyard round her neck that reads "Hills Festival" and asks Dawn if she's okay, then looks at me as if I'm causing trouble.

"Oh yes," Dawn says. "My niece needed a chaperone, so I reluctantly obliged. Can't be trusted, this one." Dawn pokes me in the ribs with a pointed finger. Smiles. The woman smiles back; a high-five with their mouths. I call Sandy Acres to let them know the location of their missing resident.

As the security guard walks away, I make a point of saying loudly to Dawn, "The nursing home minivan will pick you up out the front in fifteen minutes. They say you have to be there. This is your third and final strike." Dawn rolls her eyes. I keep hold of her elbow as we walk further down the street to wait for the van.

"Your mother called me," she explains. "I needed to blow off steam, so I came here." Sisters' relationships don't get less complicated with age, I think. "If you're going down to see her for Christmas, stop by me first. I have something I want you to give her."

"She doesn't want me to come. I'm worried. I think she might—"

"Listen, love, your mum's no more likely to top herself than I am to start playing bingo with Beryl at morning tea."

"I'm going to go down there anyway."

Dawn shrugs her shoulders in a "suit yourself" way I have come to understand. A piece of nude-colored, rippled elastic has come apart from her knickers and sits curled above her skirt. I feel a pang of intimate pity.

After the van drives away, I think about rivers and faraway lands; young bodies becoming old with nothing to lose. The women in Dawn's low-care nursing home: unapologetic women, women who are finding their voices because they no longer care about others' opinions. Women unbound by the need for approval, whose range of behavior is so fluid that at any moment they might cry, have a tantrum, or break into song. Or run away to a music festival. My aunt is a woman constantly reshaping herself to create the chaos she craves. Something that seems to run in the family.

When I get back home, I stand at my front gate and call Maggie, Mum's neighbor, but she doesn't pick up. No answering machine on the old put-your-finger-in-a-hole-and-dial-around phone. Surely someone nearby can check on her, I think. Though I've tried that before, haven't I?

A young man with a singsong voice at the Port Jericho police station asks for my name and what I'd like to report.

"It's my mother. Nora Byrnes."

"Is this Layla?" he asks.

I stop, surprised.

"I'm sorry, do I know you?" I ask.

"There's a Post-it note on my computer, ma'am. Sarge wrote it."

I try not to think about what it would say. Michael Clifton is the sergeant there. I went to school with him. He knows Mum. Knows the history. I open my mouth to explain but close it again. A flash of shame. I thank the young man and hang up.

I try to call Mum again but she doesn't pick up, so I ring the airline and charm a woman called Rosaline into changing my flight to tomorrow morning because of my "dying mother," which isn't altogether untrue. She could only get me on a flight to Hobart, but it's better than paying twice.

The last domes of orange disappear, and I'm left in twilight, standing outside my house. I've loved this time of day ever since Dad taught me about the Earth's fate. "The sun will continue to burn for millions of years, but after it burns through all its hydrogen and starts burning helium, it will expand to such a size that it will engulf Mercury, Venus and Earth. When it reaches that point, it will have become a giant red star."

That knowledge changed the way I saw the world. Saw myself. At the age of eight I became a kind of amateur astronomer, trying to find some sense of placement in the universe; became obsessed with the mysterious structures of the invisible, what lies beneath and beyond. As if finding out the facts could somehow help me prevent the sun from one day devouring the Earth. There had been nothing particularly unusual about that fact, about a distant mortality, and yet I became plagued by the thought that, although it gives us life now, the sun cannot be separated from annihilation. At dusk, the way the blues douse the burn always brings me relief.

All the lights are on in my house. I watch the bodies walk past windows. I hear Mum's voice in my head; the new resolve. Because no one else can understand, in their lives cut off from consequence, that I have no choice. What if I don't believe my mother would do something, and she does? What if I could have stopped her but didn't? I know the guilt would burn and grow until it turns into a giant sun and engulfs me completely.

THREE

WHEN WE FIRST MOVED TO TASMANIA, IN THE HEART
OF WINTER, I WAS FIVE AND WILLOW WAS ELEVEN. "GETTING OUT OF
the rat race and back to nature," Dad called it. As we stepped off the boat and
he put his arm around Mum, I heard him say softly, "Fresh air will do you the
world of good, Nora, you'll see. Good for the nerves."

When Dad had said "back to nature," I had imagined colorful flowers and
tree branches I could climb, meadows of animals and babbling brooks like a
scene written by Enid Blyton. When we drove toward the west of the island,
the wind increased from a breeze to a howl, and everything became blanketed
in snow. "Nature" started to take on a new meaning. By the time we drove
slowly up the side of a mountain and pulled in front of a bright-white homestead, I was convinced that Dad had got it wrong and the boat had actually
sailed us to Antarctica.

Our house was built on a bluff. Set atop the flat remains of a dormant
volcano. It was so white and so high up that you could see it from miles away.
Whenever we drove the long stretch of road that led from town back to Port
Jericho, I would wind down the car window and look at the building as if it
were a beacon guiding us home.

As the snow thawed and spring came, Willow and I discovered patches of
purple flowers and smooth pebbles to turn into fairy circles; we would make
cups from leaves on trees and pour the dew into our mouths like a magical elixir; and we would draw treasure maps on bark peeled from eucalyptus
trunks. Our favorite game was to run the length of the wraparound veranda,
weaving in and out of the white posts like slalom skiers.

When we walked to the edge of our dormant volcano, and stood where we could hear the waves crash, it felt like we lived on the edge of the world. Below us was the fishing town of Jericho and on the other side were cliffs, then rocks, then ocean. Despite what we learned at school, I felt certain that if you sailed a boat toward the horizon, you would fall off a flat planet and into the unknown.

At least we weren't up there alone. Ronsen's dairy farm took up half the land, while Pullman's pear orchard and our land split up the rest equally. Huon pine grew along each of the property lines so that if you were in a light airplane flying above, you'd see a giant green T.

People down in the village thought we were crazy for living up there. But at night, when Dad held our hands and walked us the fifty paces to the cliff edge, he'd look up at the dome of constellations above us and say, "I've never seen the stars so bright as they are here. There are two things in this world you can trust, girls: me and the constancy of those stars." My father's love of that place was so contagious that, even though it felt like we lived on the edge of the world, Willow and I believed we were exactly where we should be.

Dad was a king around town. They hadn't had a doctor in thirty years. They used to have to travel hours to get to the nearest hospital. Many didn't make it in time. When we walked around the streets, locals used the word "Doctor" to say hello to my father with a magical reverence.

As we settled into life, I became friends with Adara from the dairy, and her mum befriended mine; Dad joined forces with Adara's dad, Bill, and Tom from the pear orchard, to get work done on the properties. Even though Mum could be as unpredictable as the weather, I was reassured by my father's steady presence and the belief my mother was harmless.

It wasn't until I was fourteen that I realized the view from my bedroom window, out into the never-ending ocean that made the world look flat, should have taught me a thing or two about the deception of appearances.

FOUR

ONCE EVERYONE IS ASLEEP, I GO FOR A RUN. SOMETHING I ONLY EVER DO LATE AT NIGHT. A PROMISE TO MYSELF. To the kids. I turn left at our gate and start jogging the six blocks to the industrial estate. As I leave our manicured area, bright white begins to make way for gray. Even in the dark you can see the paint peeling off the weatherboard facades and the lawns become concrete, as if someone has come along and stripped the area of color. Neatly trimmed trees spaced evenly apart disappear until my only company is vacant lots and dim streetlights.

Lucas's warehouse sits between a coffee shop, which during the day uses milk crates for seats, and a steelworks yard where he gets materials for some of his sculptures. I stand in Lucas's hallway like a burglar. It's the second time I've used the key, and I'm not quite sure whether letting myself in and waiting for him to come home is exactly what he meant when he gave it to me. Should I be making dinner? Coffee? I feel like I should be doing something, anything. Even though Lucas offered the key as a romantic step forwards, it's hard to envisage any evolution in our kind of relationship.

The warehouse ceiling towers above my head. I turn on the light, the gold lacquer inside the dome of the shade casting a soft glow above me. The top of the shade and surrounds are charred black, made by an artist who survived the bushfires three years ago, with little more than his life.

Lucas and his ex-wife also lost their house in those fires. It wasn't the start of the demise of their relationship, he said, but it sealed the deal. "Sometimes I need the universe to give me a kick up the arse," he says.

I met her once, Mietta, at one of Lucas's exhibitions. He and I always keep our distance at events and so I spent my time walking the room, listening in on the crowd's comments. I was standing in front of Lucas's *Saturn's Rings* when a woman with a black bob and sharp fringe offered her opinion: "You know, Saturn is the only planet you can re-create easily." She said this last word, "easily," with an eyeroll. "Even when kids do it, they know how to make it look real." Then she threw back the last of her champagne and moved along.

The rest of the warehouse is dark, so I turn on the lounge-room and kitchen lights. Everything is open plan, except for a black timber box built in the far corner, which houses the bathroom and bed and its crisp white sheets. Bespoke furniture and lights divide the space. In the corner opposite the bedroom box is a set of steel steps that lead to a silver door and an outdoor balcony, two chairs and a telescope.

Lucas often says I love him for his telescope, which is probably true. But I also love him for why he has it. The National Museum gave him the optical instrument to say thank you for his artwork—a steel sculpture of a comet and its silk ion tail. An interpretation of the solar winds that blow the gas particles directly away from the sun. All of Lucas's sculptures are inspired by the stars.

When I called to tell him about Mum, that I think she might actually kill herself, he simply said, "Come over—I'll leave the studio early." It's this confident flick of words, like the ability to whisk the linen from beneath a set table without anything falling, which pulls me to him every time. Lucas will often spend days in the studio across town, obsessed and consumed. But one phone call and he is here.

I'm standing in the lounge area when Lucas opens the door. He drops his keys into the coconut shell on the sideboard before noticing me. "Hey," he says, pats his pockets, takes out his wallet and puts it in the coconut as well. He reaches me in four strides and envelops me in his arms. "How are you?" he asks. I shake my head. "Come and sit down." He gestures to the tan-brown leather couch. "Talk to me while I use your ankles." I raise my eyebrows at him, but don't ask any questions. I've learned to trust and delight in the surprise. Lucas swivels my body to the side and lifts both my legs onto the couch, threads a large strip of calico beneath them and fetches some water and a container from the kitchen.

"So, what did your mum say? How did she seem?" Lucas pours olive oil into his palm, rubs his hands together and smooths the warmth over my bones. As I tell him everything Mum said, and didn't, about the ways in which this conversation has been different to every other year, about the promise of a key and finding out what really happened to my dad, and most of all about the resolve in her voice, Lucas prepares strips of bandage and plaster of paris. "So, what do you think you'll find?" he asks.

"I've always thought everything that happened with Dad was Mum's fault. But no one ever talks about it." In our family, and in our town, Dad passed into that region of the unmentionable. Along with how much you earn and how often you have sex. "It's the knowing but not knowing."

"You must feel conflicted, wanting the answers but, well, not under these circumstances," he says. "And why now?"

I nod, though don't have an answer.

Lucas dips the bandages into the liquid and wraps them around my ankle. We are silent as he does this. Now and then he runs his fingers along the underside of my knee. Looks up at my eyes, holding my gaze a moment. Then looks down. Pulls the bandage tight.

"Why don't you ever make sculptures of people?" I ask.

"Because I would only want to make them of people I know. People I love." He looks up at me again. "I would never get it right. It's harder to sculpt a person you're close to than a stranger."

"Even people we love can be strangers," I say, more to myself than Lucas.

He cocks his head to the side. The way he does when he reads between my lines. "Are you glad you didn't run away from me last month?" he asks.

"Maybe," I tease. Smile. I had started to feel too guilty. Came over and told Lucas I couldn't see him anymore. It was a mess. Too complicated with everything going on at home and at work. I can't even remember what he said now, but I left with a renewed desire and a key to his warehouse. "So, I find it hard to believe that my ankles are art," I say.

"Art is just taking something ordinary and changing the way people see it, to get a reaction. You take a banana, tape it to a wall in a gallery, sell it for hundreds of thousands of dollars. It will make some people angry, but others will love it. That's art."

"Not very poetic," I say.

"Well, that's why I'm creating plaster casts of a woman's ankle and turning them into Jupiter's moons," he says, while smoothing the plaster across my skin. "But enough about that, what are you going to do about your mum?"

"I've booked a flight in the morning and—"

Lucas drops the last bandage into the container. His jaw tenses. "Tomorrow, why tomorrow? I thought you weren't flying out till Saturday?" He pulls everything off my ankles. "Fuck, this hasn't worked properly." He walks over to the kitchen and throws the bandages into the sink; washes his hands under the tap. He throws open the dishwasher. Looks into the appliance. I wipe my feet with the calico sheet and move toward him. Plates and bowls are stacked at all angles, and he divides them into ones clean enough to put away and those that need to be rewashed. "Shit," he says, and pushes down the plug in the sink, runs the water, squirts detergent in until white foam bubbles up and almost over the porcelain.

I try to bend down to make eye contact with him, but his continuous bobbing down to the dishwasher and then up to the kitchen counter makes it impossible. I stand with my thighs resting against a long brass drawer handle. I'm just about to ask him if he'd like me to leave when he spills a cup of dirty water across his faded sky-blue T-shirt; a small tear down its lower side seam, where I know he's ripped the tag off because he's too impatient to find scissors.

"Maybe you're overreacting about your mum," he says.

"Whoa, hang on. You always say people are cruel for telling me that."

He sighs. "I am just observing that you were worried last year as well." His formal diction takes me aback. He walks across the warehouse and into his bedroom, and I follow. Usually, Lucas is my soft place to fall. I want to ask him what the fuck is going on, but something has taken a grip of my stomach and isn't letting go. I feel it squeeze and then release, only to tighten again.

He pulls on a new T-shirt in the same shade of blue as his previous one, another tear in the side seam. He drops onto the bed, draping his arm over his eyes as if shielding himself from the sun. Breath shovels air into and out of his chest; a knee rises, bent, the other leg straight. I sit down on the edge of his bed and my legs dangle. Sometimes I joke that I need a stepladder to get up. He says he likes the feeling of being separated from the dirt on the floor, which for some reason I always think is a strange thing for an artist to say, as if he should be grungy and by that assumption embrace the world's dirt. The headboard is covered in shotgun-gray fabric and the mattress has no springs. I place a hand on his leg, half expecting him to pull away.

"Anyway, I…I just wanted to see you because it will be two weeks…" I mutter, trailing off.

Lucas lies quiet. An unfinished miniature sculpture sits next to the bed. He always makes one before starting something larger. It's the third I've seen in as many weeks, only small ones, though, nothing translating into a bigger work, like it usually does. "Self-portrait, uncovered truths," reads a handwritten blue pen note on paper tacked to the unfinished sculpture. The shoulders look strong, reliable, like they could carry so much more than the small half-finished head. It's the only thing I've seen him make that isn't astronomical.

"Jupiter is in opposition tonight. Brighter than any night of the year," I say, trying to find another way in, his favorite planet because it's a failed star.

"My telescope's at the art studio. Another artist needed it to look at her leaf membrane."

"Wouldn't a microscope be…?" But I stop myself; now isn't the time for nitpicking.

"You haven't asked me about my work in weeks," he says.

I think back to the conversation we just had about the moons, and then to three days ago, when we discussed his exhibition for almost two hours. Is that why he's sulking? That I'm now going to miss his exhibition tomorrow? He's never minded before. A mistress can't make promises like full attendance.

"I like your self-portrait, its proportions are interesting," I offer.

"I can't do this anymore," he mutters. I feel time fold in on itself.

I lean over and kiss the top of Lucas's forearm, but it startles him and his elbow flicks up, hitting me in the mouth. He sits upright and puts his arm on my shoulder. "Oh my God, Jesus Christ, I'm so sorry." I pull my hand away from my mouth and taste blood, see watercolor stains on my white singlet. Lucas jumps off the bed, leaves and comes back with a pack of frozen baby peas, holds them out toward me, but I push them away slowly and stand up. The scene like unplayable Bach.

"I need to get home," I say through one exhalation and don't wait for a reply as I walk out of the bedroom and across the polished concrete floor, open the door and head down the street away from him. There is something about Lucas's arm cast over his eyes, about the loaning of the telescope, about his tone of voice, that makes me want to grasp for some semblance of order. I sit down on a concrete factory step; draw my knees into my chest. My lip throbs.

I first met Lucas after a fight with Gabe about potatoes. Though it wasn't just about potatoes; no marital argument is ever just about vegetables. I was standing at the stove dropping into a saucepan oddly shaped, peeled spheres, dodging boiling splashes of water, when Gabe leaned over my shoulder and said that I should put in the potatoes at the beginning and bring them to boil all together. I stopped with my hand in the air. The vegetables were a side to have with a spinach and leek quiche, his favorite, that I had spent two hours baking. A gesture after five night shifts worked in a row.

"If they're cooked at the end, does it really matter?" I asked.

"But it won't be the same. They cook unevenly," he said.

"You've never noticed," I observed.

"I never said anything," he replied.

I put the cold, peeled potato I was holding in my hand back on the kitchen counter, turned off the boiling water, and walked out of the house and down to the beach. The bench seat I always chose was wet. I sat down anyway, trying to calm my anger as the water seeped into my white dress. I took off my jacket and laid it beneath me. The cool air on my bare arms reignited my frustration. I closed my eyes.

When I opened them, a tall, dark-haired man was walking across the sand in front of me. He glanced at me briefly.

"When you cook potatoes," I yelled across the distance between us, "do you put them into the saucepan in the beginning or do you put them all in later once the water's boiling?"

He stopped. "If they're cooked at the end," he said, "does it really matter?"

I nodded, smiling. Looked back out to the horizon. He kept on walking, hands in his pockets.

I didn't go back to the beach again until one night a month later. The evening began in a familiar way. I was standing in the kitchen, drawing funny faces on eggs with a black permanent marker before leaving for work. It had become a tradition, my way of being there, in some way, at breakfast with my family. When I would call from work, just before the kids went to school, I'd ask them what egg they'd chosen to accompany their toast. Jack would always pick the mean-looking one with diagonal eyebrows because he liked "chopping his head off and eating his brains." Audrey would act nonchalant and say she'd just grabbed one without looking, although Jack told me she stood at the fridge moving the eggs around, slowly picking each one up, looking at it, and then putting them down, before finally choosing one. That she did this every morning. I'd been in the process of drawing on Gabe's egg, my rendition of the one-eyed Scottish property owner from our honeymoon, when his phone vibrated on the kitchen counter.

"I want you, I miss you," the message said. The name at the top of the screen was "Freya (office)." With a flick of the marker, I turned Gabe's one-eyed man into a dick, left the house and walked down to the beach; sat on the bench seat.

Both feet on the ground and hands gripping the wooden edge. Too angry to cry, though my eyes were as sting-hot as my heart. I stood and looked to the heavens. I felt my grandfather and father guide my eyes to the brightest stars in the southern sky, the diamond Sirius, and then Canopus and Alpha Centauri. The navigation constellations of Orion, the Pleiades and the Southern Cross appeared as well.

My breath slowed. Even if I didn't know what to do or where to go, I was still the granddaughter of a man who had navigated by the stars and the daughter of a doctor who had passed on the tradition. My marriage may not have made sense, but the stars always do. It is them in which I have faith.

Someone stood next to me. They didn't look at me, they simply looked with me up at the sky. "Down here we have the two brightest stars," he said, "the most colorful star cluster, the largest globular cluster, the brightest double star, the nearest of the stars and the most beautiful part of the Milky Way." I felt a kindred knowledge.

"My father used to take me out on summer solstice every year," I said. "That's when we could see the sky most clearly. And when we could stay out the longest, as it wasn't so ice-cold anymore. We'd lie on the ground, nearly all the night, on the grass next to his homemade observatory." I began to say more, about Dad's story, about Sirius, but felt uncomfortable, so sat back down on the bench seat.

"Did you ever solve the mystery of the boiled potatoes?" he asked, sitting next to me. "I mean, what's more important in life than perfectly boiled potatoes?" And I laughed. We laughed together. When I stopped, with heaving chest, he looked right at me. My breath quickened; I felt the pulse in my wrist. He went to touch my arm, but his hand hovered as if asking permission. I thought about Freya's text, about the many gray situations Gabe had been in with women who were friends, when I felt there was something more but never pressed the question. When I didn't object, Lucas took my arm, slowly, and traced the thin line of my vein up my skin. With the caution of a parent moving a sleeping child's body so as not to wake them, he settled my arm back on my thigh.

We walked along the beach that night before I left for work. Lucas told me about his parents in Margaret River, accountants surrounded by winemakers. He told me about moving to Melbourne to study fine arts, and how disappointed his parents had been. Somewhere along the way he'd studied cosmology. He had become obsessed with creating sculptures inspired by the stars. "I wondered how you knew all that, about the stars," I said. We figured out we'd been at the same university, twenty-seven years ago, at the same time, he on the fifth level of Building H and me on the sixth. Something about that shared history made him feel safer than a stranger.

In the space of what felt like a second, I told him my whole story: about Mum and even Dad, and how because of him I applied for medicine, left Tasmania and completed my six years on the mainland; specialized in anesthesiology; about how, when I became pregnant with Audrey, we'd moved to Queensland where I could more readily pick and choose my hours. Gabe could run his seafood export business from anywhere. In fact, much of the seafood was caught north anyway, so it would work out better for him, better for us. Gradually, as the kids grew, I had started to gain responsibility, loved the challenges and identity the work gave me.

I told Lucas about how everything started to fall apart. Gabe got caught exporting abalone without the right license. Lawyers' fees and fines. More debt. On top of all that, an aunt I support in a nursing home because Gabe doesn't want her living with us anymore, and because I owe her so much. I ended up working more hours than I wanted, which I hated even though I love my job. When I finished and drew breath, Lucas looked at me with a furrowed brow. Tilted his head to the side in a way that felt like deep concern. My shoulders relaxed.

"I've just started work on a representation of a human body on the moon," he said. "The way a woman's hair would float as if in water, without gravity."

"It's a misconception," I said. "There is actually gravity on the moon. It's just that it's only about a sixth of Earth's." Lucas stopped walking. Looked at me with owl eyes. Raised eyebrows.

When I awkwardly said I needed to go, he said he wasn't ready yet. He pressed himself back against a wooden slat fence and pulled me toward him. As we kissed, I bit his lip. Later, he said that the bite was it for him. That the sting had been some kind of sorcery. But that first night we kissed, he told me he was revealing a new artwork in the city in two weeks. Told me where he would be and when. As I was walking away, he said, "When I saw you, sitting on the bench, before you stood up, you looked like Leonardo da Vinci's *Head of a Woman*." All I knew about that painting was that it was beautiful and incomplete. Again and again, I heard those words in my ears: *Head of a Woman*. I held the words up for inspection, turned them inside out, and reflected on the way his voice traveled down and away at the end.

The next day, I looked up the painting on the internet. The art historian Alexander Nagel wrote:

The eyes do not focus on any outward object, and they give the impression they will remain where they are: they see through the filter of an inner state, rather than receive immediate impressions from the outside world.

But it was one word that made me drive to the city and meet Lucas two weeks later: the woman in the painting was described as a "Madonna." In an interaction where I viewed myself as a whore, he viewed me as a Madonna. And that was enough.

My lip still throbs. Everyone is a stranger. Our knowledge of each other is simply a series of convenient fictions. Psychologists would call these the stories that reduce cognitive dissonance, but I would say they are the lies we tell ourselves to be able to love people.

The industrial estate is vacant. Two streetlamps the only light. A mechanic's workshop is closed in by gray roller doors; the steelworks yard is sealed by high security fencing, and the largest lot claims to hold in its hangar a machine that eats earth to create tunnels under rivers.

I stand and walk home, away from the concrete buildings and toward the shiny white houses on stilts. Wooden electricity poles eventually give way to evenly spaced, trimmed trees and I realize that, in my suburb, they must have buried the power.

At home I peek into Audrey's room and stand awhile listening to the whisper of her sleeping breath. Carefully, I heel-toe across the floorboards, remembering instinctively where the creaks are from the times I would walk her as a baby, before I lower myself onto my knees. Nut-colored hair covers half her face and I gently move it away to give her what we used to call a butterfly's kiss: my eyelashes fluttering open and closed on her cheek. I rest my head next to hers. When she's asleep she can't pull away from me, so I breathe in her familiar just-below-the-earlobe skin. It is the same place in which I would lose myself in those early baby days, when to rock her was a form of prayer.

I pull myself away, walk down the hall and into Jack's room; climb into his bed, a double I bought last year so we could do just this. Make the most of our limited time together. A hand loops through my elbow and small toes press against my thigh as if trying to perch. He nuzzles his nose into my clavicle.

I trace the inside of his ear, which coils like a burning corner of paper, and position him in the crook of my arm so that his hair tickles my top lip. The surgical scar on his hand glows white in the night light, from when he was in the pram and reached out to pick a flower for me, toppling out and onto the concrete, breaking his wrist. I wish I could freeze this unconditional intimacy. Like I do with patients. We call it suspended animation. Jack's eyes flicker open, then close again. His hair smells like the baby shampoo I refuse to stop using. His body becomes heavy.

I think about Lucas. What the fuck am I doing? Sometimes I don't even know who I am anymore. I've judged women like me in the past. Hell, I've hated them. In the way we loathe things of which we are terrified. I was so scared of women who have affairs because I knew in my bones that Gabe would probably one day get lured away. But fearing something, hating something, doesn't stop it from happening to you. Or, I think, prevent us from becoming that very thing ourselves.

I reflect on Gabe's message from Freya and on Lucas's frustration with me, on my barely living mother, my lost father, and my job and balancing it with motherhood. I've had too much time to think about things these past few weeks, which is never good for me. I'm better when I'm working. On forced leave, without work and the daily pressure and challenges I love, I haven't felt myself. Although I've loved the extra time with the kids, there is something unsettling about being in a quiet house during the day. I've spent most hours thinking about my colleagues at work and who is being given the interesting cases. And, in my most desperate moments, who might replace me. Over the years, I have sacrificed almost everything for medicine—friendships, my health, time with the kids. What happens if all that was for nothing? If I lose it all?

The rip-current feeling that I'm not doing a good job at anything pulls me away from a safe shore. And as I wrap my arms around Jack and sense the tenderness of his still-plump skin, I fall asleep holding on to him the way I would a life raft if I were stranded in the middle of the deepest ocean.

FIVE

AN ANESTHETIST'S JOB IS NINETY-NINE PERCENT BOREDOM AND ONE PERCENT TERROR. IF THERE IS AN EMERGENCY IN an operation, everyone looks to me, since the surgeon is often too focused on fixing the immediate problem. If I panic, everyone panics. And so, even when everything is going wrong, I remain calm. Gabe says that—that I "dissociate" from him. What makes me a brilliant anesthetist apparently makes me a shit wife. Eight weeks ago I made a mistake at work and experienced, for the first time, that terrifying one percent.

It was Jack's seventh birthday. I promised him I'd be home for cake. I hadn't seen the kids all week. Every day I was leaving early and getting home after bedtime. I had already missed parent–teacher interviews, a ballet recital and a tooth-fairy visit.

The day went without incident. My first patient was a knee replacement. I set up the main spinal needle and the local anesthetic syringe on a sterile tray. On another tray, I had some propofol ready to go for light sedation.

We all have our library of stories to tell people as they're falling asleep. Some of us ask questions and garner interests before choosing something that can distract the patient. My knee-replacement man liked mountain climbing, so I told him about my grandfather's regular treks through the Scottish Highlands; his walks along the pony track from Glen Nevis. As the man succumbed, I spoke softly about the way my grandfather used to describe, as only a sailor with a love for sunken things could, the geology of the area. The light-colored granite, cooled in subterranean chambers kilometers beneath the surface, which lay among dark basaltic lavas.

The surgery went smoothly. I stood in the kitchen afterward and chatted briefly with Remi, a brain surgeon who loves football and has started to crochet. Everyone in our group picks up extra hobbies. There are painters, musicians, novelists, knitters and gardeners. Anything to balance the stress and responsibility we feel at work.

I was just about to leave, pick up confetti-filled balloons and make it home in time, when an emergency came through. An elderly man's abdomen was distended, and an emergency CT scan confirmed that there was a hole and a large mass in his intestine. Cancer had weakened his colon and caused it to rupture. His abdomen was full of air and blood. Even though an anesthetic was life-threatening, surgery was his only hope.

I had seconds to find out what I could about the patient. Except nobody knew anything. Paramedics had found a diuretic pill bottle on his bedside table. Otherwise, we didn't know any of his medical history or if he was on any medications. Even though I was usually able to keep my home life at home and focus on the task at hand, in the back of my mind was Jack, sitting at our rectangular pine table, waiting for me to come home and watch him blow out his candles, Gabe saying God knows what to him about his inadequate mother. When I was pregnant and had started showing at work, an older and more experienced doctor asked me whether I was worried if I'd be able to cope professionally with children at home. At the time I had seethed, told him he wouldn't ask the same of a male doctor. I had stewed on it for weeks, the sexism, the outdated mentality, the sheer audacity and incorrectness of it all. And overall I had proved him wrong. Except for that night.

We rushed the barely conscious man away before the emergency room even finished their work. In the operating room, I ran a rapid sequence induction. We checked his preoxygenation levels, and blew all the air and nitrogen out of his lungs, replacing it with pure oxygen to buy us time between the moment I paralyzed him and the time until we started to desaturate. The nurse applied pressure on the patient's cricoid ring in his trachea, stopping any stomach content from refluxing; then, as I was planning the rest of my approach, I drew up my habitual doses of 1.2 mg/kg of rocuronium and 2 mg of the antibiotic cephazolin.

I started running metaraminol as an infusion to help maintain his blood pressure. It worked, but marginally. An oxygen mask was placed over his face while I tried to insert an arterial line. It would give me his blood pressure every time his heart beat. I got it on the fourth try. It was unlike me. A glance from the surgeon, Liam. I started giving the patient fluid and anesthesia medicines slowly to make sure he didn't tank. But despite my careful and slow induction, his blood pressure got lower. I groaned; part of me hated this man for keeping me away from my son, though I'd never admit it to anyone. No one ever does. I grabbed more metaraminol. It took me several doses, but his pressure crept back up. A quick look with the laryngoscope and I slid the breathing tube between the vocal cords. Moving as fast as I could, I put in another 16-gauge IV cannula and waited to put the central line in.

The surgeon draped up and I started to put the line in, trying to keep steady as the room was still a frenzy of activity; nurses ran for surgical supplies, perspiration formed on Liam's head from working under the hot lights. And that was the last thing I remember, watching those beads of sweat, before the patient lost cardiac output. Everything else seems to have been wiped from my mind. Only underwater-like voices telling me that the patient was wearing an allergy wristband warning of his multiple allergies to Ventolin, morphine and an antibiotic. That nurses had checked the allergies and read them out to the room during the time-out. That people had seen me check the wristband. So many steps on autopilot; we repeat them thousands of times. The words of the wristband read but not sinking into my brain in the rush of the room. I hadn't changed the drugs I drew up to take into account his allergies.

It could have happened on any day, but there was a small lead ball in my stomach rolling around with the knowledge that I resented the now deceased patient for keeping me away from my son; that somewhere in my subconscious I was negligent on purpose.

When I got home in the morning, the kids were at school. A half-eaten cake remained in the middle of the table, without a cover. Gabe had left it there on purpose. Salt into wounds. I sat on a kitchen chair. A note on the table scrawled, "You should have called." I watched a fly land on the icing and collect the sticky pink mixture in its fine hairs without shooing it away.

SIX

THE SPACE NEXT TO ME IN BED IS EMPTY AND STILL
MADE. GABE MUST HAVE STAYED DOWNSTAIRS ON THE COUCH. AGAIN.
Through a crack in the blankets, I watch the nailhead light pierce the drapes.
My alarm hasn't gone off so it must be before six. A vibration shakes my
bedside table. *Mum.* I run out and down the stairs to the backyard so I don't
wake anyone up. The jacaranda tree is overgrown. Its purple flowers fold
around and over me. Beneath it, the once-vibrant orange sepals and purple
petals of the bird-of-paradise plants have been suffocated from sunlight and
are dried down to the root.

"I need you to know I asked him to leave," she says when I answer;
breathes in through her nose like a woman taking stock. "Even though I didn't
know the whole story. I suspected something. I asked him to leave."

"I'm coming, Mum, flying out this morning," I reply. Knowing if I bite, if
I get hooked on the end of her words and ask questions, that our conversation will control my whole day, that I will replay every word and regret my
entanglement.

"Stupid, I think now," she continues. "I always thought it better you
blamed me."

"C'mon, Mum, do we have to do this now? I'll be there tonight. We can
talk in person."

"I told you, I don't want you to come. I just need you to know I asked your
father to leave," she says.

"Oh, you did enough, Mum," I say with gritted teeth.

"All I can do is hope you'll understand. I can't bear the thought of being here when you unlock the drawer. For the fallout. I...I don't want you to think, after everything, that I was," she takes a breath, "the enemy. I need you to know. More than Willow. Ever since that night with the oven."

I pull a once-orange-but-now-brown sepal from the bird-of-paradise plant and scrunch it in my hand. We fell in love with the jacaranda tree when we bought the old Queenslander; but eventually we realized that its roots were destroying the house's foundations, and its dense canopy was killing all the other plants.

When I was ten, Willow took Dad's Konica Hexar, the one he only ever loaned to me and no one else, and threw it into the oven with the Sunday roast. It landed in the chicken baking dish, splashing stock that sizzled as she slammed the rusting door shut. I tried to retrieve it, but the plastic strap melted the skin on my fingers. Mum just sat there, in the kitchen, watching. I screamed as loud as I could, until the fury flung itself out of my fingertips. I kicked the oven door so hard the left side dropped off its hinges. "I hate you!" I yelled at Willow. "You ruin everything." Mum stood and, with the weight of her whole body, slapped me across the face. So hard that her nail cut my cheek. I still have a scar. Then she just turned the oven off and walked into her bedroom. The next day, two weeks after her sixteenth birthday, I woke, and Willow was gone.

"We can go find her and bring her home, but you can't tie her to the bed. If she doesn't want to be here..." Dad said, raising his shoulders. Mum looked at him; tried to form a response but looked away. Held on to the back of the dining chair until her knuckles became crimson, then laid starfish hand blows on the kitchen counter. All I wanted to do was to escape back into my photographs. Our neighbor Maggie let me borrow her camera. She loaned it to me, probably out of sympathy. I ended up losing the camera, though I still to this day don't know how. Even when Dad borrowed it from me, I made sure he took out his film and gave the camera back, so that I could put it safely in a flannelette pillowcase, and then into my knicker drawer.

It was more complex than Dad's camera. I had to learn how to use it. Up until then I'd just point and click. Maggie's camera had gears, dials, shutters, lenses; it was a mechanical art. I borrowed a beginner's book about photography from the school library and taught myself. What I was most interested in was backlighting. I didn't have a light modifier or a good understanding of the manual mode on Maggie's camera, so usually I ended up with silhouettes. I realized this was how people usually looked to me anyway.

I often photographed Mum directly in front of windows, in front of the sun, in front of car headlights, in front of the lounge-room lamp. I never figured out how to use the manual modes, to adjust the settings so that Mum would be properly exposed. When I was younger, everything was photo worthy. But then, after Willow left, I only photographed the things I didn't understand.

The day that Willow threw the camera into the oven; the day Mum slapped me so hard she nail-scarred my face; and the day Willow left was the week I borrowed Sylvia Plath from the library. A line from her "Tulips" poem stuck in my mind. She described her husband and her children as "smiling hooks." It was shocking when I first read it, how resentful she was of the small beings that needed her to live. I always wanted to ask my mum, "Am I a smiling hook? Are we all just smiling hooks?"

I think about the peculiar, inescapable dance between mother and daughter; between wanting to rip the net she weaves around me and the desire to pull its familiarity tighter. I clasp the phone between my shoulder and ear, twirl my hair into a spiral and then tie it into a bun.

"This just isn't the time for worrying about the past, Mum."

"No, love, there is no more time."

"Mum, just…we'll talk about this tonight, okay?" I look to the sky.

"I should have told you about everything earlier. You should have known. Life isn't simple. I love you. I've always loved you. Remember that. Please." She hangs up.

I kneel to look at the dead birds-of-paradise beneath the jacaranda tree then lie back to watch the clear acres of blue above me.

Before Mum let Dad's camera burn in the oven, I tried to explain photography to her. Mum the poet. Mum the creative who "sacrificed all her dreams for us." I thought it would make her feel part of it. I explained that the word "photography" comes from the Greek *photos* (light) and *graphos* (writing), and means "writing with light."

She looked at me. Lips pursed. "Photographs rob us of the truth, Layla. When we look at them, they alter the memory in our mind. Writing does the opposite."

And so, I went to Dad, the broad-shouldered giant with a barrel chest who could pick me up in one arm and lift me atop his head, and I told him about writing with light. He threw his head back and laughed. That autumn he had two silver fillings and scattered stubble on his chin. "Well, I don't want to say I know more than the ancient Greeks but…" He shrugged his shoulders, offered his palms to the paint-peeled ceiling. "I know a few things about light." He pushed his desk chair away from the table. Pulled across the curtains; turned off the light. My opened eyes couldn't see. "Even the most expensive camera," he said, "is worthless inside a completely dark room." Then he lit a candle in the middle of his study. "Photography doesn't just write, Chicken, it determines what we remember. Photography isn't writing with light, it's fossilization with light. It's proof of life. Photographs make us believe that

36

we will be remembered." He walked around the room, holding the candle up to his vintage leather-bound copy of *Lessons on the Human Body*, up to his replica astrolabe, which in the Middle Ages measured the inclined position of stars or planets and which means "the one that catches the heavenly bodies," and, finally, up to his face.

His lips rounded and he blew out the candle. Silence, darkness. My heart beat fast. After what felt like forever, he whipped the curtains open, the light so blinding I covered my eyes.

Maggie's camera was on Dad's desk and, as I reached for the leather strap, he took it from me, explaining that he still had film inside and that, actually, he thought I was ready to graduate to a more important kind of photograph. Dad put the camera in his drawer and took out a large crackling sheet. Stuck it onto the window with masking tape.

The chest X-ray glowed blue and black. I could make out the silhouette of a torso, a rib cage and the lungs, but not much else.

"What do you see?" Dad asked.

"An X-ray?"

"Yes, of course, but what do you see in the X-ray?" he asked.

"Bones? Organs?"

"If I were to tell you there's something wrong with this heart, could you tell me what it is?" He was testing me. I didn't know what the right answer was, but I wanted, more than anything, to give it to him. I looked past the body, past the bones, past the lungs, and eventually found the heart.

"The heart is too big," I said. Not guessing, but knowing. Dad smiled. A smile that I carry around with me and replay in my mind to this day.

"Yes," he simply said. "Acute heart failure. A heart unable to pump adequate blood to provide for the needs of the body. I've just acquired funding for an X-ray machine for the community. Will make an enormous difference to everyone's lives. Would you like to come, after school, and learn about the machine?"

I was so excited I couldn't speak. Just nodded my head fast, up and down, as if any pause or idleness might make Dad take back the invitation.

"Well, now that Willow has gone," Dad said, "it's just you and me, kid."

But on the first day I was due to go to the surgery, Mum told me I couldn't go. No matter how much I complained about it being unfair, Mum forbade it. Dad said he didn't have the energy to fight her anymore. Apologized to me and said, "Let's try another day." But the force in her "no" left me furious, and I stored it away with Dad's approving "yes." Those two simple words each informed my life and my perception of my parents. The way that observation is a scrupulous teacher.

It's still early. Everyone is asleep. The neighbors have built a new deck. The distinct smell of timber oil cuts through the aromas of jacaranda flowers and soil and grass. It's the same kind of oil Lucas used on a wooden sculpture a few weeks ago. My clavicle is still marked with a thumbprint stain. I crane my head to check if I can be seen, but I'm canopied by the jacaranda; protected by tall fences. I allow the timber oil to move me, to help me feel something other than confusion and pain.

I wet my left forefinger inside my mouth before tracing a line down my stomach, through loose elastic and down between my thighs. I part my legs, graze the already swollen lips and use the short-cut crescent of my fingernail like a spoon tip, scooping mango away from its skin.

A smile touches my mouth at the knowing. At the delicious oneness between desire, action and pleasure. Even though moments with Lucas are thrilling, there is something to be said for instant understanding. There is no need to arch my back and tilt my hips to the side in the hope that a man will take the hint and move his tongue; there is no need to be silent and then groan in the assumption a lover will read my language and focus only on what fulfills; there is no need to explain the way I like long, hard strokes with a finger, only to be disappointed by a hand's interpretation of long and hard. The gaps between these things that quell pleasure.

I insert a finger inside myself, but it is too thin and the different lengths of three fingers feel too foreign. So, I use my now wet middle finger to rub the point that washes heat across my face and neck and down my spine. Slowly at first, long and hard in the way only I know I like it, until my mind whispers a "yes." Then quicker and lighter but firm enough to feel the blood pulsing beneath my skin, and a creeping prickle, then a small flush of fire, followed by a wave of weather, like a silk dress being pulled and then ripped off my body to expose it to sunlight before a cool breeze.

My body relaxes heavily onto the soil, breath as quick as a butterfly's wings. My heart reminds me of the thrill of moments. Then pause. Then sadness. I look down at the checked pajama pants the kids bought me for Mother's Day, across the garden and up to the family home.

The day is only now transitioning from darkness to light. Part of the jacaranda tree remains in shadow and part becomes exposed by the increasing glow. Gradually, I see that old layers of the trunk have shed to reveal new bark beneath, once rough but now smooth; and I watch the purple canopy cast over me, silhouetted, still in shadows in the half-light, as the sun sends its first spray of expectations across the sky.

SEVEN

I DECIDE TO RETURN LUCAS'S KEY. IT'S THE ONLY WAY. THIS SKELETON IN THE CLOSET, WHOSE BONES BEAT TIME IN MY dreams, is starting to send me mad. But I have to run, drop it off before anyone wakes up, in time to pack and catch my new flight later this morning.

My footfall becomes a rhythm for my thoughts. The quiet road widens, its blackness encroaching into factory lots as I try to push down my feelings for him.

Tonight is Lucas's exhibition. I know his routine. He would have gone back to the studio late last night, when he loves to work best, and he will stay there until midmorning. I still don't know what he expects to exhibit when he has nothing finished. Or maybe that's the point. I don't know anymore. When I get to the brass slit letterbox set into the warehouse wall, I look at my watch. It's 6:30 a.m.; I'll have to run fast all the way back home in time to get dressed and drive to the airport to make my flight. I take the key out of my pocket.

After I kissed Lucas on the beach, I went to the launch of his sculpture. On a hothouse night, at the half-lit, just-built hotel, I fell in love with him. The Zahra building was developed by a visiting Saudi king to be the tallest in the country. When I laid eyes on Lucas, in that foyer, he was standing on the middle step of a spiral staircase. The sun was setting out the window and he smiled at me midsentence as he unveiled a steel sculpture of a flower that circled above our heads across the high ceiling like an umbrella, the long petals protruding and reaching to the foyer's walls. "The artwork mirrors the building's inspiration," he explained. "Zahra means flower. The flower I have chosen to create is the orange zinnia, the first flower grown in space."

Lucas was and still is all corners and angles. On the step that night, he stood straight but tilted his head forty-five degrees to the side; he bent his knee forwards to emphasize words and, instead of just pointing his index finger when making a statement, he raised his thumb to create a right angle in the air. "The flower proves," he explained, "that life, and maybe love," he'd looked at me then, "can grow in unexpected environments."

That night, we had sex for the first time in an art gallery to which Lucas had the keys, down a city lane with no name. He stripped me slowly of my clothes then stood back and looked at me. There were no frantic boyish hands or a sloppy, clumsy tongue devouring me for its personal enjoyment. There was no quick missionary position and reluctant rollover in bed. Lucas's gaze was considered. He wanted to take me in; his eyes passed over every inch of me until the hairs on my arms stood on end. By the time he stepped slowly toward me, picked up my hand and ran my fingers down the front of his face, I thought I might explode. The next few hours, when my pleasure was just as important to Lucas as his own, were like a drug.

Afterward we lay on a large paint-splattered drop sheet on the wooden floorboards, beneath a print of the Willem de Kooning painting *Woman and Bicycle*; her bright-yellow dress, high heels and garish smile looked down on us.

I asked him about the orange zinnia. "I watched the people's faces below the petals," I said, "their looks of awe. It must be addictive, that moment."

He brushed a strand of hair from my shoulder. "Don't be seduced by that. Those people are just there for the free champagne and smoked salmon canapes. My zinnia played second to the architecture. Most sculpture is a servant to decoration."

"I can't imagine you enjoy being subservient to anything," I laughed.

"I don't," he said quickly. "I told them they could have it for the opening, but that it goes to a small independent gallery after twelve months." He smiled. "I'm robbing from the rich to give to the poor."

I stand at the mailbox with his key in my hand and take a slow, deep breath. I think about my marriage. I cannot tear myself away from Gabe for all the complex and conflicted reasons that any of us stay in situations that contract rather than magnify our spirits. And I think about my affair with Lucas, who shows me a secret world, a way to have two lives or be two selves; who makes my body thrum like a gospel choir. I grip the key in my hand and start running back home.

As my feet pound gravel and eventually pavement, I imagine Lucas's zinnia flower, its petals arcing across the hotel ceiling above my head; and I wonder if the plant, grown in space, in such a remote environment, would have survived when brought back down to Earth.

EIGHT

I'M BACK BY SEVEN A.M. AND CREEP PAST GABE SLEEPING ON THE COUCH AND UPSTAIRS TO OUR BEDROOM. I'M pulling out underwear and folding it into my carry-on suitcase when Jack walks in.

"Mum, I changed my mind," he says, lying on my bed, rolling onto his stomach and propping his chin up on the palm of his hand. "I do want to come with you today to Nanna's."

"I thought you didn't want to miss making puppets for Friday's Christmas play with the holiday program? Sweet pea, I'm walking out the door in an hour." I look at the clock. "Actually, forty-five minutes." Shit! I kiss Jack's forehead.

"Please, Mum, please?" His voice thins and lengthens.

"Sweetheart, I had to talk the airline into letting me on. There's no way I can get you a seat now."

Jack gets up on his knees on the bed, bouncing slightly as he grips the sheets, face scrunching and voice getting louder. "Mum, please, I don't want to stay here. Please, Mum, take me with you, you have to."

I walk back into the wardrobe to get dressed. He follows me with slapping soles, grips my arm and shakes it, still just young enough to have one foot in the tantrum tent, before he flings himself back out the door.

"Mum!" Audrey yells. "Jack's pulling my suitcase down from the wardrobe." Plastic wheels bang on the floorboards.

"Stop it, this is mine!" Jack screams.

"It's not. You gave it to me when you got the lady beetle you can sit on and have Dad pull you round like a baby," Audrey says.

"What the hell is going on?" Gabe comes into the bedroom. "What's all this?" His sandy hair darts off at three different angles, and his shrunken T-shirt reveals bleach-stained boxer shorts from last month's laundry mishap. This is what long-term relationships are about, I think, arguing over who put the wrong thing in the washing machine, and then who did an even worse job of trying to fix it.

"I had to change my flights," I explain to him. "It's just three days' difference. The airline said you can hand the kids over to them at the gate. I'll meet them at the other end. It will be an adventure." I pull on a T-shirt, flick out my hair.

"Really? Again? It's fine to just assume I can drop everything?" Gabe's hands clench his hips. Whenever I try to respond to him, I feel a blank in my vocabulary. He is right. I should have told him. But sometimes I just don't have the energy for the conversation anymore, the same conversation over and over again, when I ask for help and he makes me feel like shit.

"Mum, tell Jack this is my case," Audrey says, running into the bedroom, shaking her hair and whipping her head left to right, like an unbroken-in horse.

"It doesn't matter, Aud. Even if I wanted to, I can't take him with me," I say.

Jack shuffles in, dragging a suitcase, his dinosaur pajama pants three sizes too small so they sit like three-quarter leggings. I'm never quite sure whether his refusal to grow up and let things go comes from me.

"Sweetheart," I say, sitting back down on the mattress and holding each of his elbows in my palms. I look up at his wet and rumpled face.

"This is ridiculous," Gabe says. "Why can't you just call one of the neighbors to check on your mum?"

Still holding Jack's arms, I grit my teeth slightly. "I don't trust them. I'm not asking them about the weather, Gabe. And anyway, you know what the people there are like. They—"

"No, I know what you're like," he says.

I stand up and let my arms fall by my side like defeated soldiers. "You didn't hear her. She…she was different. And I think she's going to tell me the truth about Dad. Gabe, c'mon. You know what that means to me."

"I can't talk to you when you're like this," he says. "I don't exist anywhere in this conversation."

The hallway light illuminates Gabe's head so that singular sandy-blond hairs look like embers. He is a kind of sun, standing there, hands on hips, rising above us all. Audrey spins and stomps to her room, Jack throws himself face-first on the bed, and I turn to grasp the handle of my carry-on case. Gabe throws up his hands and they smack back down on his legs before he turns and walks down the stairs.

Jack, still face down on the quilt, reaches for my thigh. "You said you would make it up to me after my birthday," he says.

I grimace. "Three days," I try to reassure, but feel sick in my stomach. "And get your father to take photos of your puppet and send them to me, okay? Not to my email, my phone. Otherwise I won't get them." The internet down there is slow. Sometimes nonexistent.

Downstairs, in our kitchen, the concrete countertops are covered with hundreds of pictures of hummingbirds. Some are Audrey's attempts at tracing computer printouts, some are watercolor paintings, and some are shaded with Jack's crayons.

"Is this what you're doing for the holiday program?" I ask. Audrey looks up from printed-out pieces of paper with information from the internet and nods. "You know all they want is a drawing of a hummingbird?" After being given the assignment, Audrey became obsessed with the way hummingbirds migrate. Wanted to extend the assignment to include a drawing of the birds' flight path.

Of course, I read into this obsession everything a mother feeling absent does: a cry for help, a need to control something in her life when everything else seems to be falling apart.

"C'mon, then, let's just bang something together. Do you have anything written or typed out?"

Audrey hands me a torn-out lined piece of paper with messy writing.

Instinctively, migrating birds know where to migrate and how to navigate back home. They use the stars, the sun, and Earth's magnetism to help them find their way. They also almost always return home to where they were born.

"Don't worry, I'll do it," Gabe says, snatching the piece of paper out of my hand. "I'm the one who's here."

I look from Audrey to Jack, who is now sitting in the middle of the hallway with a cream faux-fur blanket covering his entire sulking body, and to Gabe, who is shuffling pictures of hummingbirds. I kiss Gabe's cheek and he prickles; hold Audrey close and tell her the project will be "amazing," as she stiffens in my arms; and wrap Jack up in a hug before he turns away from me and pulls the blanket over his head. When the kids were young, I was the only person they'd run to. The only person they wanted. I spent years giving them all of myself and responding to every cry and need. Now, it's as if that time never happened. As if they are rewriting the story. That act, like the universe around me, feels like it is constantly expanding, affecting more and more of our history.

I think about Mum and muster the strength to wheel my carry-on case toward the front door. Above the entrance glows a stained-glass family crest we created five years ago. Our four initials stamped in quadrants.

"Have fun," Gabe calls out flatly as I face the front door, fingers on the handle. I consider turning around to say something, but instead take a breath, open the door and close it quietly behind me.

NINE

WHEN I FIRST MET GABE, HE FASCINATED ME. HE'D GROWN UP THE ONLY CHILD OF HUMANITARIAN WORKERS WHO'D spent more time in war-torn countries than in the family home. They called it a new way to give back for their old money. Whenever Gabe had a cough or cold, his grandparents would blame it on the tear gas Meredith had inhaled when she was pregnant.

For the first three years of his life, he'd been looked after in East Timor by two nannies who took it in turns to be with him 24/7 while his parents were out in the field. Three years in a hotel room gave Gabe a lifelong dislike of room service. While a baby and still unable to talk, he learned to point at the telephone when hungry. Most of the time, war was at a distance, until a local aid worker was killed in a grenade attack close by the hotel. Gabe was sent home to his grandparents the very next day.

When we got engaged, he spoke incessantly about wanting to be nothing like his parents; about being a father who would always be there for his kids, our kids. I loved him, or loved the idea of him, and wanted to introduce him to Mum, to show her I was a capable adult who could make good decisions. So, we flew down to Tassie. Gabe wore a cream linen suit and brown loafers, the outfit he wore when he met international seafood buyers. No amount of wilderness was going to prevent him from, what he described as, "doing the right thing."

Even though I'd seen our once-grand house deteriorate over the years, in those moments we stood outside facing Mum, I saw the house, and my mother, through a stranger's eyes. The once-white exterior speckled ash, the

French doors now misaligned, the wraparound veranda, along which Willow and I would weave and run, now cracked and worn.

With trident stare, she stood on the front step with right palm placed on the doorjamb. Blocking the way, as if there was a password we could recite that would let us in.

"What do you do for a living, fancy-pants?" Mum finally said.

"I guess you could say I'm a sailor. Driving up here, I felt right at home with all these fishing boats."

Mum just looked at him.

Gabe continued, the way he overexplains when he gets nervous and wants to impress. "It's the mollusks I'm most interested in, clams, scallops and oysters. The high-end Asian markets are really after our unpolluted—"

"Seafood," I chimed in. "He's in the seafood export business, Mum."

"Well, yes," Gabe added. "But I like to get my hands dirty. Not just an office job. And I did work on a fishing boat for many years. Sailed it for a family friend who made a living off lobster."

I thought of Dad. About how much he would have loved Gabe, his business-sense coupled with a knowledge of the ocean.

Mum walked away. Gabe looked at me with raised eyebrows. We assumed that meant we were to follow. Inside, we all sat down at the bare table. Mum's welcome, so different to Gabe's parents' spread of pastries and champagne to celebrate our engagement.

"So, you met at Layla's hospital?" Mum turned to Gabe. "Funny world we live in, isn't it?"

"Hardly my hospital, Mum. I was just an intern. I'd only been there a day. Gabe brought in one of his apprentices who'd cut his hand while shucking oysters. There was blood everywhere."

Between medical school, hospital rounds and specializing, I wasn't going out much. Work was just about the only place I could have met someone. When I heard them talking about barramundi, blacklip abalone, blue swimmer crab and black mussels, just as my father and grandfather did, I felt like I had heard my own language in a foreign city.

"Layla cleaned him up, sent him off for surgery," Gabe said. "Then, I'll never forget it, she turned to me, put her hand on my shoulder and said, 'And how are you, are you okay?' There I was without a scratch, yet she still put me right at the center of it."

"Oh well," Mum looked down and brushed some crumbs off the table, "that's the most important thing then, isn't it?"

"I wish Dad could be here," I said after a while. "That you could meet Dad."

Mum's face crawled with crimson. I put my hand over Gabe's.

Then she said with the voice of a practical neighbor, "I'll put the kettle on; there's fresh bread and butter if you want. Bathroom's that way to wash your hands."

"I'll go first. You spend some time with your mum," Gabe said.

"Second door on your right," she said.

When he closed the door, Mum whispered, "Honestly, Layla, you can't be serious."

I got up, took the glass milk bottle out of the fridge, picked up the butter tray and paper bag filled with bread, and put them on the table. Mum always liked her bread as dark as Tasmanian soil. Her butter spread thick.

"I can see what this guy is like. I can see it in his eyes. Your grandmother and great-grandmother both married selfish men. The day they married was the day they also married a life of slavery. Not to the men but their egos."

"Jesus, Mum, you don't think you're overreacting at all?" I wanted to add, "Like you always do." But stopped short.

"He is the last thing you need, Layla," she continued. "I don't care what you say, he will be your downfall."

I washed my hands in the sink, took out a long knife and cut the dark bread into thick slices. When Gabe came back, I kissed his cheek; my mother's disapproval, and my ticking biological clock, two hands planted firmly on my back, pushing me in Gabe's direction.

Gabe and I were happy in the beginning. Youth and ego gave us the energy to position ourselves as the antithesis of each other's parents.

When Audrey came along, we were both enthralled; it was my first experience of love as a reflex. For the first few days, all I did was marvel at something so magnificent. Couldn't people see? A mistake of the universe to give me this small fleshy piece of perfection.

The first six months of parenting were simple. Gabe's and my roles so clearly defined. One afternoon, I filled the white plastic bathtub with warm water and placed it on two chairs beneath the window in Audrey's room. The sun ebbed and flowed on the water as I dipped an elbow in and out, happy with the heat. As soon as Audrey's naked body felt the water, she cried and thrashed and splashed me and I wiped my face, wet and laughing. Even the howling burned with the rarest kind of love and she seemed to me like something never found on planet Earth before, a girl of flesh, yes, but also of stardust.

Audrey's umbilical clamp finally became loose, and I traced the thick sinew, the once-alive cord that was now decomposing, the blood vessels made quiet by smooth muscle contraction. The remains came off. And there it was, the source of human nourishment, the connection between our bodies, sitting in my hands.

I wrapped Audrey in a towel, and we stood awhile in the sunlight, before Gabe came in restless with excitement, patting the air as he said he had something to show us. He came back into the room holding as high above his head as he could a mobile to hang above Audrey's cot.

"I've spent the last few months collecting mussel shells," Gabe said. "Pocketing ones with just the right amount of purple and blue when people on the boat aren't looking." He looked over at me and Audrey and then up again at the dangling shells, then back to us in a kind of breathless anticipation. Small holes had been poked through the shells and threaded with fishing line that was then tied upon a silver metal circle. What looked like a hundred indigo teardrops spiraled around each other and tinkled beneath Gabe's excited, shaking hands.

But when Jack came along, Gabe was pushed further down the list of priorities and I had little energy to adore him, to care, to caress his ego. He started to resent all the times I went to bed early because I'd been touched by everything and everyone all day and the idea of being touched and needed and cajoled by one more person was simply beyond me. To make things even worse, as the children began to grow up and need me less, I remembered that I was a person, with desires and passions and interests and a career that I'd spent a lifetime building. But when I decided to rebuild that part of my life, it became the final divide between me and the man who had once felt like he was the only person in the world I needed. Weariness increased resentment and the scales tipped. Neither of us caring enough anymore to compensate for each other's childhoods.

I often think about Gabe's mother, out there doing what she loved, or at least what she felt was best. The choices she would have had to make. Generations of women stuck between rocks and hard places or, in Meredith's case, the guilt of being given a privileged life and the guilt of not being at home.

Even now, when work and children and an unwell mother take up all my attention, and Gabe and I have the same broken-record argument we've been having for years, I can't help but soften; because, through his bids for attention, all I can see is a man who doesn't want to feel like a small boy pointing at a telephone for food.

TEN

I'VE VISITED DAWN AT SANDY ACRES SEVENTEEN TIMES BUT IT'S ONLY ON THE EIGHTEENTH I REALIZE THE VISITOR car park is nearly always empty.

The nursing home has a leaden atmosphere, as if surrender has soaked into the patchy carpet, the dwarfed lamps, the crocheted pillows and the plastic chairs that sit expectantly in showers. I walk through a hallway of fluorescent lights and step into the main lounge.

I have to find Dawn quickly, listen to the story behind whatever it is she wants me to give to Mum, and get into the car so that I make my flight on time. And by "on time" I mean with enough time to pick up a copy of *Monocle* from the airport newsdealer and buy a coffee and drink it before boarding—I've had that argument with flight attendants way too many times.

"You must be looking for Old Biscuit," a nurse in an un-ironed uniform says and then walks away; I follow a few meters behind. A man with lime-green socks shuffles in the middle of the hallway and we have to press our backs against the wall to sidle our way through. "That's Thomas. He used to be a doctor. Now he has advanced rheumatoid arthritis...you'll never guess what his specialty was. Now it's killing him. Ha, how's that for irony!" We pass Dawn's room, full of wigs she changes into every day, jars of brightly colored buttons used for poker money, and three Japanese kimonos hung on the walls. But no Dawn.

Through a door at the end of the nurses' station, I see her familiar stance, the elbow jutting out and palm pressed into her lower back. It looks like she's decorating the room for a party. But what I think are balloons are actually photos, printed in black and white, hanging on strings from the ceiling and moving in the air-conditioner breeze.

"You know, too many people here look through the wrong end of a telescope—life outside getting smaller," Dawn says. "Well, I'm bringing life right up to them, in their face. I call it Hung, Drawn and Quartered." She looks at me with an inscrutable squint, chewing something between tongue and teeth. She pulls a small ball out. "Sticky tape, dear; you're not allowed gum in here. Old habits die hard." She wears a redheaded wig that sticks and curls against her jawline as if wet. She collected them from operas and plays, when she used to design costumes in velvet and silk.

"I did this for you, Layla. I know how much you loved photography when you were a little girl, how your mother beat it out of you," she says.

The photographs stop moving. There's yelling down the hall. Something about "the blasted air-conditioning failing again" and "can they bloody well call Frank, not Bruce, this time." The faces suddenly still.

I have no idea how Dawn took the images, printed them out, got them up there. Though she's been known to convince the chef to give her salt and butter, contraband worse than alcohol and cigarettes, so who knows? But I know if I get into that conversation, I'll be Alice down the rabbit hole in seconds.

"I've got the cook bringing canapes at five. Speeches at seven," she says. "Does that work for you?"

"For me? What do you mean?" I ask.

"Oh you silly sausage, the opening, the gala night, tonight. I've chosen the pink crane kimono for you, of course—"

"Dawn, I'm going to Mum's, remember? I fly out, like, now."

"Bernard says he's going to play the trumpet." Dawn snakes through the photos, stopping to look at some and wipe them with a floral handkerchief.

"Dawn, please, you were going to give me something to give Mum. If you want me to take it, you're going to have to give it to me now." My voice rises with the last words.

"She's not going to kill herself, dear. But by God, she'll surely turn her back on you when you need her the most."

"Dawn, please." I take both her shoulders in my hands. She rolls her eyes and takes me by the wrist, down the hallway and into her room. A man sits in the corner armchair.

"This is Bernard," she explains. Then turns with a wink and reaches up to the top of her bookshelf, where hand-painted porcelain bells sit between piles of paper. When she can't find what she's looking for, she rifles through a drawer beneath a Singer sewing machine. "Ah. Here you go. Make sure you tell her that I gave this to you. She'll know what it means." She hands me a small brown leather box, but when I open it up, there's nothing inside. Only green silk. "She'll know what it means."

Bernard has more hair protruding out of his nose than he does on his head. He's dressed in a short-sleeved, white polyester shirt with thin brown vertical stripes, and as he waves at me, an oval sweat patch flashes. He nods and pats his knee. Everything about him is like a slow spring. Even his breathing bounces with every inhalation. "Emphysema," Dawn says, "from the war, they think."

"Burma Railway. I built it," he says. "There must have been thousands… of prisoners at…my camp." His words are punctuated by short sharp breaths, like he is telling a story in Morse code. "They were treated real bad…real bad. Tortured and abandoned."

I try to surreptitiously look at my watch. I imagine him as a young man, ferocious in his endurance, grunting from the impact of hammers and picks, surviving on the noises of toil that meant he was still alive.

"I was friends with…one of the other prisoners. He was so thin he used to…do this trick where he would…hold things, like pencils and cigarettes… under his ribs," Bernard says with a nervous laugh and a crackly cough.

"I should be going," I say, trying not to be rude, but feeling my face flush.

"He died," he continues. "Cholera. Not…enough food. I put him on the bonfire…with all the others…there were no spades to dig graves. All I remember was…the heat…on my face…they were dead…but when their ligaments warmed…they contracted. Made their bodies sit…bolt upright…as if they were alive."

"Bernard is a barrel of laughs," Dawn interjects. "I have some leftover ham from dinner if you'd like some? I squirrel away things from Beatrice's plate because she's always nauseous."

"I turned away," Bernard continues. "I just…turned…away. I looked at the ground. The black…earth. A swamp of sticky…slippery mud…from the rain."

I think of Byron's "lump of death—a chaos of hard clay."

"Ah, Bernard, eat some ham. Why live your last breaths in misery?" Dawn thrusts the plate beneath his nose. After he doesn't take any, she slides it into the bin.

"I've gotta go, or I'll miss my flight," I say, putting the small leather box in my pocket. "It was nice to meet you, Bernard." I place a hand on his forearm. He stares out toward Dawn, seeming content with the fullness of his own thoughts.

Dawn slams shut the courtyard door. Hers is the only room with an outside space. God knows how she managed that. She's like the kingpin trading smokes with prison wardens. She pulls the pink silk kimono, which she would have made herself, off the wall so abruptly that the shoulder tears.

"The color might make you look washed out, but the pattern is you to a tee." Dawn drapes the material across my shoulders like a date would a jacket on a cold night. And with just as much ownership. "Bernard, tell her about the trumpet. You can't miss Bernard's trumpet. He hasn't played since his son died, at the funeral. Tell her, Bernard."

I slip the silk fabric off my body, fold it in half and lay it on the edge of her bed. She looks more withered than I've seen her before. I try to visit when I can, especially after everything that happened. But life often gets in the way and days can turn into weeks, can turn into...

"Thank you, the photographs are beautiful. Really. You've always been the one who knows me best. Well, you and Dad."

Dawn tips her head back and laughs. "Oh, love, you have no idea. You know what? Maybe you should go. Maybe it's time you knew the truth about your dad." She always does this, tries to rope me into a conversation she knows I want to have when I'm about to leave. If people act out of love or fear, I've only ever seen fear in this place. Not much room for love. Love requires hope.

I tell Dawn I love her, kiss her forehead, and walk out of the room, but then turn for a moment to watch her after she thinks I've left; she takes off her turquoise kimono and sits on the end of her bed. Bernard has fallen asleep and is snoring.

I look at my watch as I stride down the brightly lit hallway and past the residents sitting, waiting for lunch, even though they've only just had break-fast. Outside, there are no vehicles besides mine in the visitor car park.

I call Willow's number, and it rings and rings until she answers, just as I'm about to hang up.

"It sounds like you're in a bathroom," I say.

"I'm on a platform. Up a tree. Bit early, isn't it?" Her voice is fog and far-ness.

"I'll be on the plane in an hour, so I need you to keep trying Mum until I get there, okay?"

"As much as I'd love to enable this drama of yours, Layla," Willow says with a yawn, "we've got the police coming soon, to cut me out of this tree. It's going to be mayhem."

"If you don't call her, I won't tell you what I find in Mum's wardrobe," I say.

"That's fine. I don't have any questions."

"Can't you, just this fucking once, help me out? If you don't give a shit about Mum, or finding out about Dad, can't you at least do it for me?"

"Don't be bitter. You remind me of apples in August," she says.

"What if Mum goes through with it?" I stumble over my words. "I just..." Amputated phrases. Silence on the other end. "I need to know about Dad, Willow." I soften my voice. "Can't you understand that? I need to know exactly what happened. Once and for all."

Willow breathes in. "Let it go, Layla. It's only hurting you, holding on to false hope about Dad." She hangs up.

The air outside is already a furnace and it won't be long until the heat infiltrates the building with its broken air-conditioning. I can hear the nursing home buzzers ring, wheeled carts scraping the floor, and I think of the residents—piled on top of each other—sitting in their bonfire rooms as people outside look away.

Bernard doesn't even flinch as I stride back into Dawn's room. She's sitting exactly where she was when I left. I look for a bag but then, when I can't find one, I pull out a large, multicolored piece of material from Dawn's wardrobe and realize it's the giant parachute she made when she ran the Gymbaroo class my kids went to. It was made from over one hundred kimono offcuts. Silk spiraling dragons breathe bright red fire toward shimmering peacocks; brocade cherry blossoms merge with midnight-blue clouds and mountain peaks. The children would lie beneath it on their backs while the parents stood around the perimeter holding tight to black strapped handles. *Swoosh*, they would throw the kimono parachute up in the air and then let it fall slowly down, listening to the children laugh before, *swoosh*, up it went again.

I lay it out flat on the bed and start throwing in Dawn's clothes. I add her purse and handbag, then bundle and tie the corners together like a rucksack I could thread a stick through and throw over my shoulder like Huckleberry Finn. I put the small leather box into her hand. "Here, you can give this to Mum yourself. Put on this dress." Dawn looks surprised and goes to say something but then, with a twinkle in her eye, pulls on the dress and smiles. We link arms, and with the silk parachute full of clothes over my left shoulder, we breeze past the nurse who led me to Dawn moments ago. She opens her mouth to say something, but I explain we're just going for ice cream, something we've done before. I sign Dawn out, smile at the nurse, press the code and watch it flash green.

I'm just helping Dawn into the car as my phone vibrates and my stomach lurches at the thought of Willow calling me back, calling to say she's going to help this time, but when I look at the screen, it's Maggie, my mother's next-door neighbor. The last time I spoke to her on the phone, she told me my father was dead.

ELEVEN

ON THE DAY DAD DIED, MUM AND I SAVED A WHALE. IT WAS A COLDER-THAN-USUAL MORNING. SHE WOKE ME UP WITH A smile on her face and calm in her body. Asked me to get dressed. As we walked, the ground cracked beneath a cloudless sky. Folklore in our area claimed that a sky without a cloud in sight is an omen of heavy rain. A perfectly clear blue sky was known as a "weather-breeder"; prediction of a brewing storm.

Tiptoeing quietly through the rainforest, we navigated tangled-hair swaths of sphagnum moss; further on, the forest was garlanded with climbing heath that stabbed the darkness with crimson flowers. "The only cathedral worth worship," Mum said in bird-clear syllables.

We meandered along the beach collecting sea glass, colors that looked more like jewels than rubbish. Smooth corners I would forget could once cut. We picked up soft, discarded feathers and pale-blue eggs that had cracked in half. Fragile and broken things. As the sand stretched ahead, we stood beneath the solstice sun and noticed our absent shadow.

Then sand dunes like skyscrapers. Barreling and laughing, we rolled from the top all the way down to the bottom. As the sun set, we made our way to the top of the dunes and Mum floated out a rug and made a table from a piece of driftwood and a few stones. Unpacked grapes and chocolate-covered elderberries and plums. A picnic on the lip of the sea.

From our vantage point, looking back toward Jericho, we could see the bluff where our house sat and the fishing port beneath. "Maybe our hometown's a bit like a storm," Mum said. "More alluring when you're not inside it."

We stared at the white sand on the curving shore. The wind's wet fingers running through our hair. Bird cries punctuated the beat of tapered wings: shearwaters cleaving the sky and water, dipping within centimeters of the sea's surface, as they flocked home. Mum reached for my hand without looking at me. Held it tight.

Before dark, we tightrope-walked across the orange lichen-covered rocks; I watched the sea-grape fringe flex and flow on the water. It wasn't until we rounded the cliff that we saw it: a baby whale beached on the shore.

I was fourteen years old and it was the first time I'd seen one, all barnacle skin. "They might look ugly up close," Mum said, "but if you step back and let the details blur, they're beautiful." Southern rights and humpbacks often came close to the shore, following the eastern current to Antarctica. But not this close. Never beached.

We ran across the sand and placed our palms on the rubbery skin. The whale's tail flicked up and down as its eyes darted from left to right. "It's okay, baby. It's okay," Mum crooned. She tipped out the remaining chocolate-covered elderberries and used the Tupperware container to scoop water and pour it over the calf. But it wasn't enough. I was left to keep pouring water over the whale as Mum ran home to raise the alarm and to pick up buckets, sheets, food and warmer clothes. I'd never seen a whale up so close. I stood there by myself, scooping water, a stare set on my face, a prick-eared pain. I hated the stupid animal for beaching itself, for needing us, for eliciting such sympathy and care from my mum. Most of all, I hated the whale for stopping the fleeting feeling that Mum and I were happy.

As I was pouring a container of water over the whale, a gurgle started, and I stood back from its trembling body before spurts of black mud erupted into the air. The swampy muck dropping on my head like mud rain.

By the time Mum came back, I was wet and freezing and feeling guilty about my spiteful thoughts, so took the bucket with gusto and filled and poured as much water as I could over the dying whale. Mum had tried to get other people to come, but everyone was held up in work and obligations they couldn't leave.

"When we first moved here," she said, pouring water, "we would go out looking for whales. Do you remember?" I shook my head. "I developed patience," she said. "I learned that a headland is much better for spotting them than a beach. You want to be looking out across the ocean, rather than being at eye level with the water. You look at the horizon, and work your way back in." I let her talk, not really listening, wishing the tide would come in, not just so that we could save the whale, but so that we could salvage what was left of our special day. "You know the most interesting thing?" Mum asked. I kept scooping and pouring, scooping and pouring. "One afternoon when we were whale watching, an elderly woman came up to me and told me that mother whales, to stop predators from hearing their conversations, sit at the bottom of the ocean and whisper to their calves." She smiled in wonder.

I willed the tide to come and take the whale away.

After about six hours, when the tide was in just enough to float the calf from the sand, Mum fed one end of a once-white sheet under the whale and through to me, and each holding an end we guided her out, further and further into the water, until with great strength the calf pushed away from us and swam out to sea.

When we got home that day, Mum made toast for our dinner, reheated a casserole for Dad, and told me she was going to walk down to Jericho to pick up the mail and some milk before the rains came.

Dad came home soon after Mum left and he hustled me out to his makeshift observatory to catch the constellations before they were hidden from view by clouds. He built the observatory right next to the boundary line of Huon pine, sheltered from the Roaring Forties westerly. A retractable brass dome imported from Italy sat on top of a cedarwood garden shed he'd bought from the local hardware store.

Once inside, we took our places. Him seated on a leather ottoman and me on a milk crate. Dad took out his sky map, went through the constellations we could see that night and started with the usual "Now, how do you find north?"

"Look for the Southern Cross," I began my list, "join a line between the head and foot star, and then follow the arrow to the south celestial pole. Below that is south. If I turn around one-hundred-and-eighty degrees, I've found north."

"Good girl," he said. "Good girl." Running his finger over the map and then moving the telescope, he picked out his usual favorites. Ophiuchus, the healer, with a snake wrapped around his waist; Centaurus, the centaur, with a human head and bison torso; Chamaeleon, the lizard; and Orion, the hunter, who told Gaia he would kill all the animals on the land.

He beckoned me to the telescope to take a look.

"I just see dots, Dad."

"Ah, Monkey, not everything in the night sky is what it seems. I'll show you. Draw a shooting star on the wall." My father handed me a carpenter's pencil striped red and black. And I drew, like children do, two triangles, one the right way up and another on top upside down, and then lines shooting out of the back to show it was flying fast through space. He poured water from a drink bottle over his hand and rubbed across my drawing until lines blurred. Explained that shooting stars are not stars at all, but a small piece of rock or dust that moves so fast it heats up and glows. What astronomers call meteors.

He took me outside the observatory to observe the full moon. As the wind increased, he said, "Never trust the moon because, like the shooting star, she's a trickster." The moon was low in the sky. "The moon has no light of its own; its glow is a reflection of the sun. And it looks bigger than when it's high in the sky, doesn't it?" Dad pulled me closer and bent down so that his head was level with mine. "If you hold your arm up you can blot out the moon with your finger." I raised my arm and touched the glowing disc with my fingertip. The moon disappeared. "When the moon is high in the sky, even though it seems smaller, the same finger will cover it perfectly again. Though the best way to destroy the illusion is to turn your back on the moon, bend over with your head between your legs and look at it upside down."

I copied my father, and, sure enough, the moon was small, the same size as it looks when it is higher in the sky. I stood back up. Watched Dad reach his finger into the sky and trace the lines of the healer's limbs.

"The stars are different. Reliable," he said. I watched the reassuring outline of his profile, the way the creases at the edges of his eyes smiled along with his lips. "You can always navigate life by—"

"I know. I know"—I rolled my eyes—"by the stars' constancy." I kissed his cheek.

"Oh, you have somewhere more important to be?" he teased.

"Maybe." I smiled and walked away. They were the last words I spoke to him.

That night, I went to see Jesse next door in his orchard, where our parents couldn't find us. Two weeks earlier, I'd started finding crates in our doorway, piled with apples and pears, the best of the new season. I hadn't seen him about, so I went over to say thanks. We went for a walk in the dark orchard and Jesse gave me my first kiss. Or maybe I took it. But the moment didn't last long, as what was forecast as a mild gale quickly became a furious storm. We each ran to our respective houses.

Wind rattled windowpanes. I looked around the house for Mum or Dad, but every room was empty. Worried they were caught in the storm, I went searching for them around the property. Through the shed with our four-wheel drive and tractor, down the backyard where Willow and I used to play, and around the edges close to the cliffs. I couldn't find them anywhere, until I stood about fifty meters away from Dad's observatory. They were standing next to it, yelling at each other, arms stirring the air like soup.

Under a broken sky, I watched Mum sneer and lunge at Dad, shake a fist of paper in his face with one hand and wave wildly with the other, which held a large bottle of milk. He said something to her with upstretched palms, and in response she spat and spasmed out words before throwing and smashing the glass container onto the ground. White liquid splashed and merged with rain.

The air descended and the water in it evaporated, pushing and dragging the clouds down. I tried to find the facts of what was happening around me, name the phenomena, to calm my nerves about everything I didn't understand. "Mammatus, mammatus," I said to myself as they formed diagonally: cellular pattern of pouches on the underside of the clouds. I knew the lightning was coming. I waited for the electric strike; imagined the small pieces of ice crashing into each other; all the collisions creating electrical charge.

Then a boom and light, Mum's wild eyes and screaming mouth. Dad stood with his hands on his hips and his head down. Now and then, he turned and walked away and then back to her. The wind began to howl and knock me about. In between the gusts, I caught some of Mum's words. "Bastard!" she yelled. "Liar!" I strained to hear Dad but his voice was too quiet. Only once did he yell but the wind stole his scream.

A flash of light. A bolt traveled from the cloud above me to the ground, opened a hole in the wind, and the air warmed and collapsed. The expansion exploded and detonated a shock wave that turned into a cracking sound wave of thunder. The vibrations shook me and I ran inside out of the wind and rain.

Worried about my parents fighting in the storm, I watched the scene through the lounge-room window. Our neighbor Bill ran clumsily in gumboots across our yard from his, scraped his feet on the doorstep and knocked on the door. Water tore across his face and, even though he stood in front of me, he had to yell. "Where's your dad?" I pointed to where my parents were still caught in a furious dance. Bill's face was ashen and wet, uneven as if pumiced by salt-filled wind. He looked concerned.

"What's going on?" I asked, holding the door open so it wouldn't get caught in the wind and bang against the facade.

"There's a boat sinking," he explained. "Idiot tourists circumnavigating the island. We need to head out to rescue them." Bill and Dad were members of the Volunteer Marine Rescue Services. They got called out a few times a year to pull people out of the ocean. "This one's a bad one. Kids on board, too, we think. I'll go and get your dad. We'll need all the help we can get. You stay inside where it's safe."

It took me three goes to pull the door shut as Bill ran away through the mud and wind and rain in his slapping black boots toward my parents, who were still yelling so hard at each other they didn't notice him until he grabbed Dad's shoulder.

Bill had to lean right into Dad's ear to tell him what was going on, to make Dad see he was needed. Mum paced, shaking her head. Dad said something to Bill and then they just stood there a moment. Bill shook his head. Raised his arms up in the air and then let them fall to his sides. Looked out to sea and then ran back to his property. Another burst of torrential rain. Mum and Dad were as soaked as if they'd been swimming.

I observed everything through the lounge-room window. Mum left Dad and strode away. He just stood there with a heaving chest staring out to the ocean. The front door creaked as I watched it awhile, waiting for Mum to come inside but she never did. When I looked back, Dad was gone. The rain turned to gravelly pellets of ice. It began to patter the windows like the tapping of someone trying to get my attention.

Eventually, a long time after, Mum came inside, soaking wet, and stood next to me by the window. I could smell alcohol on her, knew that she'd been accusing Dad with her paranoid delusions. God knows what. Affairs, spending money. He never did any of it. But you could never correct her. She just raged and accused. Especially when she'd been drinking.

"Did Dad go out with them?" I asked. Staring straight ahead, not looking at her.

"I don't know, love. I don't know." Then she wrapped her arms around me in a rare embrace and her wet clothes soaked into mine. I was still too angry and confused to hug her back. She started sobbing as she pulled away and then walked into her bedroom and closed the door. Through the walls, I could hear her howling like the wind.

With a twenty-kilometer view over the sea, we could usually spot a storm before it hit the coast. But that night, the storm was as sudden and as savage as they come. Cold forty-foot seas, hurricane-force westerly wind roaring at fifty knots. Once you're in a storm like that, you never forget it. The banshee moan, crests torn into foam, houses groaning, the wind cracking empty air. Raindrops large and heavy, with what seems like no space between them, falling on the roof like an avalanche.

Eventually, I went to bed, exhausted from rescuing the whale, and wanting to be alone to think about Jesse's kiss. I went to sleep with the smell of pear juice still on my hands and a child's faith that Dad would be okay.

When I woke up, Mum was sitting at the dining table with bloodshot eyes and a tired face. I stood there, watching, waiting for her to say something. Maggie, Bill's wife from the dairy farm next door, was there too. She put the kettle on the gas stove and dipped a small white jug into a stainless-steel bucket she'd brought over from the milking shed, arranged everything the way Mum usually does herself, on the table next to her purple vase. Maggie had lived her whole life on the west coast and showed her care through ritual. When the worry in the room seemed to become too much, she went to check "on the boys."

There were no lights on in the house. Just intermittent blinks of sunlight, which shone through Mum's vase and created beams of color on our kitchen table. Neither Mum nor I had moved from the positions we were left in when the phone rang. It was Maggie, who told me matter-of-factly that Dad had drowned, that they had found the boat and "a body." Not "Oscar," not "your dad," not even "his body," but "a body." I let the handset fall. Mum didn't get up from the table; she just looked at me before her face collapsed, silently.

It was her fault, I thought, it was all her fault. If she hadn't been arguing with Dad, poking him the way she always did, if she hadn't been drinking and he hadn't been asking her not to, he would have gone out with the other men, in their boat, and still be alive. In that moment a fury furnished a home inside me and never left. *A body*, I kept hearing in my head.

A strange thing happens when you hear words like that. You transform into a black hole within which gravity pulls so much that you crumple from your diaphragm and even light cannot get out. *A body. A body.* The grief a force so strong because everything that matters has been squeezed into the tiny space of those two words.

TWELVE

THE AIRPORT IS PART OLD, PART NEW, ALWAYS UNDER CONSTRUCTION. THE ROOF IS COMEDICALLY TALL, AS IF THE SPACE itself is a hangar and should hold a plane. I stand for a moment, watching the tide of movement.

Maggie's call cut out as soon as I picked up. I'm not sure whether she hung up on me or it was the phone reception—both are as likely as each other. I try to call her back but she doesn't answer, so I call Mum again; no answer. I even call Maximos, the old Greek man who runs the local fish and chip shop down in the village. No one answers, which is pretty normal, but feels ominous given the circumstances.

Dawn suggests I put her in a wheelchair to increase our likelihood of getting a ticket and because, as she puts it, "We'll be able to jump the queue and board the same time as the bastards in business."

At the check-in desk, I reach into my tote bag, where everything runs wild, to find my purse, but it falls sideways and its contents scatter across the floor. People rush past as I reach to scoop everything up: a psychologist's business card on which I hook a row of light-brown hair pins; six loose organic medium-flow tampons; a bunch of blue pens held tight by a yellow hair elastic because it's the color Audrey won't wear; and one pair of red socks because planes are always cold.

Finally, I carefully pick up an antique leather-bound copy of *Lessons on the Human Body*. I open the cover and check everything is still inside before placing it gently back in my bag.

A week after Dad died, I woke to find Mum removing everything from his study. She was pulling pictures and certificates off walls, books off shelves and a lifetime of papers out of cupboards and putting them in wicker laundry baskets. I asked her to stop, to wait, told her that it didn't have to be done now, but she pushed me away and continued as if in a trance. In a panic, I started to take things for myself, his favorite pen, his sailing cap, a few books, but she grabbed my arm: "Don't you dare. You don't want any of this. I'm not having it in the house." My eyes wide in fear of her grip on my arm, everything I'd taken fell to the floor. I walked away and stood in my bedroom trying to figure out what to do. Peeking into the hallway I watched as Mum carried a full basket toward the backyard, where Dawn was supervising a bonfire.

I ran back into Dad's study and a blue-and-gold spine caught my eye. When I put my hand to it and pulled it out of the bookshelf, I felt instant calm. *Lessons on the Human Body*; the words "sternum" and "sacral," "femoral" and "femur." My father's language. On Dad's table was a small, folded map of the constellations in the sky and a list of sea creatures fished by his father. I clutched them all in my arms as if they contained everything good and true in this world and ran out of the room before my mother could return.

Everything is in my bag except my purse. Shit. I put my hands on my hips, and close my eyes. I'm gonna have to call Gabe. And there it is again, the universe forcing me to ask Gabe for help and then him to resent me for it. Though I only have myself to blame: distracted when I left the house.

"Don't worry," Dawn says, registering what's happened. "I might be old but I'm not poor."

My glare tells Dawn there's no way I am going to let her pay for everything on this trip, though I'm also relieved she can pay for her own plane ticket. I can check in without my ID, but I'll need my cards and license to rent a car. Gabe answers after the second ring, which is a nice change. But the relief only lasts a moment.

"I thought you'd be in the Qantas lounge by now." His voice is staccato.

"I forgot my purse," I say.

"I know." His reply takes control of the conversation, reminds me that I have always felt this way in our relationship, as if he has something of value I need and he forces me to ask for it.

"I'm sorry. I need my cards. My license."

"What the hell, Layla? I not only have to be a single parent, but I also have to pick up the slack every time you mess up?"

I turn my head away from the crowds and hiss, "Single parent? You've got to be fucking kidding me."

"You're the one who wanted to go back to work," Gabe says.

"You wanted me to as well. And, yeah I did, but not like this. Not having to work every hour available to me. And then you go and fish without a license, and I'm the one who has to increase my workload because you don't want to work more hours?"

"You tell yourself whatever you need to, Layla," he says.

"You think I like being away from the kids so much? You know me. Well, you bloody well should know me better than that."

I hang up the phone. A click, like love's quick life. For a moment I see nothing. Only hear my ears drumming. Feel a thin flame run under my skin, wanting to be extinguished by Gabe bringing me my purse.

It's times like these I'd rather be with my patients. I miss their purity. When people are in desperate need, something falls away. The posing that's part of the ordinary world vanishes, that "How are you? I'm fine" falseness. You feel somehow close to the raw truth of what it means to be human. I didn't realize, until I worked in a hospital, the addictive nature of this authenticity.

"Watch out, dear, there's a scorpion under every stone," Dawn says, staring off into the distance.

A stone is one thing, I think. One's home is another.

We stood in this airport on our honeymoon. Giddy with the promise of four weeks off work and time together as "husband" and "wife." In the heart of a northern winter, we flew to Glencoe in the Scottish Highlands, a nod to my ancestry, and stayed in a small stone house tucked down into the corner of an expansive property. We intended to go walking across the peaks of Buachaille Etive Mòr and Bidean nam Bian, to visit the Folk Museum in an eighteenth-century thatched cottage and view the red deer and golden eagles. But we were so caught up in each other for the first two weeks, we stayed in bed. The second two weeks, we were snowed in.

The bedroom had a fireplace and we hauled all the woolen blankets from the wardrobes up onto ourselves. The owner of the property came and brought us food: oat porridge with melted brown sugar; roughly mashed turnips; and soup made from smoked haddock, cured using regional green-wood, with onions and potatoes and cream.

On the first night, he also brought us enough fermented honey to last us the four weeks. "That's where the term comes from," he explained when we looked at him confused. "Aye, you should know this. What do they teach you down there? You drink this honey for the first moon cycle of your marriage. That's the tradition. It's good luck but also a wink to the fact that as the moon wanes, so will your love."

We laughed at him, so smug and self-congratulatory. "We'll be different," we whispered to each other, as if our love were somehow a better ilk than others and would stand the test of time; as if we knew something no one else did.

Our flight details on the screen change to "Go to gate." I wheel Dawn and turn around just as I see Gabe walk through the automatic doors. A feeling of relief softens my body and I almost run to hug him. But then slow, take the purse and squeeze his shoulder in gratitude. He notices Dawn. His body becomes taut.

"What the hell, Layla? Dawn?" Gabe talks as if she isn't right there. "You can take her but not the kids?"

"Hang on, that's not fair. You know the kids wanted to stay for the art program." The word "fair" for Gabe is something like "menstruation." He recoils as if slapped.

"I was going anyway. I just met her here," Dawn says.

"This is Mum's life, Gabe. It's not like I'm going on a girls' weekend away," is all I can think of saying.

Gabe nods. Looks off to the side before putting his hands on his hips. "How many times have I told you about the problems we're having finding crays at the moment?" he starts. "This morning was one of those rare times when we've been able to get them. Wave height, water temp, salinity. Perfect. But I couldn't go out because I knew I'd have to bring you this damn purse. And now the wind's changed. How do I explain this to the guys in the office calling clients?"

"Who? Like Freya?" I snap the remark off cleanly but it's too late.

Gabe laughs after a short, surprised intake of air, then looks down and nods at the metal buckle on my purse. "Did you know that stainless steel was invented for cannons?"

"Are we at war?" I ask.

"I don't think we're close enough for that," he says.

"Then what are we doing?" I ask. My stormy pride breaks like a wave and falls back onto itself.

"At the moment, I'm going back to work, because it's the only thing that makes any fucking sense," he says.

"Women will settle for anything, just to say they have something," Dawn whispers to me.

"You're not helping," I snap back.

Gabe walks backwards, throws his arms up in the air and looks at me with a burning hatred, turns and strides away. I watch a stranger disappear out of sight and wonder how people we feel we know better than anyone else in the world can, almost overnight, become completely obscured.

THIRTEEN

THE MAN AT THE CHECK-IN COUNTER HAS SHORT
WHITE SHIRTSLEEVES, REVEALING SEMICIRCLE BICEPS. "HELLO,
young man," Dawn says with a wry smile. I stiffen. Stare straight ahead with
please-don't-do-it wide eyes. "Well, wouldn't I like to pretend that I'm blind
so I could touch you inappropriately." The man smiles. Asks what he can do
for us. "All jokes aside, I'm unwell. I have a letter from my doctor somewhere
I—" Dawn shuffles in the wheelchair, opens her purse, takes out pill bottles,
rattling them with unusually shaky hands. "Tasmania is the only place I can
get this treatment." Dawn continues to rummage. "Argh, it's here somewhere.
My niece is a doctor and can verify the information." I look at her. Hand over
my identification; support what she is saying.

He succumbs and puts Dawn on the plane but tells us we'll have to run
if we're going to make the flight on time. After rushing through check-in and
screening, the light on our gate's screen flashes "Delayed." We both stare at the
screen. Our bodies exhale. All that rushing for nothing.

We find a booth in Sampson's Café where we can still see a screen. Dawn
orders an orange ("the most orange one you have"), green apples, and strawberries. Everything whole. Nothing cut. I order thickly sliced raisin toast with
butter and a black coffee with milk on the side. When Dawn's fruit comes,
she smiles and peels the orange, slowly, then lines up the naked orange, apple
and strawberries next to each other in front of herself like surgical tools in a
theatre.

"Flavorless, cut up into small pieces in case we choke, that is what food is
like for us. And that's the highlight of our day. Can you imagine?" One by one,

Dawn picks up the fruit, closes her eyes, and bites into its skin as if she wishes that her whole face were a mouth. Juice dribbles down her chin and onto her hands, pips stick to the side of her lips as she bites into the apple then eats the flesh round and round as if she is devouring a corn cob. Next she kiss-bites the strawberries, sucking all the way to the green stalk. But she leaves the orange till last. Her eating seems like a personal experience, so I look out the window at the vast gray runways, the planes landing in what seems, through the thick-paned glass, like silence.

After Willow left home, Dad thought it might be a good idea to take us back to see his family. "A welcome distraction," he called it.

Mum was dead set against it. Wouldn't budge. "Too much time out of school at too important a time. And anyway," she had said, "I don't want to go anywhere in case Willow comes back."

So, Dad made solo plans and went to visit his family in Scotland.

He had spent his childhood on the island of Barra in the Outer Hebrides, a far outpost of the UK in the North Atlantic. "The weather was so temperamental, the forecast was as useful as a chocolate teapot," he'd say. It was one of the things he enjoyed about the west coast of Tasmania: how similar it was to where he'd grown up.

What I loved hearing about the most was the way you got there. Barra has the only airport where you land on the beach; the only landing dictated by the tides. Dad loved to tell people about the sign that read *Keep off the beach when the windsock is flying*. He'd pump his elbows up and down, his stomach bouncing, as he pretended to be a kid, picking up his bucket and spade and running to the grass. I often thought about that tiny airport at the mercy of the weather; the way the runway disappears at high tide.

My grandfather taught Dad astronomy. Though that's not what he called it. It was navigation. He'd used the stars, moon, sun and horizon to calculate his position when sailing. It was especially useful on the open ocean at night off the coast of Scotland, where there were no landmarks. When he got lost, my grandfather used dead reckoning, an ancient estimation technique, where all he had was his past position as a reference point. And when he was really, really lost, he would tell Dad, "Well, north is always north." And this would provide him the comfort he needed to stop, regain his composure, trust in the security of universal order, and look for the North Star. Dad repeated that saying almost every day: "North is always north."

I look up at the departures board but our flight is still delayed. "Rumor has it there's a ghost that lives in between the first and second airport floors—between arrivals and departures," I say to try and distract myself.

"Poppycock," Dawn says through bites of her strawberries. "There is nothing beyond this mortal coil."

I smile. "That's exactly what Dad used to say."

"Well, that's the only thing we would agree on."

I bite my tongue, not wanting to get into it. Dad could never just say normal words. "Life" wasn't good enough. It had to become "mortal coil." Any birthday party became a "soiree," a shudder of excitement was a "frisson," and we didn't chew, we "masticated," which always brought a giggle by the time I was a teenager. Whenever my friends and I were trying to talk between ourselves, Dad would always ask to be part of the "tête-à-tête," and when I would breathe warm air in the car on cold mornings and fog up the windows, he would ask us to please stop "suspiring." But that was Dad. Always found the extravagant in the everyday.

I sip the last of my cold coffee. I fold my paper napkin into a boat. I can sense Dawn watching me. She reaches over and takes it out of my hands.

"Do you remember," she says, examining the paper boat, "that time I found you and Willow once, in the bathtub? Do you remember?"

Memory is a funny thing. Sometimes I feel as though I've led different lives. Have been different people in the past.

"Nora used to put you girls in there, while she and your father raged outside. She'd leave a pile of paper on the floor, taught you how to fold paper boats, how to light a candle and drip wax onto them so they would float and you could play with them in the water. She'd leave you with the radio on, lock the door. Sometimes you were in there until your lips turned blue. One night I found you both freezing, picked you up, wrapped you girls in towels. You held me so tight. Tighter than I've ever been held before. Rested your head on my shoulder. I took you both over to Maggie's and she made you hot apple cider."

I look at my open hands. The same hands as in the story? I'd forgotten about those nights. Maybe survival is sometimes forgetting.

Dawn continues, "I came in another night and you'd set a boat alight, burned your fingers but had not wanted to call out." I slather a thick layer of butter on my raisin toast and take a bite. "Your mother was probably too busy howling at your father to hear you anyway." Dawn watches me. "Don't you remember?" she asks. I try to grasp at images; put them together into a memory. "That morning she'd taken you to the city, God knows what for. She never told us. But I was in the kitchen when she came home, threw a dress in the bin and put you both in the bathroom."

Mum once, with needle and thread, created a dress from a curtain she bought for the master bedroom, but never used. Dad didn't like the fabric. Mum hung that dress on the back of her bedroom door for a week. It had thin mint-green stripes. Sometimes, when I walked past, I would notice her standing there, just looking at it.

One morning, when Willow was twelve and I was six, Mum woke us before sunrise, wearing the dress. We left the house still sleepy in our best outfits and boarded the West Coast Wilderness Railway steam train, new notepaper and pens to keep us occupied on the almost four-hour ride. When the train would arch round a corner, we would poke our heads out the window to try to see the engine. Smoke billowing into the sky. Mum spent the trip pushing down the white wicks on her nails. Tracing and pressing the arcs with her thumbnail. Round and down and up. Over and over again, until her skin was a restless red.

Willow and I didn't know where we were going. Didn't ask. When we got to wherever it was, we walked to the town hall, through four concrete pillars, and up a maroon carpeted staircase, our two hands sliding along the shiny oak banister. There were four rows of seats at the front adorned with white pieces of paper. *Reserved*, they said. Mum chose us the three seats in the middle at the front. Slowly, the hall filled. When microphones were being tested and voices were quieting, three people stood at the end of our row, pointing at held cards, talking to official people in silk vests. One by one, the people in our row were spoken to until they came to us. When asked to see our invite, Mum confidently handed them a textured rectangle.

"I'm sorry, love, but you're not supposed to be seated here," they said to her.

"But I've won a prize. For my poetry." She pointed a finger to the writing on the invitation. "See, they even listed my poem, here." There was a beat of silence.

"Everyone who entered got an invite to the ceremony," the woman said. "It would state explicitly if you won." The official-looking woman then showed Mum a piece of paper folded in thirds. "Here, like this."

Mum looked at the letter. Stood without a word. Said under her breath, "I'm so sorry, excuse me, excuse me," and shuffled down the aisle. We followed, through the columns and out into the cold air. Willow and I standing, holding bunches of our skirts in tight fists.

When we got home, Dawn was in the kitchen, stocking the fridge with jam she'd made. Mum took off her dress before we'd even got through the front door, ripping and pulling until the seams split and the stitching tore and the dress was thrown into the kitchen bin.

"Go take a bath," was all she said to us. Was the only thing she'd said to us all day. When Dad came home, we could hear them yelling. Willow sat in the tub. Dried her hands on the bathmat and picked up a piece of paper, tried to fold the rectangle in half, fold the corners down, turn the paper over and flip the creases. I ignored her frustration, pretended the naked bulb hanging from the ceiling above me was the North Star. I dripped wax onto my two boats, set them in the water and blew them forwards.

Willow broke my focus by throwing her paper across the bathroom floor. She couldn't get the folds. She looked at me, stood up dripping and naked, and tried to open the door but it was locked from the outside. I handed her a folded boat, covered in wax, and she got back in. Our two boats spun around aimlessly and I picked mine up, held it to my face and whispered, "Don't worry, little boat, north is always north." And then I placed it back down, as gently as I could from my cupped hands, and blew it again toward the light.

FOURTEEN

THERE ARE FURTHER DELAYS TO OUR FLIGHT. I WHEEL DAWN TO GATE 5 SO WE CAN ASK SOMEONE WHAT'S GOING ON, BUT when we get there a long line of people stretches all the way to the desk and so we take our place at the end. "Winter Wonderland" plays over the speakers as people stand in shorts and T-shirts. The information boards flick to say all flights are canceled. What the hell?

Maggie calls my phone.

"Where are you? I thought you'd be here by now," she says, without waiting for a hello. Her words run together like colored scarves knotted and pulled out of a magician's hat. She doesn't wait for a reply. "I haven't seen her this bad since your dad died." The words prick my skin.

Dawn mouths, "Who is it?" and I mouth back, "Maggie." Dawn wheels herself away from me.

"Are you with her? What's happening?" I ask.

"She won't let me into the house."

People hustle behind me, and I realize everyone has moved along and there is a large gap in front, so I shuffle forwards.

"There are delays here but I'll be there as soon as I can. Can you just stay nearby until I get there? Please, Maggie?"

"Why would I stop her?"

I feel like I must have misheard her words so am silent.

"Why would I…of all people…stop…her?" she repeats.

"You're her best friend. And anyway, how could any human being let—"

"Don't get sanctimonious with me, Layla."

"Then why are you calling me?" I say, loudly, and people around me turn and look. Dawn looks at me too. I turn away from the queue.

"We have a different view of friendship, love. I'm not going to stop her if this is what she wants to do. She's been lonely a long time, love. And plus, there's all the other stuff weighing her down."

"Please, Maggie. I don't think I can get there until tomorrow night, and Dawn and I are just trying to figure—"

"Dawn? Is she coming down here with you?"

"Yeah, we—it's a long story—but could you please just stay nearby until we get there? I know you know she's serious this time, Maggie. Please. She's even left some info about Dad in her wardrobe drawer and I—"

"Drawer?" Maggie asks. Pauses a moment. "Alright, alright. I'll figure out a reason for her to let me in and to stay until tomorrow, but then I have to go into town. Okay?"

The first time I found Mum's locked drawer was a year after Dad died. It was late on Christmas Eve. I'd bought my boyfriend Jesse a sapling for Christmas. A new type of apple. I wanted to cover the pot with paper. "Where's the wrapping? Where is it?" I asked Mum, huffing through the house, crashing and banging the way people do when they're trying to be quiet but are desperate to find something. I looked in the hallway cupboard, and Dad's study, in all the kitchen drawers. Eventually, I stomped into Mum's room as she lay in the covers, "under the weather."

The wardrobe door shrieked as I pulled it open and rummaged through shoes and shoeboxes. No Christmas wrapping paper. Then I looked at the four rectangular drawers at the base of the wardrobe. Two on each side. One of them locked. I gave it a jiggle. Mum threw off the covers and leapt out of bed, miraculously revived, and pulled me away.

"Why is this locked?" I asked.

"Layla, stop it. Here." Mum handed me bright-red wrapping paper with Father Christmas heads all over it.

"What's in there?" I asked, while Mum ushered me out of the room.

"It's just for my personal things, you know, makeup and stuff, so you don't take them." She lowered her voice. "You're getting to that age now." It was the most reasonable, levelheaded voice I had ever heard Mum use. I started to walk back to my room but turned around, watched her touch the drawer at the base of the wardrobe, wiggling the small brass handle to check it was still locked. She stood, ran her hands over her hair like she did when she was rinsing shampoo, and walked out into the lounge room.

Later, when Mum was at Maggie's for a cuppa, I crept in and tried to open the drawer, but it was locked tight. For all I knew, it *was* filled with makeup and Mum's personal things, but there was also something in her voice that night, something so normal it was strange, that convinced me there was more to the story.

I leave Dawn sitting with the bags as I walk over to the airline's counter and stand behind a man who is furious. "You're all the bloody same," he yells at the two women behind the counter as he storms off.

"Hi, I need to get home to my mother." I try to disarm the situation to get more information. "What's going on? When can we fly?"

"Ma'am, we don't know ourselves. We are trying to find out. All planes are grounded. It's not just yours. We will let you know as soon as we do. For now, you'll just have to try to be patient."

The room is crowded with people. A woman with cracked lipstick standing near me asks a man with a toddler hanging across his shoulder if he can check the news. "Do I look like I can check the news?" he asks. I recognize the parents' mixed expression of intimacy and weariness.

"For fuck's sake, I'll do it myself," she says. The woman reads off her phone: "Some mountain in Bali is sending volcanic ash hundreds of kilometers into the air. Apparently, the ash can harm the planes and their engines."

I think for a moment about going home. After all, I don't live that far away; seems silly to stay here the night. But then what? I'd have to say goodbye to the kids all over again. I'd have to talk to Gabe. And I also now have Dawn. I'm away now. I might as well stay away. Wait until the flight tomorrow.

I envisage Mum in front of her Zenith tube television, which is encased by wood grain, the screen outlined with vinyl silver trim. Mum, always the innocent. But victims can be the most violent people on Earth. They twist everyone around them into villains because that's who they need everyone around them to be, to keep them in martyrdom. I imagine Mum watching newsreaders talk about spreading lava and incandescent rocks, smoke and dust obscuring the land, winds gathering to a violent storm.

Groups of people rush to the counter in an attempt to get hotel vouchers or refunds or just some more information. I walk against the onslaught, twisting my shoulder to slide through faster and craning my neck to find Dawn, but she's not where I left her and neither are my bags. I spin from left to right to try to locate her wheelchair and auburn-colored wig, but I can't see her anywhere.

I close my eyes and hear my father's voice, *north is always north*, and the phrase creates a space of candlelit calm in my mind. I slow and steady myself and realize that I'm standing in the wrong seating area, and Dawn and my bags are where I left them, twenty meters away. I continue to repeat the words in my mind: *north is always north*. I recite them over and over, the predictability of them, each word like a drop of wax strengthening my paper-thin emotions so that I can cast them down to float away.

FIFTEEN

THE BEST DAWN AND I CAN DO IS A MEDIOCRE HOTEL
NEXT TO THE AIRPORT, A FOOD VOUCHER AND ASSURANCE WE'LL FLY
out as soon as we can. There must be a way to get to Mum sooner. I resolve to
do some research when I get to a room. We cross the street between the airport
and the hotel. Taxis grapple for space; cars honk, brake and drive around
each other. It's like a group dance performance that everyone has learned by
themselves and not rehearsed together. Dawn grips my arm as the traffic noise
swells. My carry-on case tips on one wheel and Dawn's silk bundle falls on the
ground. I'm carrying and balancing too much. As I pick everything up, Dawn's
elbow recoils, but I gently grasp it and move her forwards. When we get to
the other side, I stop and look at the wrinkled arm I'm holding: the peaks and
troughs of a long life lived.

Just before we walk into the hotel foyer, I notice a large sculpture that
ends the ArtLink Freeway Project. Lucas worked on it as a consultant, helped
choose the artists, but turned down the invitation to create something himself. "You can't drop a few pieces of art beside a freeway," he kept muttering,
"and call it the largest sculpture park in the country just because the bloody
road is thirty-nine kilometers long."

The sculpture is a collection of colored spheres that look like they're
made from glass, piled up on top of each other so that you wonder how they
stay in place. "That sculpture reminds me of the frozen ice balls Maggie used
to make, remember?" I ask Dawn, and she nods slowly, staring straight ahead.

Maggie, who owned the dairy farm with her husband, Bill, would get
the farmwork done quickly so she could focus on creative projects, much to

his often loud frustration. We loved it when, every winter, Maggie would fill large balloons with water and colored food dye and place them around the property. She'd leave them overnight until the water froze. Wielding a bread knife in her hand, she would walk across the snow and cut the latex away to reveal colored ice spheres. They looked like giant marbles. Willow and Adara and Jesse and I would run into the snow, faces freezing, our breath a white fog swirling around our heads, as we pinballed from one giant colored sphere to the next, crunching the ice underfoot and clapping our mittened hands.

"We believed those frozen balls were something close to magic." I smile.

Dawn stops walking and turns paler than dry grass; walks slowly over to the sculpture. Places her hand against one of the large blue balls at her eye level.

"I'll go and check us in," I say and walk inside. The clerk at the desk waves me over. His balding head is sweaty, and the few remaining brown strands of hair stick to his skin like a wet feather. He wipes his forehead with a shirt cuff.

"Do you have a two-bedroom suite?"

The clerk *tap-taps* on his computer. "We have one left, televisions in each room."

I agree and he inserts cards into a machine. A pale light shines through the lobby skylight and I watch the dust specks sway in the air.

"That sculpture out there," I say to the clerk. "What's it called?"

"*A Fine Balance*," he says with a puffed-up chest, as if he's been waiting for someone to ask him. "We had a huge ceremony. The premier came and everything." The man points up to the wall where a framed picture of himself and a well-dressed woman hangs by itself.

I look out the window at Dawn's hand still planted on the blue ball. She stands and stares at the sculpture. The sun beats down. I need to get her inside, but before I can, Dawn's hand slides down the sphere, her head tilts back, legs buckle, arms become limp by her sides, and she falls like a stone to the ground. Weaving through people and knocking over suitcases, I run out to her. Even though I know it's not a heart attack or a stroke, that Dawn has sim-ply fainted in the heat, I rush to her side, the niece in me overriding the doctor.

The hotel clerk runs over to us and I ask him to help me move her into the shade of a tree. I put her legs up on a woman's suitcase to help blood get back from her legs to her thorax; tip her head back. As I kneel next to Dawn's hips, I watch her breathing and her face, so white it reminds me of bones. The thin skin beneath her eyes is slightly bruised, but not from the fall. The lines on her skin like tide marks on the sand. I imagine Dawn's body, hot and dehydrated in the sun, her brain wanting blood and oxygen, to feed itself; the trillions of simultaneous electrical impulses moving through her body like a lightning strike.

As I feel her pulse beneath my fingers—beat, beat pause; beat, beat pause—I reprimand myself for pulling Dawn out of the nursing home. Stu-pid, stupid. I should know better. Know the risks. Dawn is an elderly woman in a nursing home. Even though she mightn't have any conditions other than frailty, this trip is too much for her. Of course, it's too much for her.

Dawn opens her eyes wide. Dilated pupils dart from side to side. She tries to sit up, but I rest her back down. "It's okay, Dawn, you've just fainted. You'll be okay." I turn to the hotel clerk. "Could you please get her a drink of water?" Dawn's skin is still clammy, but the color returns to her face as blood rushes back. The brain no longer selfish. More and more people crowd around us. "Could you please move back? I'm a doctor; she'll be okay, but she needs some space."

"Should I call an ambulance?" the hotel clerk asks as he hands me the glass.

I sit Dawn up and rest her upper back and head against me, my arm an awning.

"No, no. She'll be okay." But I take my phone from my bag. Prepared to fix this and do the right thing. "Dawn, I'm going to call the nursing home. It's my fault. I shouldn't have stolen you away. I'll put you in an Uber and send you back."

Dawn tries to talk but can't. She puckers her lips a few times and finally manages a simple "Please." The phone rings next to my ear. I look into Dawn's eyes. Confusion replaced with desperation. People begin to walk away, the drama, and in turn their interest, over.

I watch Dawn and those around us, all bustling to get a room before they book out. I think about the heat that was beating down on her body; of Gabe's crayfish and the need for perfect conditions, of wave heights and water temps and salinity; I think about volcanoes erupting and ash in the sky; of snow in the Scottish Highlands; and the uneven heating of the Earth by change. The fact that weather is the great equalizer. That we are all just trying to find some sense of constancy, but that ultimately we live our lives at the mercy of other forces over which we have no control.

Even though the sisters have their differences, I know Dawn wants to come and make sure Mum is okay as much as I do. And although having a passenger slows me down, it also means company. But it's more than that. With color back in her face, Dawn looks at me with similar eyes she had the day we packed up her things from our place and moved her into the nursing home. A look that beseeches me not to send her away.

I hook my arm under Dawn's elbow and pull her up slowly, so we are standing side by side. We might not have control over everything, I think, but there are some moments in life that offer an opportunity for, maybe not redemption, but a glimmer of repair.

SIXTEEN

TWELVE YEARS AGO, DAWN KNOCKED ON OUR DOOR
WITH TWO SUITCASES AND A LIT CIGARETTE. WITHOUT SAYING A
word, she walked in and tossed her smoke into the sink, took a screaming
Audrey from my arms and headed out the back door. "Get me some olive oil,"
she shouted to me over the crying. "The good stuff." When I came back with
cold-pressed bottle in hand, Dawn had Audrey naked and squirming on a
blanket. It took only a second of my aunt massaging the writhing little body
before her for everything to go quiet. "You used to like the exact same thing,"
she said, smiling. From that day on, Aunt Dawn, who I hadn't seen or spoken
to for years, changed the course of my marriage and career.

Earlier that morning, before the sun rose, I'd sat at the dining table trying
to figure out a breast pump; screwed one end of a tube onto a nozzle but then
just held the other end in the air and let it dangle like a limp stem with no
flower. "Work, Layla?" Gabe was saying. "When are you returning to work?"
My maternity leave was fast running out and so was our money. We could
never survive on Gabe's income alone. Our life, our mortgage, our bills were
built around the surety of two wages. I looked at Gabe blankly. There were
no decent childcare centers in the area, and even if there were, I knew enough
about developing immune systems to know that I would spend the first year
being called into the center to pick up a sick child.

Things had felt simple before Audrey came along but now the pressure of
my full breasts and tired head had split the simplicity into pieces. And things
needed to be simpler for me to reply, so I just sat there with my mouth open
as if it were a valve that could release the pressure.

Gabe leaned both hands on the kitchen counter, stood and began to reorder the cupboards. He pulled cleaning products out from under the sink noisily and dropped them on the counter, then lifted a stack of dinner plates down from high above his head. "Did you know that cinnamon is a choking hazard? Seriously, a boy just died from eating it. Fine particles. Where is it anyway? Nothing's where it should be." Gabe's banging got louder and, with the noise, I heard his increasing sense of feeling out of control. Of being a little boy in a hotel room while his parents were out saving the world.

I plugged the loose pump tube into the motor and slowly covered my nipple with the translucent cup, which promised to be "gentler than a baby's mouth," then sat there, finger poised and unmoving over the start switch.

Gabe held up packets of herbs and spices. "These are just spilling out every time the cupboard's opened." He pulled out a stack of plastic sandwich bags and started tipping the contents of each spice bottle into them and slowly running his fingernail across the blue sealing lines. "We had a deal, Layla. Six months." A deal? Sounded like something that must have been discussed with a nod of the head and a firm handshake.

I had thought that within six months I would have figured all this out. Not just how to pump milk so that I could go back to work, but also motherhood, a new type of marriage. But Gabe's kindness had become a fair-weather friend.

"Did we?" I pushed the pump's start button and turned up the suction until my nipple looked like a cow's teat from Maggie and Bill's dairy farm and milk started to squirt into the bottle, but the pain was too much, so I turned the suction down and my nipple went limp.

"Otherwise, we're going to have to sell the house. Move further out," Gabe said.

Again, I opened my mouth, tried to move the muscles that used to be so sure of the answers. "I just need some more time," I said, finally. I tapped the suction dial.

"It's not as if you're on top of things around here," he said, sweeping his hand around. In the past, there's no way I would have let him say something like that to me without a rebuttal, but I didn't have any energy to argue. The banging began again as Gabe put cereal boxes, baked bean cans, muesli bars and flour into different cupboards. I looked down at my cracked and bleeding nipples, thought about the time it took to breastfeed and put Audrey to sleep during the day. I thought about how confident and competent I was in my career. How I longed to feel that way again. Taking a breath, I turned the pump back on and tried again, squinting my eyes from the pain, breathing shallow, and felt the pump and Gabe squeeze me and pull me and try to get things out of me until both I and my breast felt depleted.

The baby monitor crackled to life. Audrey wailed. She'd been up all night with her first temperature, and I hadn't slept. I looked down at my exposed chest, waited to see whether Gabe would go and pick her up. When he continued cleaning the kitchen, I stood up and went to her room, picked up the warm, pink body and hummed a song. When I came out, he'd left for work. I cradled Audrey in the nook of my neck. We stood there alone. Just mother and child. She continued screaming as the bright fluorescent kitchen lights in the dark house burned above us; brimstone, like motherhood since the beginning of time.

That was our house when Dawn knocked on the door out of the blue. For those first few years, it was her care that allowed me to return to work. That allowed me to balance being a mum and rebuilding a career I'd been working toward all my adult life. It wasn't just the gift of her time, but the gracious way she gave it, with no resentment or making me feel as if I owed her anything in return.

Her only request was that we house her hundreds of wild silk moths.

She used to make opera and period play costumes. It's something she'd done all her life. She didn't like buying the material from suppliers because most of them killed the moths before they reached cocoon stage. By using an Ahisma approach, which took longer but allowed her to harvest her own thread, Dawn let them complete their cycle. They didn't need much room.

As a child, I would watch her breaking long, continuous fibers into shorter staples, then spinning them together the way wool is spun into yarn. At a local haberdashery, she used a loom where she would weave the silk. Afterward, she would hand-embroider the creations. Parisian artist vests for *La Boheme*, Japanese kimonos for *Madame Butterfly*, black and gold Fosse dresses for *42nd Street*, and boned corsets for *Pride and Prejudice* would be wrapped in tissue paper, boxed and sent express post.

When she lived with us, she used the silk to create elaborate children's costumes. For Audrey's first-grade Easter-bonnet parade, Dawn dressed her in a green leotard, a moss-green velvet silk skirt with three-meter train, and a hat with fifty yellow and orange silk daffodils. When Jack graduated kindergarten, Dawn made him a tiny replica of Cary Grant's *North by Northwest* suit in gray silk.

Dawn also had a passion for oranges. She would walk half an hour each way with the kids in a pram to find the sweetest fruit. The ones that, when you cut them open, were so brilliantly colored you'd think you'd never known what the word "orange" meant. Every night, she would cook one over the gas-stove flame until the skin burned black, then she would sit out on the balcony under the stars and eat with a reverence I only asked her about once. "This moment, this moment is for me." Dawn loved my children the way she loved those oranges.

Everything at home ran smoothly until Jack started school and Audrey was ten. Even though Gabe worked long hours, he grew increasingly tired of having such a larger-than-life person around. When the seafood export industry took a turn for the worse because of local polluted water, he was at home more often and would not-so-gently hint that he'd like to take over the school run from Dawn.

I came home from work one day to find them fighting in the kitchen.

"I told them they were tempting fate calling the stall 'lucky jars,'" Dawn was yelling.

"You're lucky no one was killed," Gabe returned. Their argument was the last thing I needed after a long and stressful shift.

"What's going on?" I asked.

"Dawn drove the kids to the school fair and, instead of braking, put her foot down on the accelerator and plowed into one of the stalls."

I was silent a moment. Looked at Dawn. Shit, was all I could think. This was exactly the excuse Gabe was looking for. "Gabe, it's only one thing. God, I've done stupid things like that. So have you."

"The other day I came home and spent an hour looking for Jack. He was in the playhouse outside until dark. They'd been playing hide-and-seek. She forgot. When I asked Dawn where Jack was, she didn't know."

Another look at Dawn. "I think we just all need to calm down and—"

"We—you—need to face reality, Dawn. If you really love those kids, you'll…"

"I'll what, Gabe? I'll what? Think about what you want? Isn't that what we're really talking about here? The fact that you want me out?"

I knew Gabe's sarcastic comments wore her down, but she didn't have any other place to go. No money to rent somewhere, or travel interstate, let alone to another country, like she used to. I researched apartments I could afford, but that was unrealistic. Eventually, I found a lovely local retirement village, for a good price.

On the day we packed up her things, she went outside to say goodbye to her silk moths. "Just keep them until they finish their metamorphosis and die." When she opened the shed door where we'd kept the moths, the space was empty. She spun around and looked at me with an expression I'd never seen before, all bravado stripped away and replaced with a threadbare face. I shook my head. Held up my empty hands as if I was showing her that I didn't have them.

Gabe walked up, saw the look on Dawn's face and said, "What? They were going to die anyway."

"So will you," I said to him between gritted teeth. "But if I killed you now, it would be considered murder."

He looked at me with wide eyes and said, "They're…moths," in two exasperated puffs.

Dawn walked past him and then hissed in my ear, "The most generous place in that man's heart is reserved for strangers."

I still look back and wonder what I was supposed to do. I'd always wanted Gabe to be more involved and I was getting my wish. I, too, had become worried about Dawn's ability to care for the kids. Selfishly, I wanted her to stay as well. For a few years, I'd felt as if I had a mother figure: someone who I could rely on, someone who was there for me and the kids, and then it all disappeared, and I turned into looking after my aunt the way I'd always looked after everyone else. Dawn leaving settled me back into a familiar scarcity, that slinky, sinewy beast that stalks the moon shadows, and prodded a child's fear of not being enough to hold on to love.

"I'll bring you oranges," I'd promised. I think I did once or twice. Not good ones, and not often. Over the years, work got busy with staff shortages and an aging population, and the kids got older, with more after-school activities and a social life busier than mine or Gabe's.

I've played that time back to myself again and again, trying to figure out what I could have done differently, what I could have done to keep Dawn more involved with the kids and more a part of our lives. But I never came to any answers. All I know is that, since that day, when Dawn left, her hurt and my guilt have floated around our relationship like smoke from the cigarettes she gave up to live with us, not resting on anything in particular but covering everything.

SEVENTEEN

DAWN HAS ALREADY FALLEN ASLEEP IN THE HOTEL ROOM'S SECOND BEDROOM. I CHECK THE COLOR OF HER SKIN AND her breathing before quietly closing the door. Rays of soft light fill the lounge area. I slide open the balcony door in the hope of a cool breeze, but the air is still warm. We've been told we'll receive a text with new flight details when the haze clears enough for planes to fly.

Trying to find out more information, I turn on the news and watch the billowing smoke, the volcanic ash spreading across the screen. I peel the skin off my lip until a strand catches slightly and there is a sting and blood. Stand and pace the soft, short-piled carpet, open the wardrobe to take out a bathrobe, put the kettle on, and think about having a shower before changing my mind and sitting on the end of my bed. The kids will be home by now.

Their voices flutter through the phone like kites on a string. Jack's been crying. I can hear it in his voice. "Mum, can I sleep in your bed tonight? Dad said I'm a baby when I sleep with you. But your bed's empty; Mum, can I? Is that why Dad sleeps on the couch, Mum? Because sometimes I come in with you?"

Shit.

"Honey, of course—" But the phone muffles and is passed around.

"Dad won't let me go to Hannah's tomorrow after the art program. Says I need to rest for the flight on Saturday. Why do we have to go anyway? And why isn't Dad coming? You said we could stay home for Christmas this year. All my friends are."

Audrey is getting good at asking questions within statements. How much information do you give a smart kid? A child who will fill in the blanks with goodness knows what. Where is the line between too little and too much knowledge? It feels as if all the lines change every year the kids grow; as though I just get an idea of where the line is for age six, age eight and then, bang, they grow up and the line moves and I'm scrambling to catch up as the kids ask questions for which I don't have answers. Next year, next year we will stay home and Nanna can do as she pleases. Though I say that every year and yet here I am, rushing to Mum again.

"I know, Aud, I know. I used to feel the same way when I was your age. I get it, hon, I get it." And that's all I can do. Tell her I understand, all the while knowing that she thinks me clueless. "How about when we get back, I'll take you into town, to that puzzles and games shop you love and you can choose any Meccano set you like? You can choose one for Hannah too. We'll organize a sleepover, and you can give it to her?" If all else fails I stoop to bribery; it's like a safety net. She says yes, sounds happier, and I know that she will tell Hannah, that it will be a consolation prize to get her through. "I'll see you in a couple of days, okay?"

"Jack wants you to take a photo of your hotel room and send it to him," Audrey says; hangs up the phone quickly. I take photos around the room and send them to Gabe. He obviously didn't want to talk, or maybe he did and the kids hung up too quickly. I insert some emojis that I know the kids will like. It's become our thing. Like the egg heads used to be for breakfast. If all else fails, make them smile. A hedgehog, an angry monkey, two blue eggs in a nest and a snowman.

I step out and stand on the balcony, twelve floors above the concrete ground. The sun dips below the horizon. Venus appears in the sky, stars become visible. Pink and purple hues stretch like watercolor paint, but they are nothing like the sunsets down south. As it gets darker the streetlights hide the stars.

I walk back inside and turn on the bedside lamp. I flick through a copy of the *Australian* and scan pages, skipping the front few articles: "Worshipping at the Church of our Youth," "Smart Choice for Small Gardens," and "Christmas Festival of Lights." In the tearoom at work, you'll only ever find sections of the newspaper that can be removed from the rest of the news—sports, business, the lifestyle pull-out magazine. We have enough of the news arrive in the emergency department.

I turn to the arts section and a painting stops my breath. My face staring back at me. I look at myself. Sitting on the edge of Lucas's bed; white shirt and bare legs, knees knocked. A small purple bruise on my left shin. Looking up and away.

Our country's richest art prize, the Don Marigold, has been won by a first-time painter. Usually turning his hands to sculpture, it is the unpracticed talent the judges found extraordinary. "The oil strokes culminate in a lifelike image both of a person and an emotion," the judges said. "So real is the sentiment that you feel as if you could be in the room with her. Or at least be the one for whom she is waiting."

The life-size painting has a gilded frame. Standing next to it is Lucas. He's called it *In Waiting*. The paper softens between my warm fingers as I tear out the article and sit down, shaken.

Lucas's hurt, his anger in his warehouse, detachment on the phone. It wasn't just an ordinary exhibition. He wanted me to come and see the portrait. The painting I had not known he'd done. Let alone won a prize for. I try to catch my breath. I feel set up. I try to feel rage, to spear through the fog, but my anger disappears when I realize I prevented such a dramatic gesture. Though with this guilt also comes fear—fear of being found out. Why would this artist be painting me, a married woman? Surely Gabe will see this. He is far from being a newspaper reader, let alone a follower of the arts, but someone—someone—will tell him. And then what? How do I explain that away?

The exhibition starts in an hour. I text Lucas: "I just saw the article. Why didn't you tell me?" And then I wait; stand, walk into the bathroom, twist my hair into a knot on my head, pace and stand back on the balcony staring at my phone. I've never been able to handle in-between areas. Those moments when you must wait, wait to know if someone feels the same way, wait to know if someone is angry with you and why, wait to see if someone will forgive you. An enforced purgatory. My phone vibrates.

"Wanted you to see yourself as I see you. To understand that I see you in a way no one else does. But I feel like it doesn't matter anymore." And there it is. Two lines together. One after the other in blue circles on my phone. One that I want from him and the other I don't. I type one, two, three different replies. Delete them all. Begin again. I can smell the dry clay on his hands, cracked and brittle, flecks falling on my clavicle as he touches me.

People below me walk, dip and pivot around each other. We live a double life. The outer life, which is the one we observe at airports and across dinner tables, at school pickups and basketball practice. And then, the one beneath. The secret, passionate, inside-our-skin lives; the intense life that no one else sees.

Picking up the phone, I click on contacts. Look at the black text of his name. What was I going to say anyway? I call his number but it goes to voicemail and I almost hang up, before it beeps and I garble, "I'm sorry," and then, "I love you," and then again, "I'm sorry."

I hang up. Fuck, fuck, fuck. I want to untangle this mess. Indecision always has a price. I imagine the weight of Lucas's wrist across my hip bone at night.

I open *Lessons on the Human Body*, where I keep everything that stills my fast heart, and it falls open to reveal cuttings glued in from other books, handwritten notes scrawled in the margins, my father's map and list of sea creatures. I pull out the star map, the guide I turn to in times of turmoil, that has been unfolded and folded so many times that certain latitudes have rubbed off in the creases.

Walking out onto the balcony, I rotate the chart to get the correct orientation. The ascension and declination lines divide up the blue page like graph paper and I trace them with the tip of my forefinger. I'm just able to make out the southern end of the Milky Way's visible band, and some of my father's favorites: Ophiuchus, the healer, with a snake wrapped around his waist; Centaurus, Chamaeleon, and Orion. My soul catches sight of its faithful stars. After a while, clouds sweep across the sky and my celestial bodies are hidden from view.

EIGHTEEN

I CHANGE INTO A BLACK SHIRT DRESS BEFORE
CHECKING ON DAWN, WHO IS STILL FAST ASLEEP, BUT I LEAVE A NOTE
on her bedside table anyway and promise myself I won't be long.

The hotel bar is busy. Because of work, I can hardly ever drink, so I take
the opportunity to order something stronger than my usual glass of wine. A
vodka, lime and soda. There's a free table and two armchairs in the corner and
I make a beeline before it gets taken. As I slowly spin the glass, I think about
calling work. I'll have to call them eventually and ask whether they can re-
schedule my second chance. But what kind of anesthetist kills someone, asks
for their job back, and then, when the hospital gives them the opportunity,
says, "Oh sorry, actually, can we just make it some other time?"

Two glasses before me now empty, I raise my hand to order one more
and see a familiar shock of dark curly hair. Beer-on-tap drinker, football and
ice-hockey fan, Puccini opera lover, and devoted commentator on everything
you're putting into a recycling bin. My colleague Remi Brady, who has had
three miscarriages yet laughs it off because she can't stand people's pity; Remi,
whose husband ran off with a man and had three children through surrogacy
even though he always said he'd never consider that option with her; Remi,
who works at my hospital and is one of the top brain surgeons in the country.

"By the look on your face and the clear liquor in front of you, I would say
this is a pity party. Can I join?"

I smile, genuinely happy to see her. We haven't spoken since my mess-up
at work.

"You know the place has gone to the fucking dogs since you left," she says.

I've never known someone so smart to say the word "fuck" so much. I asked her about this at the work Christmas party, and she said that her potty mouth started off as a bit of fun, as a way to shock the teachers who gave her perfect marks, but then she started to enjoy the look on everyone's faces as well, and the rest is history. Became a habit. She talks while I sip my third drink.

"The roster we all knew by heart is changing constantly. Other surgeons have started to play Benjamin Bingo—anyone unlucky enough to get him three surgeries in a row has to shout Friday-night drinks." Poor Ben, I think. He's the rookie anesthetist, still a bit nervous. "And I've lost my lucky charm," Remi adds.

"Sorry?" Remi is not the kind of person to believe in luck. Hard work, yes. Political maneuvering, sure. But not luck.

"You idiot. Didn't you know that's what people called you? Evil Eye?" I knew people called me that but always thought they were referring to the look I gave surgeons when they asked me to speed up my procedures. "For years there was an Evil Eye from Turkey," Remi explains, "that surgeons used to touch for good luck in the change room, but it went missing and surgeries started to go bad until you came along and suddenly things were back on track. So, we call you Evil Eye."

"Huh, I honestly thought it was an insult." I laugh. Or maybe, I think, I've just got good at assuming the worst.

"It's the way you put patients at ease. The rapport you build with them. They go under relaxed. You're the best I've worked with."

"You know, I'm not sure if I even know what that means anymore. To be a good doctor."

"We surgeons, we have to have steady hands. But anesthetists, you guys need a steady gaze. You're the last face a patient sees. They need to trust you. Trust the process. You have it. In spades."

A relief rises through my body. People never tell you what they really think of you at work and, with everything that's happened, I'm embarrassed by how much I appreciate the praise.

"Surgeries always go better when you're there—fewer complications, steadier heart rates, better recovery. All the surgeons want to see your name on the whiteboard next to theirs."

"I bet they don't now. Especially Liam." I can still see his anger when the patient had a heart attack. The way he dropped his head, peeled off his gloves and pushed the door open before walking out.

"Well, no, probably not Liam. But he's a first-rate arsehole. Medicine is still a boys' club. And the more ego, the higher they rise—like hot air." Remi twists the beer glass in her hand. Downs what's left. "We all have something that haunts us. An incorrect cut. Miscalculations and misinterpretations. Misses. Do you really think you're the only one who's made a mistake? You aren't the first and you won't be the last. Hell, almost the exact same thing happened with Geoff the other day. Dialysis patient. And Geoff's the most experienced, and confident, anesthetist in the hospital. The only difference between you and him is that you take it on, and he chalks it up to statistics."

"My patient was wearing allergy bands, Remi. Not only that but the nurses in the room listed them. Went through the protocol."

"Ha." Remi throws her head back. Lifts her bum off the seat and leans forwards. "They're getting rid of those wristbands and the extra checks anyway, Layla. There's absolutely no evidence they prevent or even reduce mistakes. Look, you are great at what you do. Something like this happens to everyone sooner or later."

"My career is fucked, Remi. The hospital made it pretty clear that I was at fault."

"True. They have been more heavy-handed than usual. But it's got nothing to do with you. Most of their tenures are up next year. They're just making an example out of you. To make themselves appear competent." She leans forwards and whispers, "Even though they're not. No matter what the hospital says or does, you would be in demand anywhere. Not your fault if they're too far up their own arses to see that."

I nod. Four people at a table next to us get rowdy, laughing and slapping each other's backs. "Do you sometimes look around at a place like this and feel like an alien?" I ask.

"Do you feel jealous?" Remi asks. "That we see the blood and guts and death, and that other people get to pretend it doesn't exist?"

I think about this a moment. "No, I think I feel sorry for them," I say.

Remi nods with her whole body. "I know what will make you feel better." She gestures to the bartender and asks for eight tequila shots. "You have to put yourself into perspective." When the small glasses come over, Remi slides them into a group in the center of the table. "We're gonna play 'Never have I ever.' Do you know how to play? We're gonna take it in turns making statements of shocking things we might have done or seen others do at the hospital. If you haven't done it or seen it, you get a pass, but if you have, you take a shot. Clear?" I nod, slowly. "C'mon, when's the last time you were in a bar with a beautiful woman, no children, and a hotel room to fall into?"

I smile and agree, happy for the distraction.

"Okay," I say, "but you're going first."

"Never have I ever...prescribed a patient the wrong medication," she says. We both take a shot. The liquid burns my throat and I wish she'd also ordered some lemon and salt. "Okay, your turn."

"Never have I ever," I start, "given an incorrect diagnosis to a patient." We both take a shot. My stomach burns, but the weight of the embarrassment at work feels a little lighter.

"Never have I ever," she pauses, "operated on the wrong limb." We both cringe, and she takes a shot.

"Never have I ever," I look at Remi with a wry smile, "slept with another doctor." She quickly takes a shot, while I leave the glasses in front of me.

"What? Don't look at me like that," she says. "It wasn't at the hospital.

Well, it wasn't in the building anyway." She throws her head back and laughs.

"Who was he?" I feign shock.

"Who says it was a he?" Remi laughs and so do I, and she takes the two shots left in front of me and downs them herself. She becomes quiet, looks down at the empty shot glasses. Spins them in slow circles.

"You going home?" I ask.

"Yeah. Perth. Was supposed to leave a few days ago. But you know what it's like. Christmas is mayhem. Accidents everywhere. People lose their minds."

Yes, I think, they do. I'm going home to Mum.

"Last year," she continues, "I had to remove a patient's arm. Christmas Eve car accident. Today, he came back to the hospital in a lot of pain, said sometimes he felt like the space where his arm used to be was being invaded by insects. Other times he felt like his missing arm was extended straight out from his shoulder, so to avoid banging it when walking through doorways, he turned sideways. He was constantly haunted by something that was once there, and now...not. Phantom pain, poor bastard. I've never had a case that bad."

"A lot of people get hooked on painkillers because of ghost pain," I say. "What did you do?"

"That's just it. Not much I could do. He was already on a high dosage. I sent him to the pain clinic, knowing they wouldn't be able to do much either. And then I went and sat in the linen cupboard and sobbed so hard that the waffle blankets fell on my head. Thing is, I didn't really care that much about him. I mean, sure, I would have liked to have eased his pain, his discomfort, but there's nothing I could have done. I wasn't crying for him."

"For what then?" I ask.

"It was the way he spoke about that ghost arm of his. About how he felt it even when it wasn't there. That the limb still had a physical presence. I feel like that about the babies I lost. Phantom limbs, removed from my body but still there."

I reach over and put my hand on Remi's; alcohol is making her more open than usual. She's a mess like me. It's just that time of life. We're all breaking down.

"We all carry our wounds into the hospital," she says. "Sometimes they infringe upon our jobs and sometimes they don't. The doctors who seem to be holding it together are just good liars."

"Except Liam. He's just an arsehole," I say.

Remi laughs. "I actually won't have to deal with him anymore," she says. "I've been given a list at Belmont." The name makes me raise my eyebrows. It's impossible to get work at that private hospital. Still an old boys' club, where surgeons meet and develop relationships with anesthetists on the golf course, take them to football finals and sit in corporate boxes. "When you get back after Christmas, I'd like to book you for my list if you can do Thursdays?"

I'm flattered she asked but can't help but reply, "Not worried I'll kill your patients?"

"It's Belmont, Layla. Do you really think I'd put my job on the line? Do you really think I'd ask if I didn't have complete faith?"

"It's my faith I'm more worried about," I admit. "But thank you."

Remi stands up. "Have a think about it and let me know. I'm gonna get some sleep." She walks away, slow and unsteady.

I imagine Remi's patient. The space where his arm used to be and the swarm of pain that persists. I think about Remi's babies, of deceased fathers and unanswered questions. Of all the phantom limbs we carry around.

I knock on Dawn's bedroom door; start to feel as though I'm barely keeping the alcohol down. She's sitting up in bed reading a book. I point to the small leather box that she's placed on her bedside table. "Why did you give me that?"

"It belonged to our grandmother. Your great-grandmother. She was a late bloomer."

"Dawn. C'mon, why did you want me to give it to Mum?" I shut my eyes for a moment as the room spins.

"People were despairing. But she finally met someone. Lars Moller. A tiler. Settled down. After her wedding, no one saw her much. Too often she had bruises and a swollen lip the size of a forefinger. Every year, at Christmas, she made Julekage bread. Ha." Dawn laughs. "But one year—one year she changed the ingredients. I so often think about that woman, flour swirling, butter and milk bubbling on the stove, kneading her way to freedom."

"This story's going nowhere." My body slackens and I breathe out in resignation.

I turn to walk away before Dawn says quietly, "She laced the raisins, candied cherries and dried cranberries. She killed him. The leather box, it's a snuffbox. She kept the cyanide in it; it belonged to her."

I think about what Dawn said when she gave it to me at the nursing home, that Mum would know what it meant. Words that soak into your ears are whispered, not yelled. They are the ones that stay with you forever.

I lift my finger to my ear, trace the inner skin, unfold the curled-over top that always reminds me of Jack. "What are you saying, Dawn? That Mum had something to do with Dad's death?"

"You think you'll never be old like me. But you will," she says.

"Jesus, Dawn," I say. "You've always said you don't know anything about Dad's death, but this story, it means something. Otherwise, why tell it?"

"Because you asked. Your mother loved that snuffbox, and she gave it to me, even though I know she didn't want to. Kind of like the doll I made you that you gave to Adara."

My breath is hot and fast. "You move across Australia to be closer to me, but you might as well live on the other side of the world."

"And whose fault's that?" We look at each other. Dawn goes back to reading. "And close the door," she says.

NINETEEN

I'M UNSTEADY ON MY FEET FROM THE ALCOHOL AS I
STAND IN MY ROOM. THE CARRY-ON CASE OF CHRISTMAS PRESENTS IN
the corner calls to me and I crawl toward it on hands and knees. Glistening
green paper with red satin bows spills out after being held down and together
when zipped inside. I wanted to fit them all in a carry-on as they're worth a lot
of money and I don't trust check-in. The thought of giving the gifts to the kids
on Christmas morning steadies my body. It's always been like this. A drug of
sorts, giving my children what I never had. The need in me started on the day
of my neighbor Adara's tenth birthday.

I could see the large tent from my bedroom window, the sparkling montage
of the midday light. The sun made the structure's edges blur like a mirage, as
if we were in the middle of the desert. I was waiting for Mum to come home
with Adara's birthday present. I'd picked out a purple-and-white gingham
dress for her from the market last week and the lady had put it away especially
for me. Mum went to Dad's work to get some money and then the dress, and
I was to have a shower, eat breakfast and put on my outfit ready to go. Willow
was at a friend's so I was in the house alone.

When two o'clock came around and Mum wasn't yet home, I started to
get anxious. Paced the carpet; watched out the window as other children arrived next door with large colorful presents in their hands. Adara greeted
them, they hugged and ran to play. Eventually, Mum walked through the door

with glassy eyes.

"Is it in the car, Mum? Where is the dress? And did they wrap it, because I'm supposed to be there now?"

Mum didn't say anything at first. She opened jars in the kitchen, went into her bedroom and rummaged through her bedside drawer.

"Mum, what are you looking for?"

"Money, love," she said. "I'm looking for money." I didn't understand what was happening, so I just stood there, jittery and breathing fast, hating to be late. Finally, Mum stopped and looked at me. "Your Dad didn't give me any money. I tried to tell him it was for you and Adara but he didn't believe me." Then she whispered under her breath, "Bastard." As she did, I could smell a hint of alcohol on her breath.

"He did give you the money," I said. "I don't believe you." I knew what she'd spent it on, but I didn't have the words.

"You'll just have to give Adara something of yours. You have lots of things. There's wrapping paper in the wardrobe." And with that, Mum walked out the front door and away from the house and me. I went into my bedroom wringing my hands and changing my weight from left foot to right. I didn't understand why this happened. How it was that Dad worked as a doctor but we never had any money.

I searched for a present on my bookshelf. *Anne of Green Gables* looked relatively new, but there was a mark on the cover and, when I flipped through, there were well-read creased pages. None of the books looked like we'd just bought them. My wardrobe was sparse and the clothes too old and worn. The clothes Dawn made me Adara had seen. My breath caught in my chest as I paced faster and faster around the room. There must be something I can give, I thought, or maybe I could just say I was sick. But I'd only just seen Adara and helped put out the party food, and Dawn and Mum would be there and they would say I was coming soon.

My eyes rested on the rag doll on my bed. Dawn had made it for my birthday. She had soft legs and arms made from skin-colored material. Auburn hair like me in pigtails and a red duffel coat with wooden toggles and royal-blue silk velvet lining. I looked at the doll and she looked at me. Nobody else knew but I slept with her every night; held her tight, tighter when Mum and Dad fought. But I couldn't go to the party empty-handed. Adara hadn't yet seen the doll.

I picked up the small body as carefully as I would a newborn baby and laid her gently down on the wrapping paper. Smoothed out her hair and coat, slowly stroked the silk lining, once, twice, almost a third time before my shaking hands tucked her arms in by her sides. I tried not to cry as I covered her face and taped the paper down; I tried only to think about the party next door, about Adara my best friend, about the lovely food that we were never allowed in my house, which covered three whole trestle tables. The brightly colored fizzy drinks. The games and prizes that everyone would talk about at school on Monday. Adara was getting close to another girl in our class, Rebecca Woolson, and she was already at the party. Had been there awhile. If I didn't go, they might get closer. I might lose my best friend. And wasn't that worse than losing a rag doll?

Running over to the tent, I could hear laughter and smell Maggie's homemade sausage rolls. Adara moved away from Rebecca and gave me a big hug, took my gift, and walked over to the present table. Even though she hadn't opened any other presents, she began opening mine because best friends always get you the best presents. I looked around anxiously for Dawn, but I couldn't see her anywhere. As Adara slid the doll out from the wrapping, she gasped, "I love it. I love her," and gave me another hug. As she pulled away, I saw Dawn behind her looking at me. Looking at the doll. Adara sat the doll upright in the middle of that table, and before I could say anything to Dawn, Adara pulled me by the hand, through the marquee's flapping door and outside into the sun.

Every time the music stopped in Pass the Parcel, or it was someone else's turn to bob for apples, I glanced around for Dawn. As I moved between games, I saw her staring out to the sea, never focused on anything or anyone. She was always standing on the edge of the party. I hadn't seen Mum the whole time. Dad was at work, and Bill, Adara's dad, was working in their dairy. Maggie, her mum, was running the show. I'd never seen Maggie in a dress, but that day she wore floating sheer yellow crepe with large red poppies. I wore the turquoise dress Adara had given me for my birthday. It had buttons covered in fabric that had to be done up one by one. I had buttoned them myself from the front and then had to turn the dress back around to thread my arms through. Three buttons stayed undone up top, with no one at home to do them up.

We played musical statues to songs on a tape recorder. Turned up loud. When I twirled around, my skirt ballooned like an umbrella, but I always kept one toe close to the ground so that I could stop quickly and pose. Even Maggie was dancing in the sun, laughing so much that, when she stopped the music, she had to collect her breath before telling people they moved and were out. I was one of the last three left and knew that, if I could just stay in a bit longer, I'd win a set of pencils in a tin case. They shone in Maggie's basket as she started the next song.

When the music next stopped and I froze with my left leg in the air and two arms above my head, a bee stung my right foot and pain shot through my body. Falling to the ground, I started to whimper. The first person I looked for was Mum, but I couldn't see her anywhere. "Mum!" I called out, crying. "Mum!" Maggie rushed over to me and helped me up and into the tent to a chair. They put on ice and gave me medicine. All the time, the auburn-haired doll sitting in the middle of the present table watched me.

From that day on, it was as if the poison from the bee sting infiltrated all my cells, every atom in my body, with a shame and fear that could only be comforted by abundance. When I had my own children, I could never buy secondhand uniforms or clothes for them, never say no for too long to deeply desired birthday and Christmas presents, could never work so few hours that it meant I had to tighten the budget and buy discounted food, because if I ever did any of those things, I would be pained again by the sting of scarcity.

I crawl into bed in my black shirt dress. Leave the balcony door open. My phone vibrates with a message from Gabe. "Why are people at work telling me your picture's in the paper?"

Shit. I've been in denial. Of course he was going to see it eventually. There must be a plausible story I can spin. My mind flips through all the things I have done in the last twelve months to see if I can link them and Lucas painting me together. To think of some kind of excuse. After all, having your painting done by a man isn't proof of an affair. Is it? It might raise some questions, but I'm not naked or anything. The alcohol clouds my thinking.

I pick up the torn piece of newspaper from my bedside table and examine myself. I'm covered on top but not my legs. I'm on a bed. I list all the things I think Gabe will notice. But it's not my clothing, or lack thereof, that makes the painting so intimate. It's the look on my face. The simmering anticipation. I'm poised, ready to get up and press my body into Lucas and against a wall, ready to lightly bite his lip and run my tongue inside his cheek, ready to give him everything I used to give Gabe but haven't in a long time. I haven't posed for any art classes; I haven't had time to do anything except work and be at home with the kids. And be with Lucas. Even that was only a handful of times.

I lean over the side of the bed and pull *Lessons on the Human Body* out of my handbag, run my fingers over the blue leather and gold lettering, insert the newspaper clipping into the back pages, but then take it out because I realize it doesn't belong in this book of facts. I fold it up and put it in my handbag instead. Coming back to the book calms my heart. I've always found people hard to understand, to pin down, to predict. They are, as much as I am to myself, unknowable. But this book, and everything in it, is reliable. Here are the facts. The things that stay. Here, I can rest.

I underline sentences, turn down corners. There are pages where I've glued in photographs or pictures or postcards. At other times, I have crossed out sentences and written my own lines in the margin. My own arguments, my own questions, observations.

I flip to page sixty-three, looking for something to read, to distract myself. Help me get to sleep. I know every fact in this book. Even before I became a doctor, I memorized many of the sentences. In some ways they are as simple as they are remarkable. And they never change.

There are anywhere between 60,000 and 100,000 miles of blood vessels in the human body, and if they were taken out and laid end-to-end, they would be long enough to travel around the world more than three times.

I flip a few more pages before my eyes rest on,

Pound for pound, your bones are stronger than steel. A block of bone the size of a matchbox can support up to 18,000 pounds of weight.

And then, one of my favorites,

The word "muscle" comes from the Latin term meaning "little mouse," which is what Ancient Romans thought flexed bicep muscles resembled.

Another vibration. "I've seen the picture. Who are you?"

I pick up my phone to message Gabe back but don't know what to say. I can't say I haven't seen the painting, because if someone has told him, someone would obviously have told me by now too. I don't have a viable story.

I think about Lucas and him keeping the painting a surprise, about his frustration that I wouldn't be at the art show and the big reveal. And I'm struck with a simple realization. That Gabe seeing my picture in the paper will probably tear up my family and make me wholly available to someone. And this is exactly what Lucas wanted.

The darkness comes rattling; traffic outside thrums. I turn on the TV, but none of the channels are working. I flick and flick, punching the button on the remote, tempted to throw the control at the screen in the hope that the collision will make a channel appear. Mum. Dad. Dawn. Gabe. Lucas. Audrey. Jack. As I sink into a drunken sleep in the flickering light of the television static, the white noise sounds like something close enough to company.

TWENTY

THE BENCH SEATS AT HOBART AIRPORT ARE MADE FROM TREE TRUNKS. LONG PINES SAWN IN HALF, KNOTS AND CREVICES exposed, sanded and lacquered. The dark edges of heartwood, the central, supporting pillar of the tree, are the least shiny. I've always marveled at that part of a tree. The fact that, although it's dead, it will not decay while the outer layers are intact. A composite of hollow, needle-like cellulose fibers, bound together by lignin. It is, like our bones, as strong as steel.

After our conversation last night, there has been little talk between Dawn and me today. We are both as stubborn as each other and I can almost hear the grinding of each of our teeth, feel the clench of her jaw as much as my own. Maybe this is what long-term relationships are like, I think. Family. The history you've experienced together building wall upon wall until just the simple act of civil conversation requires superhuman strength.

Dawn sits down on a tree trunk, probably tired from the flight, and I put my luggage and the rainbow rucksack on the ground. "I'd like a chocolate milk," she says. As I walk to the vending machine, I take stock of the car-rental options. Driving is going to be much faster than the bus, and a taxi will cost an arm and a leg, maybe literally (local cabbies aren't ones to drive slow). A young man and an older man embrace with tears in their eyes. There isn't the same fanfare as at larger airports, with their cavernous departure and arrival terminals, red queue ropes and automatic entry and exit doors. Here, there seems little demarcation between the people leaving and the people being left behind.

I return to Dawn with a bottle of water and she eyes me. "Please," I try, "it's better for you and we have a long drive." I try to soften my voice. She rolls her eyes and I unscrew the lid for her before walking toward the car-rental booth with no line. The gray-haired woman looks between me and Dawn and starts clicking on her keyboard.

"The only hires we have left are a Toyota Commuter twelve-seater bus or a KTM sports bike. Sorry, love, this time of year everything goes fast," she says while trying to smile. "Are you from down here?"

"Port Jericho. It's where I grew up. Mum's still there and this is her sister." I gesture to Dawn, who hasn't touched her bottle of water.

The woman nods, taps the air with her finger. "Hang on a second," she says and walks outside. Fifteen minutes later, she hands me a set of keys. "Sidelined as it needs heating installed but it's better than nothing. I've put some supplies in the back for you ladies."

We walk out to see a 1970s Leyland Mini in aquamarine blue sitting on the curb. A Thermos and two tartan wool blankets in the back seat. The woman walks up behind us. "Tea's made with just the right amount of sugar to make sure it isn't as bitter as the west-coast wind."

I'm used to flying in with the kids Christmas Eve and picking up a pre-booked small car without really talking to anyone. I look at the woman and smile. "Thank you" is all I can think of saying.

As she walks away and I ease Dawn into the passenger side, my phone rings.

"Maggie, I'm nearly there," I say to Mum's neighbor, the landline number taking me back to my childhood.

"Hiya, Layla, it's Bill," a scratchy voice says. Maggie's husband. "It's your mum. There's been crying coming from the house and, well, I don't think you need me to tell you—"

"Bill, I've been talking to Maggie. I know. I'm nearly there. Maggie said she'd stay with her. I'm at Hobart Airport."

"Oh, Maggie had to go to town. I have to get the cows sorted, otherwise

I would have taken her. Want to do the right thing, even after everything." Maggie and Bill split up about thirteen years ago; she lives on the farm and Bill lives on his boathouse down at the docks; he still goes up to the property to run the dairy farm every day. I think about Mum, raging around the house.

"Any way you could go and stay with her until I get there?" A cough, then a mumble and grumble I can't make out. I can almost hear him shuffling uncomfortably in his work boots. "Well, I asked Maggie, Bill, but she left." There is annoyance in my voice.

"Layla, Maggie's not well. Breast cancer."

"Shit. God." I bite my lip. "I'm sorry." I realize now what Maggie meant when she said she had to go into town. It was for treatment. "Do you need a recommendation for—"

"No, no. She's fine. We don't need your help."

"I was just meaning that, I—"

"I know what you meant. Really, it's fine. Jesse's been a great help. In fact, you should know, every time he's come home, he's helped your mum. Checked in on her, fixed things around the house. Brought her food. He's been down here, permanent, since January. Living in the old family home. After his divorce and everything."

Jesse. Divorce. They are words I roll around in my mind; sounds that catch my breath. Jesse, who I gave my first kiss to. And then after that, the first of everything. Every woman has an unresolved man in their past. Jesse is mine.

"You know you should have said goodbye to him that night. Broke his heart, you did."

Right now, I just need to get to Mum. "Well, Dawn and I, we're not too far away. We—"

"Dawn?" Bill's voice bristles. A reaction I don't understand. There is something in his tone that surprises me. "Haven't seen her since…I'll pop over to your mum's for a second but then I'm driving to see Mags. I would have driven her to the hospital myself rather than make her catch the bus but I had to take care of them damn cows first. It's a crying shame about your mum, Layla. I mean that. She's a good woman."

I hang up.

The bags just fit across the back seat and I climb into the small car.

"Who was that?" Dawn asks.

I slam the creaking driver-side door closed. "It was Bill, said Mum's been crying. Must be loud for him to hear. God, Dawn, it's bad, it's really bad this time." I start the engine and try to figure out the fastest way there.

"Bill?" Dawn looks out the window. A Skytrader plane ahead speeds along the runway and takes off into the clouds. Because the airport is so far south, they operate flights to Antarctica. I think of the ice-covered landmass not far below and feel, even from within the car, its katabatic winds, which carry upon them a chill like ghosts from the past.

TWENTY-ONE

THE LAST TIME I SAW BILL AND ADARA WAS THE DAY I LEFT HOME. THEY HELPED ME LOAD MY SUITCASE INTO THE FRONT seat of their truck and drove me to the airport. "Better you get wet in the back than all your stuff," he'd said. "You should say goodbye to your mum, Layla. Least you could do."

Least I could do? I thought. What would be the least I could do? That would be nothing, Bill, nothing, I felt like saying but didn't, because saying "nothing" to as many people as possible was exactly what was going to get me outta there.

"Mum's fine," I said as I climbed up onto the truck's tray and then extended a hand to Adara, which she monkey-gripped before almost falling flat on her face. We sat on canvas blankets they usually put on calves in winter to stop them getting hypothermia, our backs against the cabin, our legs stretched out straight. As we pulled away and dust blew up from the tires and into our faces, I promised myself that I would create a new life. There was no way I could say goodbye to Mum. I feared that seeing her would conjure too much guilt and responsibility to care for her undressed wounds. A new life meant taking a step toward the woman I wanted to be but did not have the words yet to describe; someone safe behind the walls of her own building.

Just as we were driving out the gate, a police car pulled up next to us. Michael Clifton, a young man who'd been a few years ahead of me at school, stepped out and jostled his pants as he pulled them up by his shiny leather belt. He straightened his hat before walking toward Bill.

"It's Nora, Bill. She's in the back seat. We found her drunk, throwing glass bottles at Oscar's gravestone. Cut herself up a bit, too." More undressed wounds. As I sighed and slunk down low in the back of the truck's tray, I thought, This is your chance, Layla. You've got a scholarship to study medicine on the mainland; they're paying your board. You'll get a job. You can't stay here; you'll get trapped—you are trapped.

"Okay, Michael, okay," Bill said. "Wouldn't mind taking her back to the station for a tick, would you? Give her a cup of tea and I'll come and get her when I've dropped Layla off at the airport? If you can get her seen to, her cuts and stuff, I'll take care of the rest." Michael looked at Adara and me as if he'd just noticed us.

"Yeah, sure," Michael said and tipped his hat. "Good luck." As he drove away, I saw Mum's makeup-smeared face in the dusk light.

Bill put the truck back into gear, drove down our hill and out of town. It was my first experience as a free woman, rather than a beholden daughter, and it felt dangerous and exhilarating.

That night, I'd known if I'd climbed down from the back of the truck and returned to my mother and our home on the hill, I would have never left. That I would have been stuck with Mum. I used to think my parents fighting was bad, but with Dad's death, things got worse. What became the hardest were the moments when Mum would be sober for a few days and seem normal. Those moments when I thought things had changed. It was the hope that hurt the most, the happy nights, the quiet nights, when I let myself believe that Mum was better, that the parent I longed for and needed was really going to materialize and the beast that had a hold of her had let go. That she might take me walking along the sand dunes again. But then down and up we'd go again, left and right. It happened again and again. I was sixteen, seventeen, eighteen. Until I realized it was not Mum who was hurting me, it was the times I let myself hope she had changed. I began to accept reality. That all there is, is the parent I have and the parent they will never be. One as heavy as lead and the other as thin as air.

A further weight was the constant belief that Mum had had something to do with Dad's death. That at the very least she'd prevented him from joining the rescue boat and forced him to go out on our small boat alone. But I also always feared that she'd played a greater hand in what happened.

As we pulled onto the freeway and left the slope of sand dunes edged with sea, I turned to Adara, wanting to say something but not sure what. Words were carved in my mind and discarded. Like a broken mosaic. I had parts, shards, but they didn't make up a picture, a sentence. "Can you say goodbye to Jesse for me?"

"What?" Adara said, pulling her face away from me. "You didn't see him?"

I looked at her, with a hard stare, with the look of someone she had known for as long as we could both remember. "I couldn't," I said. "I…I'll call him when I reach the mainland."

Side-by-side houses started spreading further apart until they dotted the land and then finally there were none. As we drove, the land stretched; broad, flat fields of button grass ran to the horizon. Fields clothed in clawberry with its long trailing stems studded with yellow and purple blossoms.

The sky became dark. I'd chosen a late-night flight on purpose. Fewer people around and it always felt like Dad was close. A coin of light appeared. I held my hand up just as he had taught me and blotted out the moon with the tip of my index finger. A fog moon. Dad used to call it an Ancestor Moon.

I asked Dad once how people travel into space. "Launching requires a huge amount of burning propellants to lift off the ground. Let me show you." He'd taken a teabag and emptied out its contents, rolled the muslin fabric into a cylinder and sat it upright on a porcelain plate. Lighting a match, he'd set the base on fire and the teabag floated up into the air.

Adara rested her head on my shoulder and fell asleep, the moon on her like skin. Thin lines across her arm glowed like Dawn's silkworms. I'd had a feeling that she'd begun cutting herself but hadn't seen the scars up close. I gently traced one of the outlines with my finger. As I put my arm down and looked up, stars appeared. Spheres of gas held together by their own gravity.

In that liminal hour, I learned the importance of denial as an act of survival. Driving away from everything, my broken mother and my deceased father, my runaway sister, and my first love, all I wanted to do was take that pain away. I had always wanted to be a doctor, but when I got a taste of grief, I was set firmly on a path to anesthesia. To erase consciousness, deny memory. I wanted to blanket everyone's pain as if we were actors in *Antony and Cleopatra*, drinking mandragora so that we might "sleep out this great gap of time."

On either side of the car, bonfires burned. Farms using the last days of May to rid their properties of unwanted tree trunks and branches. Burning boughs releasing smoke and cinders into the sky. It seemed as if there were thousands of them, like mini volcanoes, erupting in the wind. Some close to the road warmed our way; others were guiding lights away from Port Jericho. Delicate pieces of glowing ash floated above and around me. And as my eyes blurred and my hometown became smaller and smaller, I imagined myself leaving behind what was heavy and using the fire inside to lift and float away.

TWENTY-TWO

WE FOLLOW THE ROUTE THE HYDRO-ELECTRIC
COMMISSION FORGED INTO THE HIGHLANDS TO BUILD THEIR DAMS
and harness the waters of the Derwent. Our car shudders; I change down
a gear to ease its way into the steep curves leading toward Tarraleah. Even
though we've been driving for two hours, the vinyl seats are still cold; my
hands ache from gripping the steering wheel, willing the car to get us there
faster.

Any signs of civilization are long gone. Stretched moors of bronze-green
button grass support rocks, pushed into random heaps, and tall cliffs fall into
deep, steep-sided valleys. The mountains are covered with so many trees they
look blanketed in moss; bright-green ferns rise from the sides of the road before we are swaddled by forest.

This island, the last place to unzip itself from Antarctica, should be a
hulking, desolate rock. If it wasn't for the warm eastern oceanic current that
cultivates life, it would be stripped of everything. The way currents are Earth's
arteries and veins. Sometimes I think, though, that a land aches to be something—an arid desert, a teeming rainforest, a lifeless stone—and that any attempt to dress it up as something else provokes a volatile response. As a child,
I would lie in bed listening to the wind sharpen itself on the side of the house,
I would think about our life of sea and rock and sky; about the ancient rocks,
wrought in volcanic fire and scraped clean by ice; about the clamoring west-
erlies, constant falling tree limbs, cold snaps in summer, and coast that turns
fishermen into wet bones, and I would imagine the landmass shaking itself of
life because all it really wants to be is a salt-washed rock.

The slack pale-brown seatbelts, which we can't adjust, billow across our bodies, and every time Dawn rolls down the window, she has to hold the glass in place when she winds it back up.

Visitors to the west coast always underestimate the time it will take to get anywhere; they think of distance as a straight line between two points. But here the roads wind around mountains and rivers and are often slippery. It takes two, three times the amount of time they think it will take to get anywhere.

I know we're halfway when we reach Lake St Clair; its surface is so still it looks like it might sound if struck. Somebody has planted flowers in a patch near the pumphouse, the same ones Mum and I would plant in our garden. Daffodils and snowdrops, flowers that wallabies and possums won't touch. The foreign plants clash with the nearby native shrubs.

Dawn has been quiet the whole way. Has only exchanged the bare necessities. I open the window to taste the Antarctic air, to have the wind in my lungs and the wind in the air all at once merge so that there is no room to breathe. The sensation makes me smile. Think of the saying "to throw caution to the wind." I think of Lucas and his painting.

"I had a bit to drink last night." My words cleave the silence.

"No kidding," Dawn says, not looking at me. Avoiding eye contact just as she did on the plane.

"I'm sorry about what I said, about you feeling far away." I grip the steering wheel. Dawn remains silent.

The road opens into wild country, running through moonscape mounds and past deep eroded gullies. On this part of the highway, you can drive for kilometers without seeing life. It's tombstone country. Where patches of ground are covered with the skeletal remains of small trees that grew for thousands of years before being engulfed and choked to death by toxic smelter fumes. Anything living on this land is a triumph of adaptation.

"Pull over." Dawn snaps up. "I need to pee." Knowing there's no arguing or even persuading her to wait until there is something like a public toilet, I pull over by the side of the road. The only tree I can see is a single myrtle, a solitary figure on the land. I point out a large boulder that Dawn can squat behind. I forever have to bite my tongue when I want to ask if she needs help, duty of care always on my mind. It's hard to shake professional care, let alone familial love. I get out as well to stretch my legs and walk to the other side of the road; twigs pop underfoot like pine wood on an open fire. Wild bracken spreads across the land.

Bleak and motionless. Brooding stillness. It's exactly what I wanted to escape when I was young. A decomposing kangaroo, hit by a car, lies by the side of the road, belly ripped wide open, guts all emptied out. Maggots eat its flesh and flies dip their feet. Across the land, beyond the trees in front of me, I know there is a shimmering watering hole.

When we were kids, Mum made a roast every Sunday for lunch. She would call us in from wherever we were—Dad in his study, Willow and I outside—to sit down as a family for three hours and spend, what Mum called, "quality time together." But quality time means different things to different people. Mum missed our home on the mainland. She never really got over leaving it and the friends she'd made. Tried to transfer as many of the traditions as possible. In our old place, we'd had kitchen windows that opened to a walled garden; the aroma of spiraling jasmine would waft into the house as Mum cooked. After the chicken was baked and eaten, she would search for the wishbone, run it under warm water, and sit it on the windowsill to dry. The next day, we would take it in turns to link our pinky into one end, with Mum's in the other, and we would break it in two. Whoever got the longer half got to make a wish.

But our new house didn't have a neat garden, or predictable weather. Even so, Mum refused to change the tradition. She would spend all morning in the kitchen cooking, windows open to the elements. Over the years, the cabinetry got so damaged from wind and rain and the salt-filled air that she had to replace it with a hotchpotch of materials. Dad refused to install a new cabinet if it was just going to get wrecked.

A slatted pine cupboard was her pantry, a white desk her kitchen island. A waist-high mint-green cupboard, a salmon-pink one and then a baby-blue one. The furniture wasn't designed for a kitchen; it absorbed water and food, and Mum was constantly wiping the surfaces so they didn't stain.

Mum would hand out plates like playing cards. We took them, heaping on food before they even touched the tablecloth. "Don't start yet, don't start yet," she'd say. "There's still sauce to come." Willow was always the one to wait. Plate flat on the table. Hands gripping both sides. Looking up at Mum expectantly.

After Willow left, Mum continued the tradition. Her way to keep Willow's presence in the house even though she wasn't there. A way to fill the space and ache with something. Anything. Just like her idea of going to university.

"I'm thinking about going back to study teaching," she said to Dad and me one Sunday. "To be a teacher. Goodness knows, they're desperate for them on the island."

"Ah, love. Do you think that's a good idea?" Dad said slowly.

"Well, you know I have everything sorted here now in the house, and Layla can—"

"But, Nora. You know how you get when you have too much on. It's not good for you. Not good for the kids—or at least not for Layla now. Remember that time you tried to go back to work after Willow was born?"

Mum. Head down. Stirring and stirring. Hair swishing over her shoulders and elbows pushing up and down like an oil rig.

"You know, this gravy used to be Willow's favorite," Mum said as she whisked the sauce in the pan, but then whispered, "Shit, it's going lumpy." She took a sieve out of the drawer and poured the gravy into the wire mesh over a bowl. Stirring the thick mixture with a soup spoon, she tried to get as much smooth liquid into the bowl as possible, but by the end of it, there wasn't enough even for one person. She tried again, stirring faster and slapping the spoon onto the lumps, but couldn't make it work, so she picked up the sauce-pan and the sieve full of gravy and threw them against the wall. Brown liquid dripped down the plaster. Mum stood there looking at it, her chest lifting up and down. I watched her for a moment as tears welled in her eyes and then looked at Dad. He sent me out of the room and told Mum that we'd give her some space and be back in an hour or two.

We jumped into the four-wheel drive and headed out to the falls, past the sign that said,

Why are you littering? a) I am a jerk, b) I don't care about natural areas, c) Mummy still cleans up after me, or d) all of the above.

There was a steep rocky path down to the falls and a slippery step made me slide and grip onto Dad's arm. I knew we were close when I could smell the sweet aroma of the honey tree; snaking down toward the water, we could hear the crash and spray before we saw the falls.

The stony banks of the river sat under spreading blackwoods and myrtles, and kids had thrown their brightly colored towels on the rocks before kicking off their flip-flops further down and jumping in. Dad always used to say that it was "the rocks not the crocs" you had to look out for down south.

Girls laughed and swung on a rope, knotted all the way up for foot-holds, screaming as they flapped their arms and fell into the water with a splash. Their bodies wet and glistening in the sun as they climbed up the bank laughing and shiny. Others were fishing downstream with buckets of worms, though we'd never seen anyone catch anything here. Sadie Armstrong, a girl from school, was chasing a monitor lizard and it took me a while to realize there were no boys around; "Down at the footy," Dad said when I asked. The football field wasn't made from soft, green, cut grass; it wasn't even made from dirt. Our field was made from gravel. There were always bloodied bodies, skin torn to shreds, wounds so deep they needed to be stitched. Every week they ended up in Dad's surgery after the game. It would be a busy night for him.

Dad got out his camera and told me to have a swing, so I clambered up the rocks and one of the girls passed me the rope. I adjusted my navy bathers that tied around my neck. And he counted me down. "Five, four, three, two, one, swing!" he yelled, and as I jumped, I could see Dad pushing the shutter on the camera and winding the film round so he could quickly take another picture before I dropped into the deep, cool water and disappeared.

I climbed up the rocks for another go, thinking about Mum and Willow and the gravy and the lumps. But then I saw Dad smile with the camera poised again. There was warm sun and a cool breeze, not hot or cold but something in the middle, when you're surrounded by air cooler than your body temperature by just the right amount. It felt something close to freedom.

I jumped again as Dad's camera clicked and the girls downstream yelled out to everyone that they'd caught something, they'd actually caught something, and this time I didn't let go, I didn't want it to end, so I kept swinging and spinning, twirling while Dad laughed and the girls bellowed and clapped as their fish sparkled in the sun.

When I walk back to the car, Dawn is leaning against it with her eyes closed.

"How long has it been since you've seen Mum?" I ask.

"Ah well, seen's a funny word in this age of technology. You mean in the flesh?"

I sigh. Feel like I'm fishing around for a small piece of shell in a bowl full of cracked eggs. I look at her and she says, "After you moved away, I came back for a little while, to check on Nora, and Maggie and Adara. But then left again and I haven't seen her since."

Dawn points across the land at a mountain in the distance. "Maggie and

I went hiking that mountain once. We came across a young girl who'd become separated from her friends, wasn't breathing very well. So we carried her out. She coughed up blood. We realized she'd swallowed a leech and it had latched on to her throat and was feeding on her; creature swelled up in there so that she couldn't breathe. Maggie went on to the hospital with her and I went home. That sums it all up, really. Always separated by bloodsuckers."

I'm unsure what she means and am just about to ask as a sudden gust of wind sweeps around our pink faces. The breeze, though wild, is a familiar breath. I help Dawn back into the car, keen to continue the drive to Port Jericho. I try to call Mum again, then Maggie. No one answers. I end up messaging Maggie that we are just over three hours away.

"I hope she's getting good enough care down here," I say.

"Maggie? I think there's lots of people who care about her."

"No, I mean hospital care."

"What—what are you talking about?"

"I thought you knew? Cancer. Breast cancer."

Dawn puts a palm on her chest. Plays with her decolletage. Looks out the window.

The interior of the car cools even more with the lowering sun. I slow down so I can reach back and grasp the tartan wool blankets, give one to Dawn and then drape the other over my lap. Unscrew the lid of the Thermos while holding it between my legs and pour Dawn a cup of sweet hot tea.

Even up until the end of spring, there is snow on the mountains. I grew up constantly cold in my bones. Pressing myself as close as possible to open fires; laughing at tourists who came here in their little cotton shorts, as if I was somehow in cahoots with the weather and we shared a wink. You can go to bed one night with stars shining in a clear sky and wake up the next morning with six inches of snow.

The car's engine and the changing gears are the only sound. I bite my lower lip. Not sure; air in my lungs heavy with whether to say something. As if trying to figure out how to negotiate my terms of surrender.

"Dawn, I…I have a lot to thank you for," I say, finally. "Looking after the kids and helping round the house." She is silent. "I didn't know what else to do. Dawn. I didn't know."

There is another silence. Longer this time.

"You're just saying that because you're pissed with Gabe. That man has always needed to chase a carrot on a stick. Only thing that's changed is that you're not the carrot," she says. I think about this. It could be true. I'm still seething from Gabe and my conversation at the airport. And with that comes resentment about how he treated Dawn. Though I'm not sure I've been much better. It's also true that I often watch the kids and think about all that Dawn has missed. All that she's not a part of. As if reading my mind, she says, "I've always lived life in the wings." I have an image now of Dawn standing in the dark, sewing silk velvets for other people, partly covered by maroon curtains, while Mum, Willow and I are on stage living our lives; then another image of Dawn walking around behind the stage and standing in the opposite wing, looking on as Gabe, Audrey, Jack and I live our lives. But it's worse than that. Because there were times when Dawn was able to insert herself into the tableau, until one of us would suddenly push her back off the stage. Mum, me. Where she would watch and wait.

"I become more and more invisible every day," she says quietly. "What I should have done is marry a rich old man and put him in wet pajamas." I look at her. "What?" she asks, pretending insult. "He dies of pneumonia, the clothes dry, there's no trace. Then maybe I could have lived the life I wanted." Dawn's is a life replete as it is spare. And in some ways, hers is the same feeling my mother could not shake. The unyielding knowledge that your life is not what you wanted. And maybe never would be.

"I'm sorry," I say, because I don't know what else to say. How does one make up for things in life? Right the wrongs?

"Sorry for using me when you needed and then turfing me out? Or, after

129

that, for pretty much cutting me out of the kids' lives?"

I look out the side window briefly, not wanting her to see my grimace; then eyes back on the road. "Both," I say. "Or you can take your pick." A wave of unease rolls through the car.

"The only person who has been a constant is Willow."

"Wait, what? I didn't know you both stayed in contact."

Dawn laughs. "You never asked. Never had enough time or weren't interested enough to be…well…interested. I flew over. Tracked her down. Helped set her up in Sri Lanka. She found her way into a group of protestors who gave her a purpose. Sometimes she'd help me with my costumes. Though she spent more time pricking her finger than getting the stitches right."

I'm not sure whether I don't know this because I never asked or whether Dawn has kept it from me, like an eye for an eye.

Blue gums tower over us on either side of the road like two giant waves; the black tarmac ahead, a path parting the sea. As we turn a steep corner, I see a hay baler, pale red and well used, in front of us, driving as slow as I would walk. Double lines in the middle of the road tell me I can't overtake. I peer round the crawling heap of metal but a car is coming the other way. Bits and pieces of hay fly through the air. Finally, there is a broken line and I accelerate to pull in front and speed away.

As we get closer to home, houses and barns spot the hills. We pass a couple with Hills Hoist clotheslines in their backyards. They probably don't work anymore; most of them just stand there, broken. On a land that gets over three meters of rainfall a year, that sends its salt sea spray far inland, it's almost impossible to dry clothes outside.

We had a Hills Hoist in our yard growing up. Mum washed the clothes and hung them out to dry, but nothing ever dried properly. Everything glazed with damp and salt. Grains would scratch your skin. I would say, "Nothing escapes the damp, Mum." And she would reply, "Your father does. Your father escapes the damp."

I only witnessed Dawn interacting with Dad once. Soon after Willow left home. Dawn was sitting next to Mum. Mum was crying and knitting me a bright-yellow scarf. Every now and then Mum stopped and blew her nose. She only ever blew her nose when she cried. She didn't bother when she had a cold. She just sniffed and went about her business. But when she was upset, she was loud and wet.

Dad struggled in with a large box on a trolley and put it in the middle of the living room. Mum wrapped the maroon velvet dressing gown Dawn had made her around her body, then unwrapped it and pulled it around even tighter, crossed her arms and stood in the corner. Dad stretched out his arms as if he was showing them how big a fish he'd caught.

"Where have you been?" Mum asked. Dad gestured at the box as if it answered all her questions. All the doubts she'd ever had. "The shops closed five hours ago."

"It's a dryer, so you don't have to hang the washing outside anymore." Sometimes when Dad and I went to the observatory, we would see Mum, the clothesline in plain sight, straining against the wind to keep the clothes pinned.

"Wow, Mum, open it, open it! Not even Stacey at school has a dryer." I remember being so excited I ran to open it myself.

"It's not going to work," Mum said.

"Of course it will. Just pull it out of the box. We'll plug it in."

"I don't want it." Mum unwrapped her dressing gown and wrapped it around herself again.

"Don't you see? It solves so much," Dad said. "You're always saying you're tired because of all the washing, trying to keep everything dry. I realized today, probably why you… And that this gift, well, you'd have more time to rest. More time to yourself."

Mum turned around, walked into their bedroom, and quietly closed the door. I began frantically unwrapping the box, gesturing wildly at the pictures in the brochure and shouting about the dryer's size. But then at the height of my excitement, Dawn came over and, without saying a word, moved my hands away. I just stood, looking at the half-unwrapped box, then at the half-knitted scarf on the couch's armrest. The yellow was too bright and the wool was too thin. I went over and pulled and pulled on the knitting until the loops began to unravel and fall, open, to the floor.

Dad sent me to my room. I couldn't hear what he and Dawn were saying. Her voice was like our neighbor Bill's hammer when he was on our roof fixing tiles.

When people are pretending to sleep, you can hear them swallow. Dawn's head might be resting against the glass and sliding sideways every time I take a corner, but she's no more asleep than I am.

We've been driving for almost three hours since we stopped and will soon see the sail masts; the ships coming into port; the old man who every day sits on the dock and mends fishing nets. A man they say has sailed so long his blood runs as salty as the sea. Growing up and even now we call him Salty. No one knows his actual name. No one asks. When I see Salty and hear the sea, I know I'm almost home; know I will soon see our house.

But as we drive the stretch of road that leads to Port Jericho and the flat-topped dormant volcano comes into view, I cannot see our homestead. The once-bright-white building that acted as a beacon seems to have completely disappeared. It's not until we get closer that I realize my childhood home has not vanished, but rather its fading facade has finally succumbed to the ever-present gray.

TWENTY-THREE

WE MAKE IT TO PORT JERICHO'S PETROL STATION
JUST AS THE CAR BEGINS TO SPLUTTER. THERE ARE ONLY TWO PUMPS;
the one I need is being fixed by a man in navy overalls and the other is diesel
for trucks. I pull in behind another car and turn off the ignition. Damn it.
I'm not sure if we have enough fuel to make it up the hill to Mum's, and
it's not worth risking; should have stopped earlier. The woman in the car in
front of us winds down her window and talks to the mechanic. "Simone, yeah,
apparently she up and ran away with one of her kids' music teachers."

The town of seven hundred people is made up of foresters, miners and
fishermen. I don't ordinarily come into town when I visit Mum; normally I
come Christmas Eve, stay until Boxing Day and then leave. Everything's usually closed. The mechanic nods at us and says it'll be at least fifteen minutes.
I look at Dawn. "Might as well stretch our legs?" She raises her eyebrows at
me and shakes her head.

I walk past the deli with its window of cheese, wild honey, sauerkraut,
relish and woodfired sourdough. There's a saying here that if you can't buy
it, you make it, and if you can't make it, you make do. I pass the chemist
from which I'd buy Mum's medication; the fish and chip shop owned by Pete
Brown, whose wife used to give us extra chicken-salted potato cakes; and the
newsdealer who paid out Betty Stevenson's three-million-dollar lottery ticket
before she ran away with Sally Brown.

The fruit and veg shop displays its usual peas and potatoes, cabbages,
carrots and cauliflower, and I peer over the neat arrays before I'm met with a
familiar face. Jesse. We stand staring at each other a moment. I'm so surprised

to see him, I'm lost for words. When I do speak, my voice sounds unnatural. "Hi. How. Are. You?" I think I should hug him, but the moment has passed.

"Dropping the last fruit off before Christmas." His voice is nervous too, a shy laugh. He puts the crate of pears down on the counter. Wipes his hands on a cloth tucked into his jeans. Then stands there bunching it up and pulling it straight.

When we were young, Jesse had shoulder-length blond hair and a clean face; he was tall and lanky. Now he has broad shoulders within a blue plaid shirt. Ripped jeans that rest flat against his stomach and taper above his scuffed brown boots. His beard is just a few steps past stubble. The rough over the smooth, the biology that separates man from boy, the texture that defines the difference between then and now, catches my breath.

I look down at my plane-ride-worn clothes. Run my fingers through my unwashed hair. Berate myself for the vanity. I always imagined this moment differently. That when I saw Jesse again after all these years, I'd be more prepared.

Finally, he says, "And made some of these for Bill's friends." Jesse shows me a stone, tied to the end of a piece of rope. "Anchors for the lobster pots," he adds.

I nod, grasping for the right words but not finding them. Something to pretend things aren't the way they are. That they're better. That I'm better than I feel, and probably look. I've spent my life running away from my childhood, building an existence that is a world away from Mum's depression and Dad's death. But now here I am, standing in front of my high-school boyfriend, rushing home to save my mum. Maybe children like me don't know how to live any other way.

"Look, I've got to run," he says. "Have things boiling on the stove. Come over to the house while you're here, yeah? Would be good to talk properly." All I can do is nod. He leaves and a million words and sentences I should have said rush into my mouth with nowhere to go.

Next door is Horton's secondhand bookshop. When I was a teenager, I

THE HEART IS A STAR

spent hours here, getting away from Mum and Dad. Most Saturdays, I would sit reading on the red Persian hall runners that lined the three narrow passages until the owner kicked me out. I hope to see old Mr. Peterson as I open the door and hear the same gold bell ding. Instead, Adara sits behind the counter, reading *The Glass Bead Game*. I gasp a little too loudly. Her once-long blonde hair is short, her body curvier than it was when we were young. But her clothes are a replica of our youth: a knee-length flowing skirt and three-quarter-sleeve mandarin silk blouse. "The material of the mainland," she used to say. Here they wear wool or alpaca, linen or cotton. But not silk. Delicate fabric is not fit for a callous climate. Adara was always one to reach for the rare.

That's why she and Dawn used to get on so well. Dawn used to make her clothes and Adara would wear them with pride. She made me clothes as well, dresses and waterfall jackets of silk velvets in deep greens and reds and blues that hung in my wardrobe and I never wore.

Adara used to watch the ocean when it was thinking. Not calm and flat or wild and wavy, but slowly undulating, the immense blue fabric of the sea rippling and rolling. "Like silk," she would say. In her final year of high school, she wanted to study subjects the school didn't offer: criminal psychology, religion and advanced biology. She traveled two hours each way to study classes at university. We lost touch over the years.

"Hey," is all I say; wrap my arms around her shoulders, but her arms stay pinned to her side. I slowly pull away.

Adara glances at the two people browsing in the bookshop; one woman looks curiously over at us. "Let's talk outside," she says, ushers me out onto the pavement and down the street a little, so that we are standing opposite the old telegraph station. I look back over at the bookshop in disappointment. "Mum told me you'd run away with the bones squad," I finally say. That's what we called the paleontologists who would find fossils and close off people's land. The town hated them.

"I did. I have. I've been in Cairo. Only here because Mum's sick," she says.

I think of the blush of wild cells diffusing. "I'm sorry," I say. Because that's what people say. I look toward the petrol station but the mechanic's still working on the pump.

I wonder if she is still cross with me for the way I left. About the fact that I started to pull away from her long before that. The years after Dad died had a shallowness to them—as if everything and everyone around me had been robbed of its thickness—and people began to barely exist. Including my friends and family. Adara, Jesse. I suppose the loss of depth came from disbelief. I felt as though if I opened my mouth to talk to anyone roughly, then I might disappear as well.

I search my mind for questions I can ask Adara that might calm the whirling wind between us. A loud squabble erupts. Two black jays fight on the ground under a myrtle tree. They are pitch black like crows. One has a worm in its mouth and is half running, half flying away from the other. Their wings are flapping so hard the soil is swept up and falls back heavy to the ground. They aren't flying away properly because their wings are broken, bent at odd angles, so that when they try to rise off the ground it seems as if they are drowning, flailing.

"Whenever I think of you," I try, "I remember that you found a bone on the beach. Ran over to my house because you thought it was from a dinosaur. When you discovered it was from a cow, you threw it, angry, across the fence and it smashed your dad's shed window. God, he was furious." I remember the bulging veins in the side of his thick neck. Adara running to her room before he had a chance to catch her.

She finally smiles. "Fossils are the only thing I believe in. I have faith in what I find. You know, in the seventeenth century fossils were thought of as tricks planted by God to test people's faith?"

I laugh. Adara frowns.

"No, not that," I say. "It's just…look at us. Can you imagine the guys down at the pub hearing us talk?"

136

"I'm trying to explain to you." Adara stands straighter, huffs, crosses her arms. "It's the opposite for me. Fossils are survivors. I have faith in a process that favors the tough and forgets what's frail."

"You were always tough."

"No, I wasn't. That's the point."

I'm not sure what she's talking about.

The weather changes; blue light turns indigo; Huon pine and eucalypt bend in the sudden wind. The sky opens and we stand for a moment in a loose girdle of rain that then transforms into large slapping drops on the land. We move further under the awning. In the distance, beyond the rolling pastures and poppy fields, the hills appear violet.

"Why haven't you called? Or at least emailed? I tried to contact you," I say.

"You're a reminder. It hurts too much…" She trails off.

I think of her last few difficult years of school, the scars on her arm. The turmoil I could see but never asked about. I had my own. I watch the telegraph station's thick stone walls and wide veranda, roof painted in government green, offering respite from the rain to a mother and her two toddlers.

"I guess I see it differently. See you differently," I say. Adara nods. Keeps her arms crossed and draws an arch in the soil with the tip of her brown leather boot. It still surprises me how the land is ever-present. In Queensland this space would be covered with concrete. To hide the dirt at all costs.

"You come back for your mum?" she asks.

"It's bad this time," I say.

"Yeah, I heard." I wonder if Adara knows more than I do. "Maybe you should just let her be?"

"Your mum said the same thing. Would you let your mum be? Under the same circumstances?" I feel my temperature rise in the cold air; sense a crawling dread of things unseen.

"Your mum's different," she says. "A few weeks back, she got drunk and almost walked off Bennet's Cliff." I nod. It's not the first time. The birds come back, fighting and flapping their broken wings under the trees. One of them knocks the other into a trunk and it falls to the ground.

"I can't just leave her to top herself." My stomach constricts, the way it learned to do when I discovered people could believe whatever they wanted to about you. Or any given situation. Even if it wasn't true. And nothing you say or do can change their mind. I look up at the petrol station.

"The pump's fixed," I say. "Better go." Adara nods. I step toward her, and there is an awkward moment where she pats my shoulder. I hurry toward the car beneath a broken sky, rain falling hard.

I read so many books on the night sky in that bookstore. My favorite one taught me that the only thing an astronomer can do is decipher the past. That when we look at Sirius in the night sky, we are not seeing it as it is now but how it was 8.6 years ago. I think about Adara's fossils and my stars. The faith she has in the land and I in the skies. The way that, when I look above me, I'm looking at cosmic fossils from thousands and millions of years ago. The way that fossils and stars are the marks history makes. When Adara looked at me, it felt as though she wasn't seeing me but history's scars. And I don't understand why. I think of prediction, of control, of history, but it all falls away, intangible, and muted by the urgent pull to get to Mum.

TWENTY-FOUR

A DRUMROLL OF RAIN SOUNDS AS WE ASCEND TO MUM'S. WATER BLOTS OUT THE LAND, RUSHES ACROSS THE DIRT ROAD in driving sheets. There's a sheer drop down to the ocean and I grip the steering wheel tighter. The wharf below is a jumble of motorboats, seaplanes and schooners. The water is serrated, pounding at the stubborn shore, convulsing in the lightning strobe. Milk foam boiling over a saucepan sea.

Dawn leans against the window and twists her hands in her lap. When we reach the property gate, I unhook the chain, open it up just as much as I can until it drags, a perfect arc inscribed on the ground. There is just enough light without headlights to make out the old place. We follow the Huon pines along the property fence line, a ragged silhouette, a narrow, dark, torn strip laid under the galvanized sky.

The once-grand Victorian homestead, which was built to survive a harsh environment, to resist the Roaring Forties, snowfall and howling wind, doesn't seem to have been able to withstand my mother's sadness. I face Dawn to see if she's coming in, but she simply looks at me with wide, unblinking eyes.

The stone path to the door is cracked and broken. Inside, the house is dark; cold. The perpetual freeze of sorrow. The curtains are drawn. There is the familiar smell of wet wool, like the odor of our school jumpers after a rainy recess.

"Mum!" I shout through the house. "Mum!" There is the stillness you get when no one is in the house, although I start to worry the house might feel like that when there is a body but no life. I run through each room. "Mum!" I shout again. I check the bathroom first, the bath where Willow and I would fold boats and onto them drop wax, the shower with mold-dappled curtain.

Through the kitchen, past the mint-green, salmon-pink and baby-blue pantries, into the lounge room with its corduroy couch, the armchair where Mum cried and I uncoiled the yellow wool. I rush into my bedroom, the pine bed pushed against the wall, a purple bedside table, now-hard Blu Tack, chipped paint, a bookshelf with every yellow-spined copy of *National Geographic* from when I was born until I left home. Willow's room is empty: all the pictures on the walls have gone, even the jewelry box and old teddy that were here last year have been removed; her bed just a frame.

Lunging into the corridor, I stop and pick up the wall phone's pale-yellow handset from the floor and place it back it on the receiver. In the garage is the old Mazda that Mum rarely drives and the red ride-on mower she uses weekly. In the gathering darkness, my body deflates. She's probably at Maggie's or gone for a drunk walk, as she often does. Fuck. I can't believe I've been sucked into this again. A familiar fury burns inside me, but also a slight disappointment that I have to push away; a letdown from the rush to get here and the preparation I had to do in my head and my heart in case I found a body.

There are so many silhouettes on this property at night. A sliver of moonlight slides across the ceiling. A leafy shadow across the white walls like gray lace; lightning claps and flashes it away, filling the sepia room with color.

I open the back screen door. On the wooden deck, a terra-cotta pot has split in two, a Moreton Bay fig's roots shooting through the cracks. Most of the pots Mum owns are broken. Rather than buy new pots, she's drilled holes either side of each rift and threaded copper wire through the holes, pulling the pot together like a tight corset.

Another boom of lightning and I see something sticking out from our playhouse down the end of the fenced backyard. Dawn has come into the house and stands looking at me, frozen. I run the twenty meters down to the edge of our yard. I'm yelling, "Mum! Mum! Mum!" but there's so much ringing in my ears, I can't hear myself.

Mum's body lies slack on its back inside our playhouse. On the walls she has stuck our childhood drawings: Willow's colorful long-legged people with large heads and big smiles; my wrongly ordered rainbows with "I love you Mum" written jagged beneath them. Hearts and animals and houses and flowers in carefree crayon.

Licking my palm, I wet my cheek and place it close to Mum's mouth. Her breath is faint, a moth wing's flutter, but I feel it. I push two fingers onto the side of her neck, searching for a pulse. I ask her to open her eyes, and I pinch her earlobe, but her body remains lifeless, so I place a hand on her forehead and tilt her head back to make sure there's nothing blocking her airways. With my head on her chest, I listen to her breathing, then roll her into the recovery position, and look around the playhouse to try to see what she's used.

I pick up the pill bottles. Different brands of benzodiazepines. Maybe she's taken only enough to make this a cry for help, but I roughly count in my head how many she would have ingested if the bottles had been full, and it's pretty clear she wanted to finish herself off. I stick my fingers down Mum's throat. She dry retches a few times before vomiting all over the ground. Trying to stand up, I hit my head on the roof; slide myself, bowing, walking backwards, through the small doorway.

Running into the house, I grab my phone; my voice, halfway between groaning and silence, says to Dawn, "Alive. Barely." I whip off my soaked jumper and throw it onto the couch. Running outside again, feel as if I'm stumbling across unlevel ground.

Standing under the house's eaves, I watch Mum's body; give emergency services the details. Raindrops are thick and heavy on the ground, and although most of Mum's body is under cover, the wind pushes the water in through the playhouse windows. The temperature is dropping and the last thing her body needs is to be cold. The Western Hospital is about forty minutes away—twenty-five if they're speeding. Too long to leave Mum outside. I grab a rain-soaked blue-and-white-checked tea towel that's been draped over an outdoor chair and run down to wipe her face. I check her vitals. Her breathing is still faint, her pulse weak. As I run back into the house, Dawn is arranging food and jars on the kitchen island desk.

"Why are you cleaning out the fucking fridge?" I say as I lunge into the room.

"I'm reordering. God help me, if I'm going to be here awhile, I need to at least be able to find things in the fridge. I mean, who puts peanut butter in the fridge anyway? And in Tasmania, of all places?"

"I need you to come out the back and help me get Mum inside." She doesn't stop. "Dawn, please, I know you won't be able to lift too much, but—"

"Girlie, I'm not going out there and seeing my sister's body. I have lots of mental images in this noggin of mine," she pats her head sharply, "and that is one I don't need. Old age doesn't give you much, but it gives me the right to say no, so…no." Dawn returns to moving chutney, jam and pickle jars, milk bottles, butter and salami out of the fridge onto the kitchen island desk.

I run outside and look at Mum's body, my mind flashing back to the beached whale we saved the day Dad died. I sit Mum up, resting the top of her body over my right shoulder, but I'm not strong enough to stand up. Shit. If I had another person, I could roll her onto a blanket or sheet and carry her in a makeshift stretcher, but even if Dawn wanted to, she's probably not strong enough, and dropping Mum on the backyard lawn would be even worse than her lying in the rain.

The only person I can think of calling who will be close enough and strong enough to help is Jesse. There is part of me that doesn't want to bring him into this intimacy after not seeing each other for so many years, but I know he is the only one who can come quickly enough. I don't have his number in my mobile, though, and I can't remember it off the top of my head. I pace up and down and then walk over to Mum's telephone. Look at the pale-yellow contraption, the handset hung up on top, the round, clear dial with individual holes for numbers and fingers. I close my eyes and think back, all those times I called his number growing up. Placing my finger in the nine, it comes to me and I twirl each number around and let the dial twirl back, giving my body time to remember which number to choose next. He picks up after the third ring.

"Jesse, it's Layla. It's Mum, I..." I don't know how to explain. But somehow he seems to understand.

"I'm running over now."

Back in the house, I open the hallway linen cupboard. There are two large yellow woolen rugs, bright-yellow satin ribbons running around the edges. When I return to the playhouse, I throw one over the roof, making sure it drapes to cover the windows, and then put the other on Mum. I kneel next to her. Lean down to her ear. "It's okay, Mum, it's okay. I'm here. It's going to be okay," I croon. Rubbing her back with flattened palm.

I hear Jesse's footfall outside and yell to him, "Out here! Out here!"

He lifts the blanket. "Oh Jesus..." he says, before helping me up and reaching down to Mum. "It's okay, Nora, we've got you. You're going to be alright, hang in there." We roll Mum onto the yellow blanket, carrying an end each; the rain cascades down our heads and shoulders. We move her inside to lie on the lounge-room carpet, put a pillow beneath her head, and Jesse finds another blanket to put over her body. I turn off the bright lights and sit down next to her.

"Nora," Dawn moans and her body crumples down to the floor. "No," she cries. "No, what are you doing, baby, no." A cry like falling water. She picks Mum up in her arms and rocks her backwards and forwards. "We're here, baby, we're here now, stay with us, stay with us."

"I'm gonna stand at the gate for the ambulance," Jesse says.

Dawn places Nora back down on the ground and curls up next to her like a child. I rub Mum's wrists, right on the pulse points where the blood vessels come close to the surface of the skin, trying to warm her body. Mum's face twitches with signs of life; I keep checking her pulse to make sure it's there, to will it to keep beating. Dawn strokes Mum's hair.

Crunch on gravel and red lights flash and flicker through the window. Two paramedics come into the house, controlled and calm as they always are. As I usually am. The male paramedic opens the flip-top bag; Velcro rips as he asks me if I'm family, and I explain who we all are, let them know I'm a doctor. They change their language. Ask me what I've done, what I've performed. They check Mum's vitals. "Looks like she's going to be okay, but we should get her to hospital."

It takes only a second for them to get her onto the gurney, roll her outside and slide her into the back of the small ambulance, where the female paramedic climbs in too. I step onto the back, ready to hoist myself up. "I'm sorry, there's not enough room," the woman says. "We'll meet you at the hospital. She's in good hands." Moving away, I look at Mum's small frame, more like that of a child than a woman. Her bare foot juts out of a waffle blanket, her heel cracked and toenails long.

Jesse runs inside the house and comes back just as the ambulance door slams and the vehicle pulls away. He is left standing in the wake of mud spray, holding Mum's other navy-blue slipper in his hand. The three of us stare straight ahead, marooned between the decreasing sound of the ambulance's engine and the silence of an empty house.

Jesse puts his hand on my shoulder. "You okay? Want me to drive you to the hospital?" All I can do is study the unending tire tracks disappearing into blackness and slowly shake my head. Dawn doesn't move. "I'm right over there," Jesse says. "If you need anything." He crosses the driveway, then turns around. "Maggie told me you usually come down on Christmas Eve. Thank God you came when you did."

Dawn and I are left alone. Came early, I think. Yes. And then I remember all of the reasons I did. I turn to look at my aunt; she pauses a moment before saying, "Not now, Layla. Please don't do this now."

TWENTY-FIVE

THE KITCHEN IS HALF-LIT BY THE HALLWAY LIGHT. THERE IS A TEACUP TIPPED ON ITS SIDE WITH TEABAG AND SUGAR spilling over the countertop. Dried remnants of food not properly wiped make shapes on the counter. Even in the limited light, you can see dust covering the floor. I look at Mum's broken kettle. Take a deep breath. Lift it slowly to find a small gold key. Hold it in my hand. It feels heavier than its size suggests. I hesitate.

"Give yourself a break, Layla. Us a break," Dawn calls around the corner. "At least for tonight?"

In Mum's room, her bed is perfectly made but the rest is a mess. Clothes are thrown everywhere. Books are open on the floor. A smashed silver picture frame lies on the carpet: the four of us on the deck of the car ferry that brought us here from the mainland.

I fall to my knees and stare at the Wilhelminian wardrobe. It seems so much smaller than when I was a child. The four panels on the two ash doors are uneven in color, but the curves of the honey-colored crown at the top are shiny and smooth. Jumpers, cardigans, dresses and skirts are piled in front, so I have to move them aside to reach the two drawers just above the floor.

"Your mother's been through so much and—" Dawn says, walking into the room.

"Mum's been through so much?" I say; my glare stops her talking. The drawer on the left has always been unlocked and I open it to see the usual array of folded handkerchiefs with lace edging and suede boxes housing jewelry. I jiggle the gilded handle on the right; look at the key's teeth: little slopes cut in between the drawer's pin positions. The spring-loaded lock begins to click but the key gets jammed halfway. I try to twist it left, then right, but it won't budge. Sitting up on my knees, I press all of my weight into the key's hexagon head and it finally turns and comes out, but the drawer doesn't open. My rough handling has broken something. When I try the key again it spins loosely.

"That's fine, I don't need a key anyway. I'll just…" I walk back into the kitchen; hinges rattle as I open drawers and leave them hanging. I pick out a butter knife and open the fridge, removing a red-and-white-topped jam jar. Striding back into Mum's bedroom, I charge toward the drawer, wedge the blade into the thin gap at the top, breathing quick. I bang the bottom of the jar on the end of the knife to crowbar the drawer open, but it takes two, three, four goes until the wood pries apart. I'm hoping to find what Mum promised, anything that resembles answers to the questions I've had since I was fourteen years old. I clear a circle free from clothes next to me on the floor, the space serving as a set of crossed fingers. My hands shake as I slowly pull at the drawer, every faculty twitching. The wood sticks a little without runners and I shake the drawer from side to side to dislodge it before I can pull it completely free.

I kneel back on my calves. It's empty. The clean wooden rectangle laughs at me. Perfect in its proportions. My fury at Mum returns as I stare at the hollow space. Willow was right. She was just trying to manipulate me. "No!" My voice breaks the silence like a cracking whip. Dawn lets out a sigh before walking out of the room.

I follow her into the lounge room, where she scrunches up newspaper and covers it with kindling in the wood burner. It's the first time I've noticed the house is freezing. She lights a corner of the paper and then blows oxygen onto the flames, before making a tepee of red-gum logs. Secures the glass door shut.

To the right, close to the warmth and on the floor against the wall, is Willow's old single mattress with its pink-and-green paisley duvet cover. I hadn't noticed it before in the dark, tucked out of the way. Mum must have pulled the mattress off its wooden base and slid it through the house. There's a circular imprint on the pillow and the covers are pulled down. My heart pounds. Mum's been sleeping there.

Newspaper clippings of Willow saving trees are stuck on and fill up the large rectangular wall mirror; photographs of her face are circled in thick red pen. Words are highlighted in yellow: "Months-long saga," "Military raids Sri Lankan protest camps," "unnecessary use of brute force."

Five or six pairs of women's underwear are strewn across the coffee table. I hear Gabe's mum telling me about her work in war-torn countries, about the fact that suicide bombers often wear two pairs of underwear. An attempt to hide their fear before they act.

"I can't. I can't stay here," I say. "I need to get out of this house and off the mountain. Come with me?" I look at Dawn, who falls into the nearby armchair.

"I'd rather stay here. Sleep here. To be alone. For a while. Anyway." She chips off the ends of her sentences, snap, clip, her lips like scissors.

"I don't want to leave you here alone." Now I'm about to leave, I feel guilty for every time I've been impatient with her over the past few days. Especially tonight.

"Really, it will do me good to be alone awhile. Come back in the morning and we'll have some tea."

I nod reluctantly, too tired and angry to argue.

I take my bag and step outside. Listen to the reliable pulse of the tide; sense its contrast to the erratic wire of nerves inside me. In the sky, Mars is hanging high in the west. Dad's favorite position for it. Passing the Pleiades cluster

Tennyson described as stars that "glitter like a swarm of fire-flies tangled in a silver braid," I breathe in the night's atmosphere to replace the stale air in my lungs from Mum's house. Walk across the property. Dad's observatory is covered in leaves and twigs, but the structure is still standing.

I open the door to find the familiar milk crate, Dad's ottoman, the telescope, and my drawing of a smudged shooting star on the wall. I sit down and look through the telescope to find my faithful constellations. I still struggle to see the lines between the stars that turn the dots into a picture. I think about moons that seem to change size depending on their position in the sky, but which really remain the same; I think about shooting stars we think are magic, but which are really nothing more than dust.

People think there's only one dusk, but really there are three. Facts are heavy nets that stop the butterflies in my stomach. I try to focus on the angles to distract myself from images of Mum's body in my mind.

When the sun's disc goes six degrees below the horizon, it's civil dusk. Venus appears in the sky, stars become visible to the naked eye. As it gets darker, in dimming light, the sun at twelve degrees below the horizon. Sinking. Nautical twilight. The stars in the sky brighten.

But now, at eighteen degrees, it's astronomical dusk. The sun stops illuminating the sky. Stops interfering with observations. Or is supposed to. It's the best time for navigation.

As I step back out of the observatory, I look up at the spiraled stars, constellations reaching for light years across the transparent sky; I arch my head backwards and feel the Earth move beneath my feet. When I lift my head, the stars are still exactly where they've always been. I place my palm against the side of our observatory and then into my bag to run a finger along the blue leather binding of *Lessons on the Human Body*.

Aud and Jack will be sleeping now. I'd rather be home with them than in this darkness. I search for my phone and think about calling Gabe, but what would I say? The thought of explaining everything that's happened tonight is too much. Even if we were still close. And tomorrow is supposed to be my chance at work. I need to call them, email them at least. Dwarfed by the dark, I can't stand still. I still don't remember Jesse's number and I can't bear the thought of going back inside that house to the old phone to jog my memory.

I've done the walk a hundred times before, and just like when I get into an operating theatre, and the Mozart music starts playing, I move on autopilot. Orion, a magnet in the sky, will be situated over Jesse's house. First, I find his belt, the three bright-blue giant stars, Alnilam, Mintaka and Alnitak. Then the tip of his sword, Hatsya, and the top of his head, Meissa.

Although it's dark, I follow the stars and my feet find their way. I place a palm on Huon pine as I weave through the thick, tall trunks of ancient trees. In daylight, I know I'd also be walking past heart-leaved gum, white trunks, blotched with green-and-purple patches. A few logs carpeted with mosses and lichens. Once on Jesse's property, there are smaller trees with loose hanging bark, corrugated leaves that form rosettes toward the ends of branches. Yellow flowers. In the distance would be rugged hills and deep gullies verdant with forest and fern. I know I'm getting close to the house when the air becomes musky from blowing over orchards, heavy with fragrance, the breath of harvest.

I hold my hand up to knock, wait a moment and then tap twice. Jesse opens the door with a look of surprise.

"Hey, thanks for tonight," I begin. "There aren't many people who would have understood…all that. Actually, I don't think there is anyone else."

Jesse stands, silent a beat. And then a moment more. "Sorry," he says. "I think I'm still getting used to the fact that you're here."

I nod, not knowing what else to say, except the sentence I've replayed in my mind all these years. "I should have told you I was leaving."

"Yeah, you should have. But now's not the time to talk about that."

I feel a sickness in my stomach at difficult conversations delayed.

"Do you want to come in?"

I look past Jesse's shoulder at the familiar lounge room with sturdy wood-fired stove, large timber kitchen island, industrial steel oven, and pared-back soft furnishings in charcoal and tan. Coming inside seems too personal for now, with too many memories.

"I don't suppose you know anywhere still open for a drink?" I ask instead.

Jesse laughs. I realize the sound is less innocent and more world-weary than the last time I heard it, when we were young. "I think I might know a place," he says.

TWENTY-SIX

THE AIR IN TOWN, UNLIKE ON THE MOUNTAIN, IS STILL. JESSE PARKS THE CAR IN FRONT OF A LARGE RED-BRICK building, the shape of a barn. A backlit gold metal sign above our heads glows with the word "Bramble." Jesse scratches the back of his head.

"Looks closed," I say.

"You know, when I started this place," he says, and I raise my eyebrows, realizing why Jesse's brought me here, "I thought of you. By tradition, most stills have female names." I look at him with wide eyes. "Don't worry," he says, laughing. "I would never do anything that hokey. No, no. I thought I'd turn it on its head. Name the distillery after a famous cocktail and my drinks after famous women."

"Oh God, you didn't name a drink after me, did you?"

"Don't get too ahead of yourself. Since when are you famous?" He smiles. "Come inside and I'll show you."

Jesse creaks open the doors. Inside is a steampunk dream of copper and steel, along with handmade wooden tables, leather couches, tartan blankets and an open fire. It looks as though the brass, woodwind and timpani sections of an orchestra have been moved into a country barn. Right in the middle, a copper genie bottle as big as an igloo, polished to a blinding shine. I sit at the bar while Jesse walks around the other side.

"Looks like you're running your own nuclear reactor," I say.

"Only someone from the mainland would say that," Jesse says with an "I'm not being serious" grin.

"So, I know two things about gin," I say, giving back my own smirk. "Firstly, that gin wasn't sold as a drink to start out with, it was sold in pharmacies as a kind of cure-all."

Jesse holds up the crystal tumbler he has pulled from beneath the bar as if to say a "cheers" to me and my correct fact.

"And, secondly, I don't like it."

"That's only because I bet you've only ever drunk it with tonic." He takes another glass out. "I'll make you my signature—a Bramble—first." I watch as Jesse pours gin, lemon juice, sugar syrup and crushed ice into a cocktail shaker. I appreciate the distraction. "Elderflowers and juniper berries grow wild on our property. So I forage for them at home. The other fruit too. Pears and apples, obviously." He strains the mixture into our glasses. Drops in more crushed ice. Drizzles purple liqueur over the mound and tops the drinks with a sprig of mint, pale-purple flowers and four plump blackberries.

The night we had our first kiss, the night Dad died, Jesse took me walking through his orchard. "We usually pick pears before they ripen, because if they're left on the tree, they ripen from the inside out and the fruit become mushy. They're harvested when fully formed, not quite ripe. But the only problem with that is you can't eat them straightaway," he said. Walked me to the far end of the orchard. "So I saved this tree for you. Left the pears with a bit of blush, so they drop easily when picked." I cupped the bottom of a pear with my hand and it fell off. He looked at me and nodded as if I should take a bite, and as I did, the juice ran down the side of my mouth and I laughed breathlessly; dropped my head as I wiped the juice away self-consciously. He leaned in and kissed me.

After that night, we were inseparable. For the four years between Dad's death and the night I left, Jesse's love got me from one day to the next. Through the funeral and the days after, through Mum's ups and downs and through high-school exams. His company was my constant in a complex mathematical equation with lots of unknowns. When I found out I'd been accepted into medicine and received a full scholarship and board, I never said a word. He would have been happy for me, encouraged me, but I knew that if I'd looked at him, told him, if I had forced myself to say goodbye, even though it was the right thing to do, I would never have been able to pull myself away. And in some ways, I needed to escape him at that point in my life as much as everything and everyone else. I came to realize my love for him and my grief about my father's death were all mixed up and mingled together. Everything was a reminder. Every time I looked at him, he made me think of Dad's death. When I held the university's letter in my hand, I knew it was my chance and that if I stayed a moment longer than I had to, I might not survive.

"How are you?" he asks; holds my gaze. "Do you want me to check in at the hospital?"

"I gave them my number; they'll call if there's a change. She'll be okay." I say this even though I'm not sure. Jesse nods and knows not to push. We stop to drink our Brambles until the glasses are empty. He understands the fine balance I tread between vulnerability and control. Strange how, even after all these years, he still knows me better than anyone. "Can we talk about something else for a while?" I ask. "Tell me more about the distillery."

"When I came home after my marriage broke down, I needed a distraction. I always wanted to use the fruits and berries around our property in another way, a different way than Dad does. So, I started making gin. Bought this dinky gin-making kit from town. Started to enjoy the process. The steps to distilling were one thing, but then when I started to add botanicals and experiment with the citrus and cardamom and cinnamon, I'd start to lose time. I still do. I know I really love something when I start in the morning and then look up at the clock and it's almost dark." He says this in an easy, almost be-mused tone, the way he used to speak about everything.

"But you know what really got me?" Jesse takes a cloth and wipes down the bar. Stops and holds the rag in his hand. "Finding the sweet spot. Dur-ing the distillation process, different alcohols boil and change into vapors at different temperatures and pressures. We call it the heart—the part of the process that provides the best quality spirits. I became obsessed with figuring out, using taste and aroma, how to capture it. That, and I needed to get drunk a lot to forget my train wreck of a life." He laughs.

"Speaking of which." I point to the two empty tumblers sitting on the bar. Smile. He takes out two new glasses, along with an array of ingredients. Ber-ries, apples, eucalyptus leaves, plums and pears.

"Right. So, I've named my drinks after local, historical women, using the famous gin drink White Lady as inspiration. We have Lady Jane, an explorer, Lady Louise, an artist, Lady Constance, a doctor, and Lady Gwen, a poet. Each drink's ingredients inspired by the woman and her life. Each drink, like each life, has its own story to tell. Whenever I make a Lady Constance, the first female doctor in the country, I think about you."

"Because she was a doctor?" I ask.

"Not just that." He smiles. "She was stubborn, audacious." He laughs. "Opened a hospital encouraging other female doctors to join so that female patients wouldn't have to be examined by male interns. I like her style." Jesse holds up the bottle of gin. "The liquid looks clear, but it's infused with corian-der, riberries, rosebuds, wild rosella flowers, strawberry gum, lavender, pep-perberries, pear. All from our property. Oh and…" He hands me a ripe piece of fruit. "From your mum's property." I hold the split plum, the purple-black flesh pushing out of its open skin and staining my palm.

Jesse aerates an egg white and puts it on top of the Lady Constance he's just poured. I take a sip. It's like being kicked by a cloud. I give a full-body laugh, the way I do when something has taken me so much by surprise that it knocks the self-awareness out of me. "Jesus," I say, before I take another sip. "That's, well, it's wonderful." I hold up the gin bottle and look at the clear liquid. Think about the fact that things are not always as they seem.

"Some I make using a lockable metal hatch, which swings open. I tip in a potpourri of ingredients. Inside, they mingle with near-pure ethanol and demineralized water. Once heated, the mixture emits vapor, which steams out of the top of the hatch and passes through a network of pipes, cooling as it goes, and eventually emerging from a column on the right, as clear liquid. This I dilute, and that, give or take about a thousand adjustments, is how you make the gin. But my drinks named after famous women, I make them using vapor infusion. I hang the botanicals above in that basket," he says, pointing over and above his head. "The steam ascends and…" Jesse makes a *poof* action with his hands. I follow his hands with my eyes. Marvel at how much he has grown since I last saw him.

"I fell in love with infusion too," I say. "We call it intravenous."

"Your mum tells everyone you're a doctor," Jesse says. I'm surprised, since she always seemed against the idea. "She's proud of you, Layla."

I think about arguing but want to escape her and what happened tonight a little longer.

"I'm an anesthetist," I say. "One of the things I fell in love with was the concept of sedation and time. Anesthetics work within one arm-to-brain circulation time."

Jesse squints, no doubt trying to discern the relationship between arm and brain.

"When I inject drugs into the vein," I explain, "it's the time that it takes for the drug to travel from the injection site in the arm to the brain, where the drug takes effect. It's usually less than a minute. I love that. Always imagine the anesthesia finding the body's brain. I once had a little girl wake up from surgery and thank me for making her disappear."

Jesse finishes his drink, puts down the glass and spins it between his fingers. He is quiet for a moment before saying, "Maybe in some ways you've spent your life searching for the brain to run away from your heart."

I'd forgotten about this. The way that Jesse can lull you into thinking he is simple and then deliver you a complex truth.

"And maybe," I counter, "you've spent the past few years finding the heart in something, to try to quiet your brain."

We look at each other a moment, the way we did when we were young.

He looks down at his palms. "I heard you got married. Kids?" he asks.

"Audrey is twelve and Jack is seven." An ache, of missing, of life pulling me away. Shame in the fact I let it. "I'm not doing a very good job," I say, eyes stinging, blinking. I tap my heels on the barstool. "And my marriage," I say, looking up to the roof. "Well, that's complicated and I'm not sure I'm doing or have done a good job at that either. Neither has he." Jesse nods. And I continue: "I always had this idea that I would give my kids the childhood I never had, show them a marriage like I never saw. Security, love, dependability. But I…I think I might be failing at life." Clasping my hands together, I wring my skin. Jesse separates them gently, unfurls my right hand's fingers so they are flat. Runs his hand across my open palm as if he is smoothing crumpled paper. I slowly take my hand away.

"How about you?" I ask.

"Yes. Complicated too." He smiles, but then the upturned sides of his mouth fall. "Your mum? Sorry, I know you don't want to talk about it, but—"

"I knew she was going to do it, Jesse. No one else did, but I knew."

"I'm so sorry," he says, looking me right in the eye. Not claiming me as Lucas does, but simply sitting with me. For a second, he softens my sadness.

"I'm the one who should be saying sorry. Sorry to have run away," I say.

Jesse nods. "I deserved better, Layla," he says. "We deserved more than that." I see it now, the hurt he's been working to hide from me. It slides across his eyes like a veil.

"I'm sorry. I ran away." I say it again just in case he hasn't heard, because

I need him to hear me. I need him to know of all the nights and days that I regretted the decision.

He places his hands on the bar top. His chest rises and falls. I look out the distillery window, worried I shouldn't have brought it up.

"It's just. I don't understand. I've never understood. Didn't I support you? Love you?" he says.

"I…I didn't know how to live with my father's ghost. And, because I was with you around the same time it happened, I think you felt like a ghost of sorts, too. Everything felt haunted by that night. I just didn't want that to be all I ever knew. I was…I was barely surviving." I finish with a quick breath, stopping tears.

Jesse comes around the bar and sits on a stool next to me. He reaches over and I think he's going to stroke my cheek, but then he runs his fingers through my hair, reaches a knot made from the wind and rain, and begins gently untangling the strands, lightly pulling here and there until the hair eventually unravels.

"What's that?" I ask, pointing to a tattoo, half exposed above the open collar of his shirt. He pulls his T-shirt down slightly to reveal a fine and intricate drawing of two overlapping concentric circles.

"One of Mum's sketches. She'd left it on the table the night she died. I kept it for years and was terrified I'd lose it, so…" Jesse runs his finger over the tattoo.

Jesse's mum had been a mathematician. She responded to Hilbert's twenty-third problem, an invitation for people to further the work in the calculus of variations, by applying it to string theory. A theory I've always thought of as beautiful and true: replacing all matter and force particles with tiny vibrating strings that twist and turn in complicated ways. She'd been on her way to collect an award in mathematics from the University of Tasmania when her car skidded on black ice. Jesse was seven. When we were older, I was curious and looked her up. The sketch on Jesse's skin is her version of the theory of everything.

"I got it last year. It was my first tattoo," he continues. "After that, I looked forward to the feeling of the needle prick." He laughs. "Sounds kind of masochistic, doesn't it?"

"It's addictive," I say. "Feeling something else for a moment. Something other than grief's pain." I think of Lucas. "I'm sorry you had to go through losing your mum."

"It was a long time ago. We've both had our tragedies."

"Do you have any others?"

"Tragedies?"

"No." I smile. "Tattoos."

"A couple." Jesse rolls up his sleeve to reveal a eucalyptus tree on his right forearm, then, further up, anise myrtle. I try to distract myself from the closeness of his skin by imagining him as anatomy: his skein of hollow organs, the globes and bulbs of great tissues; the sheet muscle strapped around the trellis of the bones; the intricate house of the heart, veins and arteries radiating, curling, branching into tiny tributaries. The last tattoo he shows me is of a naval ship on his forearm.

"It's my most recent one. Represents how we measure the strength of gin. Ours is navy strength. Back in the day, they knew gin was strong if it ignited the ship's gunpowder. Otherwise it was diluted."

I sit back on the stool. Mull over what I'd like to ask. "That night, when your dad and Bill and the guys went out to rescue that boat," I say and take a breath, "what happened?"

Jesse crosses and uncrosses his ankles. "It's so long ago, Layla." The sound of him saying my name makes my cheeks flush. "It was the worst storm we'd seen in years. Even the best sailors would struggle if they got caught in something like that, and, well, your dad, with all due respect, he wasn't really..." He trails off.

I nod, trying not to let my frustration, a general animosity I feel toward everyone there that night, creep into this reunion. Jesse is the last person I should be hounding, even though I crave answers more than ever. So, I change the subject. "What's happening with you?"

"Well, Dad retired. Went traveling overseas and left me the orchard." Jesse runs a flattened palm down the side of his jaw like a blade.

"I thought he'd have to die before he let you run the orchard. He hated it enough when you suggested grafting fruit trees, rather than growing them from seedlings."

"God, I remember." He laughs. "After I told you what Dad said, you came over with reams and reams of printouts, graphs and academic studies that proved that it increased production. Dad said it was 'rubbish' because the west-coast Tasmanian soil was different. So you went away and found new studies based solely on local farms." Jesse laughs again and shakes his head. "You know, that moment when you took Dad through those pie charts. It wasn't the fact you were doing it for me, it was the way your mind worked. You could have been talking about anything, but that way you lit up. The look in your eyes. I fell for you that day."

I sigh. "I know, Jesse, I know I should have said goodbye. Or at least called you later."

"It's hard to have a conversation with a *ghost*," Jesse says. His voice swells. I shouldn't have called him that. "It's okay," he says. "Really. I understand a bit better now we've been able to talk. And what were you supposed to do? We do the best we can with grief. But there are always other casualties, beyond those who died."

I think about Willow, Mum, about mentioning the key and box she said she'd leave me. But I still feel so angry and confused, I don't even know where to start. Instead, I pause before vocalizing my next question, as if forming my vaporous thoughts into solid words could somehow make them true. I lower my voice even though there's no one else around. "Do you think that Mum could have had anything to do with Dad's death?"

"No, no," Jesse chimes in straightaway. I nod, but am unconvinced.

"You have to admit, though, that if he hadn't been arguing with Mum and had gone out with the others instead, then he would probably still be alive."

Jesse puffs out his breath between pursed lips as if blowing out a candle. "Not sure if it helps to go to places like that, Layla. At the end of the day, it was your dad's decision. Your mum wasn't holding him hostage." Not with her hands, but maybe with her heart.

"Even so, nothing about that night really makes sense. She didn't come home till late that night, and Dad was a sailor, Jesse. Even if he was alone, he knew what he was doing."

Jesse's brow furrows and he shifts in the seat. "Maybe the problem is that you've only ever seen the storms from up on our bluff. That bird's-eye view is misleading, makes the waves look small. When you're down there, in the water, they tower over you like the sand dunes. Everyone was lucky that night."

"Except for Dad," I say. We are both silent a moment.

"You must be exhausted," Jesse says, finally. "You should get some sleep. I'll call the hospital."

"I'm sorry. I'm pushing," I say.

Jesse's tense face relaxes. "No, no, honestly, it's okay. After the night you've had, I'm surprised you're not completely falling apart." He puts a hand on my shoulder. Grips it tight.

There is part of me that wants to crumble right here, to scream and fall apart, to let myself sink beneath the heaviness of everything that's happened tonight. Instead, I try and stand up off the barstool but lose my footing. Jesse catches my arm. I haven't had that much to drink but the alcohol mixed with exhaustion is a strong combination.

"I'll take you home," he says.

"It's not my home."

"Back to your mum's then."

"I can't, I can't go back there yet," I say.

Jesse looks at me, then around the distillery. He nods, picks up my bag and leads me to another room, lined with wooden barrels.

"It's black gum," he says. "For the gin I age. Most of the flavor comes from the type of material alcohol's stored in. Some people use oak. I use fallen trees from around the area. You know what it's like after a storm." Although it's called black gum, the wood is honey-colored and the amber glow warms the room; a smell of maple syrup and mandarins.

There's a day bed in the back corner of the room. "I like sleeping here sometimes," he says. "The smell of eucalyptus. Sorry, it's not much, but—"

"No, really," I say, stopping him. "It's exactly what I need."

He nods. Comes toward me and hugs me, past the moment when people usually pull away. I rest my head on his chest. Breathe him in. My neck and torso stiffen, but then our shared history and his understanding of my family make me relax and sink. Worried he might have brought me in here for more than sleep, I pull away. More complications are the last thing I need. I make my way to the bed, away from him; don't have the energy to get changed into anything else so lie down in my clothes. Too exhausted, even, to pull the covers up and onto my body. But Jesse puts my bag next to the bed and tucks me in. "I'll leave you to it," he says and walks out without looking back. I feel the weight of the heavy wool blanket, relieved and tired, but with the familiar feeling of a swirling mind pulling my body from sleep.

I reach down into my bag and take out *Lessons on the Human Body*. There is just enough light from the glow of the distillery's main room to see the black words on white paper. "Sinews," I read, and my breath softens. "Tendrils." I roll the word across my tongue and my pulse slows. Toward the back of the book is a piece of paper, folded in half, a handwritten note that was going to be my medical interns' next assignment.

All valve surgery and most coronary bypass surgery is performed on a non-beating heart. Because the body requires oxygen, which is carried by circulating blood, a machine temporarily takes over the function of the lungs and the heart to pump blood around the body. Specialist anesthetists and cardiac perfusionists may work together to manage the machine. How? How do we help perform the role of the heart?

Putting the book down, I try to sleep but feel restless. Jesse walks back in. "Sorry, just thought you'd like to know your mum's gonna be okay. They're gonna keep her there for a couple of days." And he waves goodbye before leaving me alone.

A heavy sadness fills me when I think of Mum's limp body in the playhouse. The image collides with other anxious ideas about beginnings and endings. About the fact there's part of me that wished my mother dead. At least then she'd *be* gone rather than just *feel* gone. I count the exposed wooden beams above my head and with them the number of times my mother taught me you can be abandoned without being left.

TWENTY-SEVEN

DAD'S FUNERAL WAS HELD ON A COLD SUMMER AFTERNOON. I DIDN'T SAY ANYTHING AT THE SERVICE. EVEN THOUGH the priest wanted me to "say a few words." He asked me in the same tone of voice he used later when he asked if I'd like cream on a scone. I just watched the way the light reflected on the shiny coffin; thought that if I walked right up to that diamond shape and looked into it, I'd be able to see my face. Mum got up to speak. The syllables sounded like an endless tremor rolling off her tongue.

When there are no words for a
life there are the things left
behind; a shadowed yew tree
lit up finally by letter and law; a
foot in a shoe who ran away; a
fat gold watch who does not
know who set her going; and a
moon who aches to, but cannot
find a way to, be a door.

When the smell of the scones and the cream and the strawberry jam and the mini quiches with too much egg became too much, I walked out of the small, carpeted side room and back into the church. It was there I saw Willow.

"Plane delays," she explained, while standing below leadlight. Crimson carpet held ribs of colored light. Next to us, the organ, still turned on, gave a low-throated thrum.

We stood in silence. Looking at each other. Her broomstick limbs static;

her flaming hair brushing the planes of her collarbones; body half-shadowed by the falling sun, as if she was grief's after-image. She smiled, the way she had done as a child, head crooked to the side, tip of her tongue resting on the roof of her mouth. It was the type of look, along with her childlike wonder at beginnings, that made people fall in love with her. She loved the first of everything: first breath of any season, first light, first kisses and first blossom on a tree. She loved the potentiality of things. But not the follow-through. Not the work. She wasn't one to stick around.

"How's the commune and the rainforests? Sri Lanka?" I asked.

"We basically climb up the trees and scream at the loggers for days on end. Until either they back down or take us away," Willow said.

"Living the dream, then," I said.

She laughed, looking down at her shoes; gave a small quiet nod. "You know, the thing is…I'm not even sure I care about the trees. I just like the yelling. Screaming at the top of my lungs until my chest burns and my heart hurts." The stained-glass light shimmered around Willow's body.

"I want to find out what happened to Dad," I whispered.

"It was an accident, Layla. You're the only one who has any doubts."

"How would you know? You weren't there. Aren't here," I said, slightly raising my voice.

"Dad couldn't pilot that boat to save himself. Let alone in a storm."

"Yes, he could. And it still doesn't make any sense," I said.

"Life rarely makes sense, Layla."

When she was younger, Willow had spells. They became worse just before she left home. The one that frightened me the most happened among the Huon pine trees on the perimeter of our property. We were playing hide-and-seek between the trees. I yelled out to ask Willow to say, "Ooo woo." The way we always did when we were trying to get a clue as to where the other person was. But she never made the sound. I finally found her, frozen, unblinking, staring into the distance. I couldn't get her attention.

The priest walked in and saw us talking. Stood a moment. "Your father used to come to church on a Wednesday night," he said, with an exaggerated voice that demanded attention. Willow and I looked at each other, differences aside for a moment, sharing in the shock of Dad going to church. "Had the loveliest voice. Always sat on the pew right up the front, harmonizing with the choir." Then he picked up a book from a table and walked away.

"They were the nights Mum thought he was with other women, Willow. Having affairs. She used to berate him about it. That's what she was probably doing that night. Don't you see? He never deserved anything she dished out."

"None of us are what we seem," Willow said. I felt someone standing behind me. Saw Willow's eyes flick over my shoulder. I turned to see our mum. "I shouldn't have come," my sister whispered, and hurried down the church aisle and out the two large wooden doors. By the time I got outside the church all I could see was Willow running off into the distance.

People started to leave. Walking out and down the steps. Hugging each other. I watched one woman's head rest for a long time on another woman's shoulder; a man hold his son with wraparound arms; then my mum, staring away from me, arms limp and empty by her side.

TWENTY-EIGHT

EARLY NEXT MORNING, I LEAVE A NOTE FOR JESSE AND
TAKE A WALK IN THE CRISP AIR TO CLEAR MY HEAD. LOCATED ON THE
far edge of the village, the distillery is nestled in the middle of trees, down the
road from the post office. When I walk past, the sign across the weatherboard
building is the same it has always been: "Mail, School Uniforms, Craft
Supplies, Newsagency." Shops in small towns must be more, do more, than
one thing. A bit like its people.

Only the bakery's light is on, as staff take trays of bread from an oven and
feed them into the shop's display. Steam fogs the glass.

A woman unlocks the hardware-store side door. Port Jericho is still the
kind of place where people need to buy screws and nuts, nails and hammers.

Buildings tremble on the verge of color. The sunrise begins in a fire of
orange and crimson that merges into soft pinks and changing blues. The light
spreads over the nearby mountains and reaches the sleeping shops. The sun
sends steamy vapors from the tarred road.

I make my way down to the wharf. A long time ago, it was a place where
convicts built ships' hulls by hand. Lobster traps sit stacked on top of each
other, ready for the day. Fishing still matters in the community, and moorings
in the harbor are split between lobster boats and single-masted sailing boats.
The vessels of various shapes and sizes line the wharf, moving backwards and
forwards on the water like rocking chairs. A woman throws crates of rope
onto a boat and two men in peacoats stand outside the closed Fisherman's
Wharf restaurant.

"There's no kitchen in her, but I tell ya, she sails straighter than any other

I've sailed," one says, before clapping his hands and rubbing them together.

"Well, Jim," the other one says, "all boats are a compromise."

The pier, extending out perpendicularly from the port, has been repaired and extended since I was young. Metal cleats and springs now hold boats tight. The first ferry out glides upon an even keel. My breath smokes in cold puffs.

In the distance, the train station comes alive. I stop for a moment when I see the forest-green engine, the black-lacquered boiler, brass lettering, and blood-red carriages. When I last rode the train with Willow, I spent the trip counting the stitches in the seat above Mum's back.

Today, the fireman scrapes his shovel into a container of coal and feeds the boiler; steam billows from the vibrating valve. At this time of year, the train transports bees from the east coast to the west, where they can drink the nectar of the flowering leatherwoods.

A Christmas market is being set up in the grounds of my old public school. One classroom window is filled with primary-colored paintings and the other with crayon rubbings. We used to do the same. Collect leaves, feathers and twigs from around the schoolyard, put them in envelopes and then ask classmates to color over them with crayons. They had to guess what was inside.

I think about Dawn sleeping alone at Mum's house all night. The least I can do, after the night we've just had, is cook up a hot breakfast. I look around the market for supplies. An acoustic guitar player has already started plucking steel strings as stall holders flick open wooden trestle tables and laugh and talk about whether enough people will come to make braving the morning cold worth it. "Everyone leaves buying presents till the last minute," a man with a wooden-toy stand says.

The coffee van already has a couple of people waiting; I take my place in line before ordering a long black with a splash of cold milk. As I stand and wait, the stalls are nearly up and ready for the day. Westside Garlic has bulbs, bags and glass jars of salts; Mumma More sells relishes, pickles and preserves; a bright-yellow tent with "Join Our Honey Club" across their marquee has so many jars of honey they spill out in front of the table and onto the asphalt. Next to that is Nicola's Olive Estate, Portuguese tarts, mosaic-covered bird-baths, and sheepskin boots and rugs.

While I wait for my coffee, I check my emails. A red exclamation mark catches my eye and I take a breath before I click it open. It's from the hospital where I work. Nausea fills my body, the same sick sinking I used to feel when I got in trouble in this very school. Does every woman feel like this? As if they are half woman, half little girl?

"Layla, please call me about your post-review surgery at your earliest convenience. Dr Madden," is all it says. I look at the time. Too early to call. Fuck Mum for putting me in this position in the first place. I should be visiting her. Should. *Should*. It feels like she waited for me to come home to try and kill herself. And then promised me answers she had no intention of giving. What kind of mother does that? It's a question I've been asking myself my whole life.

With coffee in hand, I try to distract myself and walk around; collect an open carton of eggs, a still-warm loaf of sourdough bread, small marshmallow-soft mushrooms in a paper bag and local butter. My arms laden with produce, I stop and put some of it on the ground, eggs still in my hands. I look up to see bright-red flowers filling half a table, the rest covered with pamphlets, T-shirts and stickers. The stall holder locks eyes before walking over and wrapping her arms around me. She smells of orange rind and rose oil. As she pulls away with a broad smile, I rack my brain trying to remember where I know her from.

"Elizabeth Lanyon. I was your sister's best friend," she says. "Holy moly, I miss Willow every single darn day. How is she?"

I must still have a confused look on my face, because she laughs, but in a way that warms me on this cold morning. Finally, I remember her; grasp an image of Willow and Liz laughing together at the shops after school.

"I feel like I should ask *you* how Willow is. We don't talk much." I say this last bit more to myself.

"We keep in contact. I even sent her a T-shirt. But it's not the same, you know? Willow and Dawn have been pretty—"

"Dawn?" The name from her lips takes me by surprise.

"Oh, she joined our group years ago. I sent T-shirts to the aged-care home as well. Some of the nurses come and do our tours when they visit. You know, word of mouth being the best form of marketing and all that."

I look over Liz's shoulder to the stall. "What is it that you—"

"First of all..." She hands me a wicker basket and helps pick up the bread and mushrooms and butter and put them inside. Adds one of the black T-shirts. "We're called Save the Dark. Been running for about fifteen years now. Me, my partner and a few friends. Maggie is a member. It's part education, part eco-tour." Dawn, Willow, Maggie. There are whole worlds I don't know about. "We try and teach people that light pollution is as bad as any other pollution. People are so keen to turn a light on as soon as their world dims but, truth is, everything needs the dark—plants, animals, humans. Part of the reason we and the planet are so messed up is because of 'light worship,' as I call it."

"What do you do on the tours? I can't see Maggie doing anything like that," I say, balancing the full basket in my arms.

"She's our most requested guide." Liz laughs. "We take people out to see a proper night sky, stars, planets and the Milky Way. People smell the white-and-yellow flowers opening their petals for nighttime pollinators. We listen to owls, try to spot bats, and watch the fireflies flash their secret signals. We believe the dark night sky should be as much a part of our natural heritage as wildlife and bushland."

"Sounds like something they should do up where I live," I say.

Liz nods and then picks up a potted poinsettia. "That's why I have these beauties. They only bloom—"

"Oh, I remember your science project now." I smile and place a hand on Liz's arm. "Sorry to interrupt you, but I remember you standing in the gym. With your posters, saying that in the future kids will learn about stars from photographs in books. You're probably not far off being right. Kids where we live use computers and apps to explore the sky. But it's not the same as being able to go outside and see, with your own eyes, your own small corner of the universe."

"Wasn't just my project. Was your sister's too. She was a whole lot smarter than me. I just came along for the ride."

I've never thought of Willow as being smart.

"She was on track to win a university science scholarship," Liz says. "But then her marks got bad, and she just, I don't know…retreated. We don't talk about it, but yeah, for a while there she was destined for some pretty amazing things."

Liz puts down the plant and claps the dirt off her hands. "I often think of you, Layla. We all do."

There's a warmth from Liz I haven't experienced in the town before. All these visits, when I've come just before Christmas, my hometown and its people have seemed cold and quiet and inhospitable. Apart from Mum, something feels different this time.

"You're always welcome to join us. At the very least for the wine and cheese we have at meetings," Liz says, before picking up another poinsettia and putting it in my basket.

TWENTY-NINE

I MAKE MY WAY OUT OF THE SCHOOLYARD AND DOWN THE ROAD BEFORE COMING TO THE TOWN'S CEMETERY; OPEN LAND, braceleted by trees. The graveyard looks like a sea of empty beds. Older headstones are cut from Huon pine. Lasts longer than concrete, they used to say. Bright-green grass has grown like blankets on the older graves, and crosses above beds cast long shadows in the morning sun.

Some of the newer graves are concrete with marble covers. Dad's, a combination of cement and pine. He lies between a teacher I had at school and a man named Lawrence Stanley.

Here lies beloved wife, mother, grandmother, and teacher to the community, Yvonne Marre. 1918–1988. The world is a richer place because she once lived.

Lawrence's headstone reads,

In loving memory. Beloved by family, treasured by friends, parted by death but we will be reunited in heaven. Good night, dear heart, good night, good night.

I recall the last line from visiting Mark Twain's daughter's grave at Woodland Cemetery in New York; the words slightly altered from a poem by Robert Richardson called "Annette."

Both graves either side of my father's have new fresh flowers in metal vases attached to the headstones. Weeds have been pulled and any dirt recently dusted off. There is a small square of fake grass placed in front of Yvonne's, with worn oval patches in the shape of knees; and Lawrence's has had a park bench erected opposite his burial plot, with a small gold plaque identifying that it was donated by the Council for years of service.

I look back to my dad's grave.

Dr Oscar Byrnes. 1938–1985. Husband to Nora, father to Willow and Layla.

It's a mess and the grass is wild; weeds with prickly gray edges sprout everywhere.

I haven't visited Dad's grave since he was buried. I always felt closer to him in the hospital, being a doctor. I never thought of coming here. But now, looking at the clearly unloved and unmaintained grave, I feel embarrassed and ashamed of my selfishness. I breathe a quiet "Sorry" to my father.

When I look at the three graves again, and read some of the surrounding headstones, it strikes me that it's not just the unkempt-versus-loved look of the graves that differentiates them, but also their dedications. I feel a match spark and burn in my heart. Would be just like Mum to give Dad these flat words. Dad's unacknowledged legacy plays on my mind.

A few meters away, the children's graves with rainbow pinwheels constrict my airways. I've seen too many children die at work. Last year, I ran a research project into reducing children's pre-surgical anxiety. We found that those taken into the operating theatre in playful, remote-controlled rockets had reduced preoperative stress and better postoperative recovery. My supervisor, Dr. Phillips, couldn't argue with the results and signed off on developing the program further. I even asked an old university friend who was now at NASA to design the kids' rocket to look exactly like their current ship; hospital gowns were replaced with astronaut suits, customized with the patient's name, "Astronaut Mary" or "Oneida" or "Aki." I look at the time. I need to head up the hill to Dawn, but call Dr. Madden, head of anesthesia at the hospital, and he answers straightaway.

"Layla, I got your email and—"

"Doctor Byrnes. It's Doctor Byrnes," I correct him. "I just wanted to ask first, about the rockets, whether Darsh is remembering to print out the names for the gowns. It's important the kids see their own name."

"Rockets?" he asks. "Oh, you mean Dr. Phillips's preoperative project?"

"My project. I…it was, is, my initiative. I spent two years on it. I published an article about it."

"Co-authored with Dr. Phillips."

"Well, yes, but only because you suggested it. Because it increased our chance of publication."

"You'll have to forgive me. He is here day and night. So, I see him implementing the project more often." Heat rises up in my arms and face. "I received your email and we are all disappointed that you didn't appear for your surgery."

"I've had a family emergency, as I explained. I also have an impeccable record and I know that in the future this won't—"

"Layla, Dr. Byrnes, look." He lets out a sigh. "You know, I have children of my own and understand how they can be...derailing."

I bristle, knowing he has his wife, Margaret, at home, who does everything for him. He starts a spiel I've heard a million times before in meetings and public presentations. "We pride ourselves on being equal opportunity. It's something I myself have"—I see him in my mind wiggling his fingers in the air as he always does, as if playing an imaginary piano—"orchestrated."

People are in awe of Madden because he brings in so much money from donors. They also say there's nobody like him for having a memory for people's mistakes. I wonder whether there's a connection between soliciting donations and holding grudges.

"This is a profession that, rightfully so, demands focus, consistency and excellence. All is not lost; I'll still write you a glowing—" he starts but I hang up before he gets a chance to finish. Which is probably the worst thing I could have done, but I can't listen to him patronize me anymore. All I can think about is having sat in that waiting room ahead of appearing before the medical tribunal and hospital board, looking at the thickly framed oil paintings around the walls. The men who have been commended. The hospital wings we walk down, named after men; the classical music we listen to in surgery, men. Their honors and careers seem less impressive when you realize they had full-time free childcare, a cook, cleaner, launderer. They had wives. All so they could focus on "consistency and excellence." I don't envy them. There's not a minute I've spent with my kids that I would have given up, but still. I miss my job. I love my children. And I have no idea how to reconcile the two. When I was little, I believed I could *have it all*, that in fact I had an obligation to all the women who lived before me to take advantage of as many opportunities as I can. But I'm not sure I really *have* anything. I'm just *doing* everything. And none of it very well.

I look at Dad's unkempt grave; drop to my knees and start pulling out the weeds with my hands, prickle and scratch ignored, and I throw the leaves and roots across the site and away from my father's bones. My breath heaves as my body strains, and I wipe my face with the back of my hand, leaving what I'm sure are streaks of dirt. When all the weeds have been pulled, I wipe down the grave top with my flat palm, in sweeping motions, until my hand flinches. Blood shocks bright. I look down to find a piece of glass.

And I'm suddenly eighteen again. In the back of Bill's pickup. Watching my mother's face in the police car as Michael describes seeing her throwing empty wine bottles at my father's grave. I suck the slit in my hand. Saliva the best medicine. I stand, dirty, breathless and angry.

Picking up the basket of food, I look up the road and to the extinct volcano I have to climb to get to Mum's house and Dawn. A not-so-silent reminder of destruction.

THIRTY

MUM'S HOUSE LOOMS. MY HAND IS STILL BLEEDING FROM THE GLASS CUT. IF I DIDN'T NEED A BAND-AID, I WOULD probably delay entry longer. Every time I stand in this spot, I am a little girl all over again. The nausea of not knowing what I'm coming home to, paralyzing. Even with Mum out of the house and in hospital, the feeling is still there. The fear. Sometimes my childhood seems like one long night of dreams. Until I come home and I am very much awake.

I expect to walk into a ramshackle mess, but inside it looks like Dawn's been up all night cleaning. The house is quiet. I peek into Mum's bedroom and Dawn is asleep. I've been a doctor too long for sleep not to conjure death, so I creep up and make sure she's breathing before finding a Band-Aid for my hand and unpacking the market produce onto the kitchen table.

I wash the dirt from Dad's grave off my hands and arms before starting breakfast.

Butter sizzles in the pan as I fry the mushrooms and then scramble eggs, mixed with cream rather than milk, which separates. Hot, thickly sliced toast. I look out the window and realize Dawn has also cleaned up the playhouse, where I found Mum. I see the drawings are still taped to the inside walls. I close my eyes in pain from the memory.

As I heat water in a saucepan for tea, Dawn shuffles into the kitchen. No wigs or silk kimonos or makeup. Her eyes are half open, still tired. She resembles the elderly woman who collapsed at the airport hotel.

"Have you heard? Is she going to be okay?" Dawn asks.

"Right as rain," I say through slightly gritted teeth. "I would have helped,

Dawn." I gesture to the clean room. "You should have waited."

"I should have done a lot of things in my life, Layla. The *shoulds* and the *should nots* have become harder and harder to decipher."

"I'm just saying, you collapsed only two days ago."

"Are you saying that as a doctor or my niece?"

"Dawn," I sigh. "Both." Though I wonder myself.

In the lounge room, the only thing left to tidy away is Willow's mattress, which Dawn wouldn't have been able to move. It has no handles, so I try to grip as much of the material as I can to hoist it up on its side, but it buckles in the middle and falls to the ground. I sandwich it between my palms then, to lift it up and slide it along the ground, stepping forwards and dragging my outside leg as if I'm injured and limping.

"Layla, Layla, leave it. We can do that later. Come and eat outside with me—I am never allowed to eat outside at the home. I've been dreaming of it."

I bring the plates out and she sits slowly at the white wrought-iron patio table and chairs. She picks up a fork; knuckles white-and-blue knobs in a setting of stretched skin. I pour tea the way she likes it: "strong enough to bend a spoon."

I say, "There aren't many problems in this world that can't be—"

"Solved with a strong cup of tea," she finishes. "I know I used to give you girls that advice but, like things parents say to their kids, I'm not sure I believe it myself. It's supposed to be more comfort than truth."

This side of the house gets the morning sun and Dawn closes her eyes and tips her head back.

"Hey, I need to ask you something," I say. "Who gave the cemetery, or whoever creates those things, the words to put on Dad's grave?" I move the scrambled eggs around the plate with my fork.

She looks at me and sighs. "I don't know, Layla. It was a long time ago. I don't think anyone was in the right frame of mind to be particularly poetic."

"It reads as cold as the cement looks." We take grape-sized sips of the hot tea. Cups on saucers clink.

"I always think of Nora knitting when I sit in this chair," Dawn says. "She'd love to sit here in the sun. Made her own yarn. Like I make silk. Spent days cleaning the wool, separating the fibers, turning it into something she could use. Dyed it with spices she bought in town. Once, a really popular girl at your school wore a yellow scarf. Do you remember? The one that befriended Adara, Rebecca someone…"

"Woolson," I say.

Dawn nods. "Yes, she walked around boasting to everyone that her parents had bought it overseas. You talked about it for weeks. Nora went out and picked the softest fleece. Oscar never gave her much money but she used what she could scrounge to buy the knitting needles, and the most expensive turmeric to dye the wool that vibrant color. Knitted you the most beautiful scarf."

"She didn't have to do that," I say.

"No, love, she didn't. She didn't have to do that." A length of bark hangs half torn off a eucalyptus tree like a small thread clinging to a sweater, waiting to be pulled free. "Are you going to visit her today?" she asks.

"Sorry?" I ask, distracted. Still thinking of Dad's grave.

"Your mum, are you going in?"

"No. I'm not going."

"Layla, no matter what, she's still your mum. She's your family, and even though—"

"Please don't," I say. "None of you understand. You didn't grow up with her—you don't know. Honestly, after everything, she can go to hell." Now that I've started, I can't stop pulling the words out from the heat in my heart. "And how dare she wait till I got home to do it. So that I would find her. I should never have messaged Maggie when I'd be home. She would have told her. Mum timed it so I would be here."

"Nora's holding on to a lot, Layla. She never worked out how to be happy after your dad drowned."

I recoil from the words, still reluctant to hear "Dad" and "drowned" in the same sentence, even after all these years. "She wasn't happy before Dad… it doesn't matter," I say. "She still makes everything about her. It's the ultimate selfish act. How dare she not think about her grandchildren or Willow or you, how dare she—" I stop, short-winded. "How dare she never, ever think about me. She can rot in that hospital, for all I care. I'm done, and I'll be damned if I give her one more second of the attention I should be giving to other people."

"Layla, please." Dawn looks at me, beseeching. "After I saw Nora last night. I saw my little sister in that moment and I…I want to explain." Dawn puts her cup down and pushes her plate away. Clasps both hands together and offers them on the table. "She deserves that from me at least."

My tea has gone cold. I nod and sit back. Hoping I'm going to hear some truths about the night Dad died.

"After you left for university, I came back to keep Nora company," she says. "Over the years, Maggie and I became close. It was just before you had Audrey that Bill and Maggie separated. Bill was fine at first, happy to have some space down on his boat at the harbor. But then one day he found us in bed together."

"Wait, what?" I say. My mind races. "I didn't know that…you…" I search my heart for the right words.

"You were always too caught up in your own life to get to know me. It's okay. Most of us live like that."

"But I don't…" I rack my brain for any memory of them together, but can't.

Dawn holds her hand up as if she wants me to stop and listen to what she is saying.

"Bill…" She pauses a moment, twirls her cup on her saucer. "Shit." She takes a sip of her tea. "Bill, he found Maggie and me in bed together and he lost it. It was the heart of winter. He bolted out the door. We watched him from the window. He took a machete from the shed, stormed round the property like a man possessed, smashing her beautiful, colored ice spheres to pieces, spilling the color across the snow. We were terrified. Maggie ran out and was screaming, yelling at him to stop. 'Please, for the love of God, don't do this,' I can still hear her screaming in my head." Dawn pauses and brings her hand, now shaking, to cover her mouth. Looks off to the side toward the ocean. Her hand is wrinkled and the veins blue. "I'll never forget the sound of her voice that day. After destroying all the spheres, Bill ran back into the house, pulled me out of bed and dragged me down the steps, into the yard, and threw me naked onto the snow. The patch was covered in red dye from one of the smashed spheres, so that when I stood up, it looked as though he had beaten me with the machete as well. Might as well have. I ran to your mum's place to get warm. I was naked, stained red."

"Oh my God, Dawn. Why didn't you ever tell me this?"

"A whole lot of truths wrapped up in that story. And shame, but worse. Shame you know you shouldn't feel, which has a way of muffling the heart."

"I'm so sorry." I think about the airport sculpture that reminded me of Maggie's spheres. The way Dawn had stared at it before she collapsed.

Dawn turns to me with her ever-dry eyes. "You know, when your mum and I were young, we were inseparable. We had each other's back. I never thought that would change. But time does change things. Your dad's death first, then that day."

"But why that day? Wasn't Mum's fault." I can't believe I'm defending her.

Dawn makes a sucking sound. Looks at me for a moment, taking my measure. "Ah, love," she says, then shakes her head. Looks toward the heavens as if asking for help. "That day. When Bill pulled me from Maggie's bed, threw me into the snow. When I was naked and stained red, I ran to your mum's for help, for...love. Your mum, she sided with Bill. Told me I had no right being in bed with a man's wife, that I deserved everything Bill dished out." I stop to think about this. "That's when I came to live with you," she says. "When I turned up on your doorstep. I just couldn't bear the thought of being alone after that." I think about what Dawn gave us over those years and how we put her in a home. Alone again.

I stand up slowly, pick up my iron chair and put it next to Dawn's. Wrapping both arms around her, the way I used to do as a child. I want to say something meaningful. Words that explain how sorry I am for not fighting to keep her in our home, our family. Dawn has only ever given to everyone in her life. Only ever wanted to be loved.

"I love you," is all I can think of saying. I haven't said those words to her in years. Her body softens for a moment. Rests in my embrace.

"But I need to tell you something else, Layla," she says, gently pulling my arms down and looking into my eyes. "It's important. I was thinking about it all night when I was cleaning. Your mum, she didn't have anything to do with your dad's death. You can't blame her for that anymore. Some blame she deserves—God knows we take our comeuppance when we need to—but that, that she doesn't deserve." The quiet pulse of history sounds through what she is saying. And not saying.

"I don't understand," I say.

"When I saw Nora last night. I…I've been hard on her, Layla. I just don't want you to be there too. What I'm trying to say is…"

"Why does everyone talk in circles around me?"

Annoyance clouds her face. "I'm just saying stop, please, stop blaming her for your dad's death." Dawn starts coughing. Takes a sip of her cold tea. "You know, in my day, people just kept to themselves. There wasn't this endless self-indulgent searching. These days, the world is run on the fuel of truth-seeking. Most people go for most of their lives without caring. Out of sight, out of mind. A bit like old people in nursing homes." Dawn looks down at her plate as she talks, presses her toast flat.

"I hate the deception more than I would hate *you* for telling me." I make the point of saying the word "you" like an arrow. To make it personal. I look at the food on our plates. Mine merely moved around. Dawn's toast flattened as if someone has pressed it between the leaves of a book as a keepsake.

"Your dad's death was not her fault. That's all I'll say."

But that's not all she is saying. I think of her running over to my mother. The humiliation. Dawn, as naked as a pin. Even though I want to push her to tell me more, I let it go. All I can think about is her then turning up on our doorstep. I hug her again.

"Alright, alright," she says, gently pushing me away, "these eggs smell amazing."

I smile, pick up my plate and go into the kitchen to scrape the food into the bin; watch Dawn for a moment out the window, carefully guiding yellow clouds onto her fork. Some things can only be known with age and most of those things that have to do with love require a fair amount of amnesia. But then I consider Bill and his rage. His anger at Dawn for taking something he saw as his. The way he broke everything and anything in his line of sight that was valuable to the women. And something does not sit right.

In medical school we learned about the way memories are stored. That they only exist in our short-term memory unless they are rehearsed. Repeated. Then they move into the long-term stage. If we do not pay enough attention to events, they fade away. But memories create our reality. They are the only truth we know unless told otherwise.

I hated Mum, for many things. Not least for telling me she would leave the truth in her drawer but then not doing so, for hurting herself just in time for me to find her almost lifeless body. But maybe with Dad's death, I've been focusing on the wrong events. Her yelling at Dad, preventing him from going out in the boat with the other men. Driving him to danger.

Pay attention, I think. Pay attention. I see Dad in his boat. The full-moon night. Even with the storming clouds there was light. My father, the trained navigator. The waves were ten foot, maybe twelve, yes. But boats are only obscured when waves come in between them and someone's line of sight. Like any wave, there are troughs precisely as many times as peaks. Dad would have found their boat; it wasn't that far out; they must have seen him. What I didn't understand was what happened in between the time when he reached the capsizing vessel and when he drowned. That, I realize, is the missing piece. I have no way of knowing what happened, but I do have a memory, which I have paid attention to over the years. Every time I visited a butcher or deli, the flashback played again. Moving more and more firmly from short term into long term. And it occurs again to me now. A memory of the time Bill slaughtered a lamb.

THIRTY-ONE

I WAS THIRTEEN YEARS OLD WHEN I FIRST HEARD ABOUT BILL AND DAD'S FEUD. WHEN BILL AND MAGGIE'S SUPERMARKET distributor said they needed almost double the milk or they'd go elsewhere, to Jackelby's farm in the Derwent Valley. Bill was desperate to increase his herd from two hundred head to five hundred. To do that, he needed at least three more acres per extra cow. The only way he'd be able to get that was to cut down the Huon pine trees that ran along the perimeter line between our properties.

Bill didn't think Dad would mind. "Wasn't even going to mention it," he said to anyone who would listen. "Was just gonna cut them down." He was shocked when, over a friendly tin-mugged tea, Dad threw the last bits of sweet liquid into the bush and said, "No. I can't agree to this." They didn't speak again until the night Dad died.

Bill shared his anger toward Dad with anyone in the town who'd listen. "How many animals am I gonna have to kill, Jerome?" he'd say to the man who owned the bakery. "Since when does someone get to tell a man what he does with his own trees?" he'd ask Bob Davis down at the wharf. Sometimes we would overhear him. Sometimes people would tell Mum at the supermarket or me at school.

Even with the dispute, we still bought meat and milk from Bill. He was nice enough to Mum and me but maintained a fire-in-the-belly rage toward Dad. "Do you think I want to be doing this? I'm a milk man, not a meat man," he said one day as he climbed up and stood on his workbench with a lamb. I didn't know what was happening. I stood behind Mum, who hadn't seen me run up behind her midway through their conversation. The light winked through the barn slats. "Meat will only bridge the divide for so long," he said. In between words he grunted, as if the sentence was hard to say.

I watched Bill's triceps. His hairy, bent knees peeking through thick, ripped work pants. He held the lamb's chin in his hands before running a knife swiftly along its neck, as simply and gracefully as if he were up there with a baton conducting an orchestra. I should have looked away but had no warning. My body let out a high-pitched whimper and Mum turned around to see me there, my palms turned upward to the sky. "Layla, what are you doing here? I told you to stay and hang the washing out." I just stood there, watching the limp animal. The blood fanning across the table and onto the concrete floor. "Ah well, love," she said to me, "we see these things sooner or later. You're not that young anymore. Maybe delay only makes it worse."

"We'll sort this out, Bill. We always do," Mum said to him.

He climbed down from the table, gripped the lamb's forelegs and pumped them up and down. Emptying the small animal's body of blood. I stood there watching, knowing in that moment that I would never be able to get the imagery out of my head but still not being able to look away.

Adara and Maggie were outside, stringing up bales of hay. I watched Maggie attempt to show Adara how to tie the hay bale, creating two loops with square knots on each end and then connecting them with a slipknot. Untying and retying again and again. "Adara. Look. Please, I need your help with this," I heard Maggie say. "You can't live on a farm and not pitch in. You think this is my idea of fun? It's not, so watch again."

Mum stepped toward Bill. "What if we let you farm some cattle on our land?"

I turned from Adara and Maggie to watch Bill roll his eyes. "You don't think I thought of that? First of all, there's boundaries to contend with, and then there's Oscar. He flatly refused to that as much as the trees." He poked the lamb in the back of its leg and then inserted a shining metal hook. With a grunt, he hoisted it up and hung it in the middle of the barn. Blood, darker now, dripped to join the rest.

"Thought of moving to a bigger farm? Or the guys at the bank could help you out? They have in the past."

Bill stopped, the lamb still. Maggie and Adara threw the last hay bale onto a pyramid just outside the barn and looked at Mum.

"Here we go," Maggie said beneath her breath.

"My grandfather came here on a boat, only one of five to survive the trip, and worked in the coal mines to buy this piece of land. Crawled inside a trap-door the size of a fucking fairy house for twenty-five years." Bill wiped his hand across his forehead and left a streak of blood. "And anyway, the banks believe a productive property is a cleared property. Simple as that."

Maggie and Adara came into the barn. Adara just looked at the lamb like it was as ordinary as a piece of household furniture. "Bill, it's not Nora's fault," Maggie said. "What is she supposed to do? Just let it be."

"I have half a mind just to cut the bloody things down. Should have done that in the first place. Rather than mention it to that mainlander-dressed-up-as-islander husband of yours." At the sound of Bill's raised voice about Dad, Adara and I exchanged blushed glances. "Don't get me wrong, Nora, you know I'm not like them loggers down at the ridge. But if it comes down to my family's livelihood versus a few pieces of wood. What am I supposed to do?"

With the hay bales tied, Maggie took Adara back out of the barn and to the pasture where the cows were grazing. They clipped a rope onto a large black-and-white cow and led her to the gate, separating her from a calf who ran back and forth and cried in a high-pitched bellow. The sound didn't stop until the cow had been led into the milking stall next door to the barn and was out of view.

"Okay, okay, I get the picture. I'm just saying. It's not just the trees—the wind up here has already knocked over those old stalls twice," Mum said.

"Only someone who's come here from the mainland would say we should sell. My father always said, the mainland is full of snakes." In the stall next to us, the milking system began to whir to life. Slowly at first but then with a marching rhythm. Mum took another step toward Bill, who had started separating the skin of the lamb from its flesh.

"Then why don't you, Bill?" Mum said, quieter now. "Why don't you just cut the fucking things down?"

"Because, since Oscar put the petition into Council, the greenies are onto me, men from Council are driving past every few days. I see their silver station wagon slow right down at the base of the bluff. The fine would do me in as well. I'm not between a rock and a hard place, I'm lodged between two hand grenades, choosing which pin to pull."

"Don't you think that's rather—"

"You're probably in on it," he said. "Heard you were one of those chained to the trees when they wanted to build the hydro."

"That's different. And you know it, Bill. There's a time and a place."

"Didn't strike me as an enviro guy, your Oscar," Bill said.

With that, Bill pulled the last of the skin off the lamb's body and severed the head; it fell to the concrete floor and rolled to within an inch of my feet. Mum turned and walked out the barn door, leaving me there. Adara stood nearby. I froze, looking at the lamb's face, then ran after Mum. Trying to escape. Trying to outrun the thought of my best friend and her parents losing everything and having to move; trying to outrun the fight between Bill and my father; but most of all, I was trying to shake from my mind an image of the lamb leaping around only hours ago, naive to its place in the food chain.

THIRTY-TWO

IT TAKES ME THREE GOES TO GET WILLOW'S MATTRESS BACK ON ITS BED FRAME. DAWN NAPS. I PULL ON MY OLD NAVY-BLUE gumboots. Once I leave the driveway, I find that the path Adara and I made when we were girls, running back and forth to see each other, is still there.

I walk toward the Huon pines that tower over our properties and act as a more obvious land divide than the farm fencing. Hoof-churned mud sticks to my boots. Silage ferments under a large green tarp. The smell of cow manure gives the air shape.

On Adara's property, the cows are in their barn after their morning milking and feed. They don't even raise their heads as I walk by. When I look back on to our property, the once-dense forest is now sparse and I can see our previously obscured observatory.

"Layla, how are you? How's Nora?" I turn to see Bill standing in overalls, knee-high gumboots, carrying a stainless-steel bucket. "Drove Maggie back home from the hospital this morning. Farmhand did a right old job messing up the morning feed, so I'm playing catch-up." Bill is still tall and broad, though he has softened in the middle, his gut sloping forwards under his plaid shirt. There are bruised bags beneath his eyes, as if he hasn't slept in all these years.

"Mum tried to kill herself. But she's alive. She's in the hospital." I speak the words as if they're being punched out on a typewriter for the morning news. My mind is on other things. Of questions to ask and answers I want.

"Nora." Bill's eyes tear up. I've never seen him get emotional. "I don't know what I could have done. Oh, Nora," he repeats. His hands shake; he takes a handkerchief from his pocket and wipes his face. I don't feel anything for either Bill or Mum.

"You know what I'm learning, Bill? The way time always reveals the true nature of things." There is so much I want to say. "You cut down the trees," is all I can muster.

The line of Bill's lips curve, hard as a blade's edge. "Well, yes, of course, the change."

"Change meaning that the person who stood in your way happened to die?"

"Whoa, now hang on, missy, I didn't mean—"

"It just doesn't make any sense. It's never made any sense. How Dad, an experienced sailor, could go out, even in a storm, and never come back."

"You should probably check yourself, love, before you go throwing around accusations like that."

"Convenient, though, isn't it?" I say.

"You don't know what you're talking about." Bill sets down the bucket. Puts his hands in his pockets. Takes them out again.

"I'm not saying you killed him with your bare hands, Bill, but there are lots of ways to kill a man."

"Layla, we were busy saving people's lives," he says through gritted teeth, as if at the mercy of a ventriloquist.

"All I know is that Dad went out. He would have found you. What I don't know is what happened afterwards. Either way, you were there."

"There were kids, damn it." Bill's voice rises. "Frank was giving mouth to mouth to a three-year-old," he says.

I try not to let the image derail my questions.

"You cut down the trees, Bill. You cut them down."

"Nothing to do with your dad, Layla," he says. Every time he takes his hands out of his pockets, they eventually creep back in like fish sliding back into water.

"Why would I believe a word you say?" I ask.

"Listen, Layla," he says, as he steps toward me. "When I was a boy, we had huskies. Sometimes, I used to play and forget they were sleeping. I might whack a stick against a tree or come barreling round pretending to be an airplane. When dogs wake like that, they're unpredictable. More than once I got my arm chewed into. That's when I learned where that saying comes from."

"But, Bill, I—"

"To let sleeping dogs lie. It's not my place to have this chat, Layla. Never has been." A resolved expression is stapled to his face. We stand staring at each other when Maggie joins us.

"What's going on? Hey, Layla, how ya doing?" She's holding a tea towel; wrings the fabric in her hands. Ties it into a knot. Maggie still has the appearance of a little girl grown old. A brown bob of wavy hair, freckles across her nose and cheeks; slim and swaying, as if at any moment she might close her eyes and wave her arms above her head, dancing to music only she can hear. The only parts of her that give her age away are her neck and chest, which sag within her denim shirt, as if her heart is so heavy it draws what's outside of it in. Maggie's body doesn't yet show the signs of disease, signs I know all too well. Soon she will be raw-boned, hair and weight and color fading away.

"I found Mum," I say. "Almost dead in our playhouse. She's at the hospital. They say she's going to be okay. She'd taken a whole lot of pills."

"Jesus," Maggie says. "I stayed for as long as I could, Layla. Lord knows I would have stayed longer if I didn't have chemo at the hospital. You know better than anyone I can't miss those."

I nod. "I know. I know. It's not your fault. I think she waited for me, wanted me to find her."

"Ah, love, I don't think she was in the right frame of mind to think that clearly. I was with her, then Bill was, and then I think, as soon as she was alone, she just…"

My head pounds and I rub the side of my face with my fingers. "That's not why I'm here anyway." I turn back to Bill. "All this time, I thought it was

Mum's fault, for fighting with Dad, for delaying him so that he had to go out alone, and maybe in some ways it was, but you were the one who was there, Bill. You. Were. There." I shout each word.

"Layla." Maggie steps forwards.

"Don't you defend him," I say, turning to her. "Dawn told me what happened." They both look confused for a moment, before they realize what I'm talking about. "How can you not hate him?"

"Well, people are hard to hate up close, sweetheart." Maggie unknots the tea towel and folds it into a small square. Her face clenches.

"I'll tell you something, Bill. You either didn't help Dad when he needed it or you did worse, but either way you've got blood on your hands."

"Whoa, whoa, hang on for a second," Maggie says.

"I don't want to hear it," I say. "I've had a gutful. I'm going to tell the kids not to come and I'll fly home as soon as I can tomorrow. Leave me the fuck alone." I turn and walk back toward Mum's.

"Wait!" Maggie yells and I stop. Turn. She stands there, arms by her side. I wait. She is silent.

I raise my shoulders at her as if to say, "What?" When she doesn't say anything I turn back around and start walking away again.

"Wait, Layla, wait." I stop walking but keep my back to her. "I can't bear the blame you place on your mum anymore. And, now, I can't have you blaming Bill either." She sighs. "Enough's enough." She walks toward me and talks more quietly, so I need to turn around to hear. "Your mum, she was going to leave you everything in that locked drawer, but I, we…" She looks to the ground. She turns away, puts one hand on her hip and the other across her mouth, as if she's deciding whether to open it again. Turns back again to face me. "I've never wanted, we've never wanted the truth to come out. Bill more than anyone. And Adara—it was the only control she had left. So, when you told me where everything was…"

"Maggie…" I stare at her.

"We unlocked the wardrobe and pulled out the box. Moved it over to my place. We were going to burn it. Your mum, she would have thought everything was still in there."

"What?" I choke on the word.

"I...I need a moment first," Maggie says. "Come sit on the porch. I'll make you a hot drink." We walk over to Maggie's house, past the pots of rosemary and up to the sweet smell of creeping jasmine. Maggie and Bill walk inside and the screen door slams behind them. Then the hardwood door. I crane my neck to try and hear what they're saying but I can't discern anything.

The unpainted veranda posts have dried to silver in the sun. As I sit down on the porch seat, I look out over the land. Cows in the distance low. I grate my nail along the white wicker armrest, scraping off white flecks. Ahead of me, a nest sits in the crook of a eucalypt. A baby bird stands on its edge, small wings flapping, looking down, leaning over an abyss from which there will be no return.

THIRTY-THREE

EVENTUALLY, AFTER MAGGIE, BILL AND ADARA SEEM TO HAVE BEEN DEEP IN CONVERSATION, THEY OPEN THE SCREEN door and beckon me in.

When I was young, Bill and Maggie's house was filled with the necessities. A cream couch. Caramel coffee table. Brown wooden spoons in a white jug on the kitchen counter. Farmyard scenes painted on cork placemats. Neutral tones. Now, in the hallway, are vases in all shades of color. Translucent blue rectangles and solid purple squares, moss-green flutes and burnt-orange hourglasses. Maggie's creations.

I pass Adara's childhood bedroom and, sitting upright on a pillow, is my rag doll. Its red duffel coat not as bright as it used to be. The off-white calico smudged by love. The doll looks at me with a permanent, black, sewn-on smile. I think of grabbing the doll and running out of the house but instead force myself into the kitchen with its waxed linoleum floor. Adara sits at the kitchen table and Maggie stands at the stove. She stirs the white enamel saucepan, with its alternating yellow and orange sunflowers, and blue and green roosters, just as she did when Dawn brought Willow and me over after finding us freezing in the bathtub.

"The place is…it's different than I remember," I say to Maggie as I sit down.

"You know, in his late etchings," she says, stirring, "Rembrandt would erase most of the detail he had drawn, leaving just a few important lines. I often think that's what I've done these past few years. Emptied the house of most details, kept only the most loved things. Added the new." The smell of hot apple cider on the stove and the Wild Strawberry teacups on the table are some things Maggie has kept. She only ever poured her cider into "good china, with a thin rim and white inside" because "appreciating the color is all part of the experience." The furniture may have changed but the rituals haven't; habits like gold coins thrown over a shoulder and into a wishing well.

Everyone is silent until Maggie finishes at the stove, strains the liquid into a teapot and serves small bowls of ginger, star anise, cinnamon and brown sugar on a wooden cheese board. Maggie passes me a glass of water.

"Please drink something," she says. "Did you know, most people are dehydrated? Listen to me, telling this to a doctor." Maggie puts brown sugar into a cup and pours the cider over, hands it to Adara. "It's just, I often think about the world and all those thirsty people." I take a sip of water, more for Maggie than for me. I've bitten the inside of my cheek so much it's ulcerating. My body is knotted and stiff with tension.

Maggie looks at her daughter. "Are you sure you're okay with this, hon?"

"We shouldn't have taken the box," Adara says; breathes out a long sigh that seems to deflate her entire body. "It's time." She tries to take a sip of her drink but her hands are shaking so much she has to put it back down.

"Don't, don't do this," Dawn says, coming into the kitchen. When she sees Maggie, she stops. Her chest heaving from the walk over.

"I thought you were sleeping?" I say.

"I woke up and couldn't find you. I was worried. Though now I know I should have been worried about something else."

"This isn't about you," I say.

"Dawn," Maggie says and stands up. Although they're the same age, the years haven't taken their toll on Maggie the way they have Dawn. Well, not on the outside. Looking at them together is a lesson in half-lived lives. Dawn sways and Maggie sweeps in and holds her arms for balance. They linger, give each other a long look before Maggie lowers her arms.

"Come sit down, Dawn, please." Dawn doesn't move. "Have some cider; I just made it."

"You always put too much ginger in."

Maggie offers a small smile. "I did used to need a little extra spice. It's more balanced now. I add more cinnamon, sugar."

Dawn looks around the house as if she's noticing other ways Maggie has balanced. "I, I didn't know you were sick. I didn't know," Dawn says, the side of her mouth twitching.

"I'm just coming to terms with it myself. I haven't really told my own heart, let alone others."

Dawn nods. "Well, we can talk about all that later, I suppose," she says.

"We will, Dawn." Maggie looks into Dawn's downcast eyes to draw them up so that she knows she means it. "We will, okay?"

Dawn nods again. The room is silent awhile. When nobody speaks, I can't help myself.

"I'm sorry, everyone, I know there's a lot of…history in this room, but can you please, for the love of God, talk to me?"

Dawn looks at me as if she's just remembered why we were talking in the first place.

"We didn't just promise Adara," she says to Maggie, leaning forwards, "we promised Nora. She didn't want Layla to know any of this, didn't want it to be part of Layla's story. It's only because she lost her senses recently, lost them completely, that she was going to let Layla see that stuff. You can't just betray her, not now, especially when she's flat on her back in hospital."

I feel a tightening in my chest.

"Dawn." Maggie places a hand on her forearm. "It's time, Dawn. It's time."

Dawn crosses her arms over her chest and breathes out a few times, quickly, looks to the side out the window. Shakes her head. "I can't. You didn't see…" Words get stuck in her throat, and she has to swallow them to continue. "You didn't see Nora, Maggie. You didn't…see…her."

"I'm so sorry, Dawn. I—"

"I can't. I can't do this," Dawn says, crossing her arms and then opening them up as if defending herself against an invisible threat.

"Stay, Dawn, you're not steady on your feet." Maggie places a hand on her shoulder. Dawn looks at Maggie's hand and reaches to hold it for a moment, but then picks it up and lifts it off.

"I'm going for a walk." Dawn leaves and lets the screen door slam shut. I watch her walk away and see Bill out with the cows. He must have gone out the back earlier. He's never been one for difficult conversations.

There is dust on the kitchen counter. A minute ago, I didn't notice; it's easy to get distracted by the colorful objects. But now the light shines through the window at just the right angle. The streaming sun showing all.

"That night your dad went out," Maggie says. "He didn't get lost." Her voice is confident and monotone, as if everything she is about to say is the unvarnished truth. "Bill and Tom and the boys, they saw him. They were pulling kids out of the ocean, little ones that couldn't swim. Seconds more and those children would've drowned."

"I knew it," I say. "I knew they saw him."

"It's not that simple," Maggie says. "In the middle of the mayhem, your dad arrived in his boat. He looked Bill straight in the eye. There was a moment when everyone stopped, froze. They were about to direct him to help, but before they could say anything, Oscar turned his boat around and headed straight out into the storm. That was the last they saw of him."

"That's ridiculous," I say. My fists clench so hard I can feel my nails making crescent indents in my skin. "Why are you saying this? Why?" My voice rises and my breath is quick and hot. I stand up.

Adara stands too. "Please, Layla, just hear us out, okay? You're the one who wants to know."

"Your mum suspected for a long time," Maggie continues, "that your dad—that he was having an affair. He'd be out late at night after work, he'd often lie about where he was—"

"Jesus, Maggie, Mum's got to you too, hasn't she?" I say. "She's been spin-

195

ning this paranoia my whole life." Adara and Maggie look at each other again.

"We can't watch your mum cry out for help anymore," Adara says. "Mum and Dad are often here with her, help her, Jesse too. But she's so alone, Layla. Believe me, I didn't—don't—want you to see the truth. I wanted to burn everything in there. Just be rid of it all." Adara walks out of the room.

I watch her leave, then look back at Maggie. I start to pace the room, past the colored vases, and glance at Maggie's Christmas baubles in the lounge room hanging with such promise.

"Your mum," Maggie says, "she found something out the day your dad died." I place a hand across my heart as if it will help protect me from anything they say. "Bill and I found out a few days later. After he drowned, Nora searched for more proof, opened all the locked drawers in Oscar's office, got his safe picked, rifled through the surgery. Collected everything. We all swore not to tell you. I mean, what would have been the point? Your mum didn't want to ruin another life. She is far from perfect, Layla, but she loves you fiercely. She wanted to protect you."

Fear spreads through my body and flows with a rush to my head. I feel faint.

Adara walks in carrying a wooden box in her arms like a baby. "She wanted to prevent any of this from being part of your story."

I look at the box in Adara's arms. We stand there staring at each other. She holds it tight. I walk over and try to take the box from her but she resists; finally, she hangs her head and lets me pull it away.

Maggie looks at Adara. "Are you sure you're okay with this? It's a lot, sweetheart, and things that are seen can never be unseen."

Adara shakes her head and looks like she's about to cry. Lifts her hands up. "I don't know, Mum. I don't know. But having this secret from Layla, it's too hard now."

Maggie nods and puts her arm around Adara. I feel a pang of jealousy at their easy intimacy. Realize I always have.

"You'll need some space, hon," Maggie says as she puts a hand on my shoulder, before she and Adara walk out the door. "We'll be outside if you need us. We're right here, okay?"

I take the box and walk cautiously into the lounge room. Sit on the ground to feel something firm beneath my body and lift the lid. Even as I start to rummage, I'm still thinking, *Fuck you, Mum, fuck you.* But then the atmosphere in the room takes on a heavier weight, more liquid than air. My hands are shaking as I reach in and pull out a pile of paper and faded photographs, all different sizes, so some fall out and onto the floor.

There are girls in school uniforms, some people I recognize from my class and others I don't. I can't make out where most of the photographs were taken. The backgrounds are blurry. But then others are as clear as day: a topless young girl holding up a fish; one of a group of girls half naked, swimming in the river.

My heartbeat quickens as I come to photos of Adara. The first ones just look like images I'd have in my photo album: her wearing a dance-recital costume; her standing on their porch in a teal silk sundress. But then my breath flinches as I stare at Adara, looking back at me, naked. My hands are trembling so hard I drop some of the photos and have to pick them back up again.

Sifting through, I find photos of Adara in a darkened room. There is something about the images that looks familiar. In one, she's in her teenage, soft cotton bra with the small purple flowers. The photo is full of shadows. Behind her are lines like those of wood slats. I run my finger over Adara's face, so young.

And that's when I see it, behind Adara's right ear: two triangles, one the right way up and one upside down on top, and then long lines trailing out the back. My drawing of a shooting star. The glowing meteor that is nothing but specks of dust. She's in our observatory.

Hundreds of bees start to buzz in my head. I close my eyes to try and stop them, but they only get louder. I open my eyes and breathe out through trembling, pursed lips.

Beneath all the photos is Maggie's camera, the one I thought I'd lost. I breathe, in and out; slowly take the camera, lift the device out of its case, and it feels heavier than I remember. It weighs down my right hand.

There is one more item in the box. Two pieces of paper folded in half. I take them out and open them up. They are crumpled and water damaged. Almost torn. At the top is a logo, a small blue map of Australia and the words "Medical Board of Australia."

15 December 1985

Dear Dr. Oscar Byrnes,
You are hereby notified that your practicing license has been suspended due to a number of serious allegations of sexual assault at your Melbourne surgery between the years 1970 and 1973. These allegations will be investigated and further information will be sent to you if charges are to be laid and a court appearance is scheduled.

I stop reading and let out a muffled whimper. Clasp my hand over my mouth. I pick up all the photos again. The girl with the fish; the ones half naked, swimming in the river. I remember these people from that day, the same day Dad was smiling and taking photos of me, counting down as I swung off the rope and fell into the water. I will myself to keep going, all the while slowly knowing, Dad took these photos. Dad took these photos.

I look again at the photos of Adara. She is smiling. *Smile for the camera.* My father's voice inside my head: "Smile." The way the word started low, then singsonged in the middle and came down at the end. The word sounds in my head, repeats again and again. I feel my insides turn choppy; whitecaps in my stomach.

I flip through all the photos, wanting to make sure I'm not imagining the images, the half naked and naked bodies; and, I realize, because I'm trying to see if there is a photo of Willow. When I've seen them all again and again, I drop them on the floor and run into the toilet and fall to my knees. My body lurches, contracting and contorting; I haven't eaten, so nothing comes, but my body still heaves and heaves. I try to cry but all that comes out is a low-throated exhale of a wail. Wrapping myself into a ball, I rock backwards and forwards, unable to let myself think of all the truth in that box. I shake my head as if I can somehow make it stop, make the thinking and realizing and understanding stop. I try and try to not let myself unravel what the photographs mean, because I know that if I pick at the thread, everything I've ever known will come undone. I tap my head in a final plea; *please*, I tell myself, I tell everyone out there, I cry to anyone who will hear. I beseech some power greater than myself to wipe this information and the images from my mind. But then my body sags in a reluctant acceptance that I have to play this out, knowing that the truth will enter me like acid, be carried through my capillaries and into the furthest reaches of my being.

I make myself think of the photos. Ideas swirl and spin in my mind as everything I thought my father ever felt for me or did with me or said to me joins in a cacophony of confusion, and the off-white tiles and the off-white shower and the off-white walls in Maggie's bathroom blur into a dirty snowstorm, until I fall completely onto the ground, planting my cheek on the floor to feel something solid.

Those girls at the watering hole, when I thought Dad was taking photos of me, when I was jumping and spinning on the rope, when I felt free and as if I was the focus of his attention. He had known the boys would be playing football. Known it would be just the girls down there. I'd been his excuse to go. His decoy. He wasn't pointing his camera at me. He was pointing it at them. At them. The lies gorge on themselves.

Adara in the observatory, in my special place, shivering in the cold night air as my father looks at her, photographs her, makes her...I stop. And girls at school, girls I played with, who I shared parties and playtimes and secrets with. How many? I think, how fucking many? I try to cry again but I can't get the tears to release. I can't get anything to move; it's all caught inside me so the only sound I can make is a vibrating growl. And Willow. Willow. Her throwing the camera in the oven, running away the next day.

The shame comes like a lightning strike. How could I not have known? Why the fuck didn't someone tell me? The world contracts and I'm lassoed to the here and now. A wave crash of noise and I realize it's me, screaming. It travels out of my mouth, down my body and along the ground like a flood. But even as that old voice rings in my head, new vocal cords are forming, twin infoldings of membrane starting to stretch horizontally across my larynx. They can't speak for the moment but make little puffs of sounds like steam. I hear them whisper, *Bastard. Fucking, fucking bastard.* And with those words I hear my mother screaming the same things to him the night he died, in the wailing of the storm, waving a piece of paper in the air, waving the medical board letter. *Bastard!* I hear us scream together. *Bastard!* And the mighty fall. Oh, how they fall. I crawl on hands and knees across the bathroom floor; sit with my back against the door, my legs out straight. The room spins. I scream again at the top of my lungs, willing the knowledge to leave my body with my voice.

THIRTY-FOUR

THE DOOR AT MY BACK SHIFTS AS SOMEONE TRIES TO
GET IN. I SLIDE MY FEET UP, PLANT MY SOLES INTO THE FLOOR AND
push back. One voice becomes two, becomes three, before the door pushes
with greater force than I can resist. I scream, "No!" and then again and again
until it is no longer a word but a gust of air that comes from the deepest
parts of my belly. I scream again and again until my throat hurts and the
pain cancels out my confusion. Hands wrap around me and I look up and see
Maggie and Adara and Dawn. "Why?" I yell. "Why didn't you tell me?" Then
I ask it louder, "Why didn't anyone tell me?"

The women try to hook their arms under mine, but I pull away and sink
down to the floor. But they keep coming, keep trying to lift me up. I push
them away and stand up myself, walk unsteadily back into the kitchen and
then look directly at Dawn. "You. After everything. Why didn't you, of all
people, tell me."

"We promised Nora. Promised Adara. We promised," says Maggie.

I look at Adara, and she looks like the little girl in those photos.

"Adara," I whimper. "God, Adara."

Her face crumples up. She starts to cry, softly, brushing the tears off her
cheeks in hard strokes, as if willing herself to stop.

"All those times we were together. I told you everything. You should have
told me. Or when we were driving away in the back of your dad's truck. Why
didn't anyone tell me? Who else knows? Am I the last one?" I think about the
school market and people I've seen since I've been back. I think about people
looking at me, knowing, knowing; all the while me, smiling, smiling like an idiot.

"No one, Layla, no one else knows," Dawn says as she reaches for me, but I push her hand away. My head shakes as if trying to rid itself of walked-through cobwebs.

"You lived with me," I shout, and Dawn recoils from the rage in my voice. "You helped raise my children. How could you not tell me? All those times I wanted to know, you knew I needed to know." I'm yelling and trying to keep standing, though I know that soon the truth will become too much, too heavy, and I will surely collapse.

Maggie takes Adara's hand. I think, Oh God, Adara.

"Just tell me," I say, standing in the kitchen. "Tell me everything, so I know there's nothing left."

"Nora opened the letter," Maggie says. "That night, when she went down to the postbox. He may not have been seeing other women, but it confirmed all her suspicions. Worse—it was worse than anything she'd ever thought."

Questions flash through my brain and I try to grasp them so I don't let them go, so I don't forget any of them, because I need to know everything, I need to know everything now. One question burns brightest and, even though I can't bear the answer, I have to ask.

"I need to know," I gasp. "I need to know what it means. I need to know if it was just photos or—"

"Don't," Dawn interjects, "don't do what my generation did and put the word 'just' in front of heinous things."

"I need to know whether the truth is…" I pause for a moment. "Whether it was photos or more, if it was…" I can't bring myself to say the words.

"I can't, I'm sorry. I want you to tell her, but I can't be here right now." Adara runs outside. Everyone is quiet.

"Layla, Adara, she…" Maggie now has tears in her eyes. The usual confidence in her voice falters. "It wasn't just photos. That's not all it was. It was more."

"What?" I gasp, shaking my head, ridding the truth from my ears. "No, oh my God, no." And I allow the truth to bear down on me and I fall to the floor again. Dawn and Maggie come down with me too, and while the three of us are on our knees, they put their arms around me, and even though I feel a rage through me for the betrayal of not knowing, I let their hands rest on my back. We are quiet a moment as my body shakes and my breath catches in my chest. I can't breathe. Winded. I think about the lines on Adara's arms.

"That night," Maggie finally continues, "at the start, when Nora confronted him, he was crying. Ashamed, pathetic. Adara and I could just make them out from our kitchen window, though we weren't sure what was going on. Nora said that he became angry that she had opened his mail. He never hit her, he was too controlled for that. He hurt her in other ways. Never gave her any money. Made you all live like you were poor. Used to question her memory until she was so confused she thought she was going crazy. But that night he slapped her, hard, when Bill was talking to you—I saw it with my own two eyes."

"When she would put you in the bath, Layla," Dawn says, "it was because he would stand over her and call her names. Names I can't repeat. Say awful things to her."

"Stop, please," I plead. "Just stop for a moment…" I heave, trying to catch my breath; no tears come. The weight of it all too much. I think about all the times Mum didn't have money. The times when she bought me secondhand clothes and scrounged for food. I think about Adara's birthday and the rag doll. My father was supposed to give her the money, but he wouldn't. He made me give that doll away, not Mum. Every single memory gets washed away like a map drawn in sand.

"I want to tell you the story again so that you can hear it differently, so that you understand," Maggie says. "Your dad, he got in his boat and sped towards the idiots that had tried to sail in the weather. Bill and Tom said they saw your father come up to them in his boat. He cut the engine for a moment and just looked at them. God knows what was going through his head. He must have known then that everything would come out. He gave Bill one last glance, started the engine and tore off into the ocean." Maggie pauses in what seems like an attempt to let this image, this truth, sink in.

"People think that daylight brings calm," Dawn says, "but the only difference daybreak brings is that you can see the monstrous waves coming at you, see the fury of the raging sea. The men still went out looking for your dad. You don't know that, but they did. Risked their lives. At the time, they didn't know what had been happening, or they probably wouldn't have gone.

"Once the storm died down, your mum stood at the lookout, watching the water. For hours," Dawn continues.

I remember watching Mum, leaning on the rail, staring into dimpled water the color of motor oil.

"I'm going to go check on Adara," Maggie says softly. Stands slowly, putting one hand on her knee. Before she takes a deep breath and walks out the door.

So many questions swirl in my head, carried by the loudening bees. There is nothing I can say except, "Please, just leave me alone. Please."

Dawn looks at me and opens her mouth to say something, but then closes it.

"I couldn't, Layla, you have to understand," Dawn says at last. "Nora and I might have been through a lot but she's my sister. Not only that but I thought—I thought at the time I was protecting you too. We never did a very good job at protecting Willow."

"Willow," is all I can say. And then ask directly, "Willow? What about her? Did he?"

"I don't know, love. I wanted to ask. I always did. I always thought that if she wanted to tell me, she would. So…I don't know. Your mother might. You need to ask her."

I nod. "I need to be alone," I say, before standing and leaving Dawn on the ground. By the time I push out the door, no one is around, and I walk, unsteady, back over to Mum's.

The air is cold, afternoon transitioning to evening. I take a blanket from the lounge room and head down to our playhouse. On hands and knees, I crawl into the space where Mum laid unconscious last night, lie down under our childhood drawings. I curl myself into a ball and pull the blanket over my body. In anesthesia, we learn about loss of consciousness, how to stop pain. All this time, I thought Mum locked us in a bathroom to get us out of the way, as a kind of punishment for simply existing. But I realize now that she was being an anesthetist. She placed the radio next to the bath so that we could not hear Dad. She gave us the paper to fold into boats and the candles to burn for wax, because it was her way of distracting and protecting us.

But anesthesia is temporary. You might not feel the intense, in-the-moment pain of surgery, which would surely kill you, but there will always be the pain afterward, and your body's memory of what has happened. Pain catches up. It always does. As does truth. You can't outrun it, out-busy it, outsmart it. Even though you delay it. The body knows.

I look at one of my childhood drawings, of me and Mum under a rainbow; another of a garden of flowers and fairies; another of a nest with small, blue birds. When I drew that bird picture, I remember Mum singing her favorite nursery rhyme, clasping her fingers together and turning them inside out: "See my little birdies grow, day by day, day by day, until they spread their little wings, and then they fly away."

These pictures that I drew before I began to believe that my mother and her gnawing needs and paranoid mind were the fist that squeezed our family out of shape.

I have been numb to the truth. I brace myself for the inevitable withdrawal. Wanting to shed everything, my body trembles. As I feel the form of the ground beneath me, the salt-washed rock that shakes itself of life, the island whispers to me, "What if part of you has always known you've been living a lie?"

THIRTY-FIVE

I WAKE WITH A START. UNAWARE OF WHERE I AM. THE SKY IS DARK. A MOUSE HOLDS ITS TAIL UP IN AN ARC AS IT RUMMAGES through leaves looking for insects. Droplets of rain on blades of grass blink in starlight. Rolling onto my back, the cold in my bones adds to gravity's weight; I look up at a wooden ceiling. It's the sight of the drawings on the wall that brings everything back. I can no longer feel the cold or the damp or the shape of my body.

As I roll into a ball, a voice in my head screams, *No, no, no*, over and over like a wooden rolling pin tenderizing meat. Carrying this knowledge around with me for the rest of my life is beyond my strength. I push the blanket off me and crawl back out of the playhouse. Although the moon is new, the stars provide just enough light to guide my way across our property, the soft soil cushioning my feet toward the cliff's edge.

The view looks different from what I remember, and I struggle to find the opening to the steps Dad built down to the sand. Overgrown grass hides the stone until I find the path and zigzag my way down the cliff. The tide is out, and the sand is covered in shells, seaweed and driftwood carved by the ocean. Streaks of starlight in the sea shine like electric eels. The cliff looms behind me. Small waves loll into shore.

I walk to the water's edge. On any other night the temperature of the ocean would take my breath away, but I am immune to the cold now. I step on stones and wade until the water is up to my knees, grit my teeth and push myself forwards until the water is up to my waist. The current sweeps my skin.

My body falls forwards and into the sea, freestyling out as far as I can, past where I know the seabed drops, past where I know you can turn and see the safety of the shore, past where what is beneath the water is known. I dive down, deep, through the water, pushing further with breaststroke arms and fish-kick legs. The ocean is clear at first and then pale blue, and I see an image of myself as a little girl listening to her father be revered by the townspeople for his title; then royal blue, an image of myself under the night sky, learning about the stars and their constancy; and then navy, an image of myself as a bride, marrying a man of the ocean; and then, deeper still, until the water is pitch black, I see myself falling for a sculptor, a man of the stars. All the parts of my father I put upon a pedestal. Darker and darker in gradients, the ocean's viscosity mirrors my descent, becoming thicker too, firstly like bathwater, then as heavy as molasses. I succumb to the strata.

All the decisions I have made, to become a doctor, to marry Gabe, to put my kids second to my career, even to see Lucas, have been based on my reverence for my father; my desire to be like him and nothing like my mother; the desire to acquire, somehow, the magic with which he seemed endowed. I feel a grating in my heart vanish and then appear again, vanish and return, like the history of something, like the story of all things.

My arms pull my body deeper and deeper through the water until my lungs hurt and I become disorientated in the darkness. Shadows swim around me and beyond me and I'm not sure if they are seaweed or animals or a play of light. An outline appears below me, murky at first but then clearer. A man's body, brown hair made soft by the water, fear gushing out of his mouth in silver spheres, panic constricting his throat, a scream trapped in his chest, choking him. Thrashing, contorted, eyes bulging.

Dots of light emerge and swim around the drowning man—small, luminous spheres of gas that create an underwater cosmos—and for the first time I can see the silver thread connecting them. All the familiar images form: Ophiuchus, Centaurus, Chamaeleon, and Orion.

The submerged stars swirl around the man's flailing body until he clasps one silver string after another in his swollen hands. I reach out and grab one of the threads and try to pull it from him, propelling backwards with kicking legs, but he only pulls harder and descends further, trying to drag me under in a celestial tug of war. String after string tangles around me until I am trapped.

I stop fighting and let him take me down. I give up; no longer have the strength or the hope to fight. I sink with my eyes open. My father like a large stone at the end of a rope, tied around my ankle. But as if they are there next to me I hear my children, laughing, calling my name, *Mum, Mum*; I feel my wildfire love for them and yearning to hold their bodies; I think about how angry I was at my mother for giving up so completely and I thrash my head and my body and my arms and kick my legs and fight with everything I have left inside me until the silver thread finally snaps and slips from my body. The sinking man holds tight to the constellations, taking them down with him, and he and the stars fade from view.

My chest constricts and I push myself back up through the water's gradients to lighter ocean and thinner weight, and when my head bursts through the foaming surface I gasp, each breath knifing my lungs.

I float forwards and let the small waves carry me so I can touch the sandy bottom with my toes and eventually fall onto my palms and then elbows and drag myself onto the shore. All the women in me are tired. The wife, the mother, and the daughter, the doctor, the lover, and the friend; the list goes on. I go on. We are tired. All those versions of me have been made to please others; have been constructed in response to the myths of dead men. My father, my grandfather, hundreds of years of powerful dead men. My decisions have come from deception. So many choices based on idolizing lies. Who am I? I let out a whimper at my father's hand-me-down dreams.

Lying on my back, the tide taps my toes. In the darkness, my skin turns into sand and sand turns into water and water turns into an ocean that expands for thousands of miles until there is no delineation between me and anything outside and beyond my body. This is what I wanted. Exhaustion.

Oblivion. An ocean filled with endings. Death. And not just of my father.

I look up and behind me and side to side. All my ways to navigate the world, gone. I'm not sure how to find the steps that climb the cliff, not sure I could scale them in such blackness even if I did. And if I were able to feel my way, once I reached the cliff top, I would have no way of knowing how to get home. I look to the heavens for help, for the constancy and a guide to calm my racing heart, but now all I see is a dark and starless sky.

Waves roll, crash onto the shore. My body has made an imprint in the sand. Eventually, I stand. Walk. Just walk. It is all I can do. And barely. The ground is too hard beneath my feet, as if gravity has increased in strength, Earth pulling me to its center with greater force. I wish it would try harder. Draw me down into its depths, through grass and dirt, through the rocks and fossils, through the layers of hot magma and silvery liquid of nickel and iron, until it pulls me all the way to the solid, heavy inner core, where I can stay, stuck and away from the world forever.

Sounds make me flinch. A gull's cry. A dog's bark. Waves continuing to crash, though that sound decreases as I put one foot in front of the other. A crackling glaze of frost beneath my feet. I hear everything. Feel nothing. I breathe, in and out, in and out, though I know that if I think about this too much I might just will it to stop.

More sounds, though human this time. Men yelling in the distance. A child laughing. A woman singing. The weight of my body calls me back to my own inescapable, solitary existence. I see a bird. I see a horse. I put one foot in front of the other.

I must have been walking a long time, because there is more light now. Outside of me. But inside of me there is what feels like an eternal darkness. A body made from the genes of a monster. I have always feared I was broken, and now, when I think about the molecules that make me, I can't help but think that something bad is inside me as well.

I start to imagine myself as a seashell. Worry that if people now come close and pick me up, place me to their ear, they might hear the sounds of the places from which I've come. Hear the heinous actions that are my history, that have influenced my decisions and that have made me who I am. Any ear tuned to the pitch of pain would know my truth, know me, and put me down.

Eventually, I come across a park. I stop and stare at a child being pushed by her father on a swing. A creak and she flies up, a creak as she comes down. A scream to be pushed higher and higher, and so he does. The man notices me. Looks at me, and something flickers across his eyes. He slows the swing. Takes his child by the hand without taking his eyes off me and walks away to a car. Now and then flicking his head back at me and then to their destination. They get in the car. He must know the truth about me, I think. He must know.

I walk over to the swing and sit on it. My legs are too long, so I just push myself backwards until my legs are straight and then draw myself forwards with my toes until they are bent again. Backwards and forwards. I listen to the creaks, over and over. Look down at the soil at my feet.

A small terrier runs up to me wagging its tail. Panting. Tongue hanging out its mouth. It looks to me for attention but when our eyes meet, the dog's ears drop, its head bows and it shrinks away from me.

Layla, oh Jesus, Layla. Disembodied voices. Hands on me. *Oh my God, we've been looking for you everywhere. How did you get here, and in this town? If the police hadn't have called, we'd never have found you.*

Then someone else: *She must have walked, it's miles. She's freezing, sandy, muddy.* Something heavy wrapping around me. I'm leaning on shoulders and shuffling my feet until I sit down in the back seat of a car and finally close my eyes. Rumble of the engine in my bones; I melt down along the back seat without worrying about a belt.

Before I know it, I'm in a bed with voices around my head. *We can't put her in like this, she's filthy.* And someone else: *She's no good for anything else at the moment, except rest.* And my body, heavy from the weight of no going back, sleeps.

THIRTY-SIX

EARLY THE NEXT MORNING, I STAND IN THE BATHROOM; REALIZE GROGGILY THAT I'M AT MUM'S. DAWN TURNS ON the bath's hot water until steam fills the room and the window is silver. Like a mother with a baby, she turns on the cold and dips her elbow in to test the temperature. As I slide my body in, I close my eyes and wince with pain. I draw my knees up to my chest as Dawn fills a jug with water and pours it over my head and body. The tub fills with clouds of sand and dirt.

I don't usually let people do this: look after me. I push hands away, shake my head. Say, "I'm alright." Even when I'm not. Even when I'm far from it. Would rather have to take care of myself than feel indebted to someone's kindness. Care that can turn to resentment. But here I have no choice. No energy to do the task myself. No energy to even say no.

Who mothers the mothers with absent mothers? People like Dawn, I guess. If you let them. Though goodness knows, I don't feel I deserve it. Her gentle hands squeeze liquid from my hair. The warm water across my body like grace. This bath holding more than just water. Pain. I run my finger along the porcelain edge, imagining folded paper boats, lit candles, screaming. Close my eyes. But here in this moment, Dawn and this bath are medicine.

"Growing up," Dawn breaks the silence, "my father used to play a game with your mother and me. Well, he called it a game. We would pick the fruit from the garden, oranges mostly, and carry them inside in our skirts. Mum would make them into marmalade. Out of nowhere, Dad, your grandfather, would appear from round the back of the corrugated-iron shed. He didn't do it always. Just sometimes. It was the surprise of it he liked, I think now. He would tickle us as we walked. And if we could keep that bundle of oranges in our skirts without letting one drop as he tickled us, he would give us a penny. For years I associated that citrus smell with fear. Powerlessness." She scoops and pours water across my back.

"Then I met Maggie. And she had this habit of cooking an orange over an open fire, usually outside. She'd section the fruit and put the pieces one by one in my mouth. It was the closest thing to love I had ever tasted. Ever smelt. Then when I lived with you and I would eat those same oranges over and over again, it was as if I was trying to conjure her but never could and so the oranges tasted of longing. Last night, Maggie made me one over the fire and there it was again. The taste of love, but this time different. Gratitude as well." She stops a moment. Takes a breath. "But soon she'll be gone. My beautiful Maggie. And I know that when I eat oranges then, they will be made of grief. Those oranges made me scared, made me feel loved, made me sad, made me feel loved again, and will help me grieve. The whole human experience wrapped up in that one piece of fruit." Dawn takes a white washcloth, dips it into the warm water and runs it across my shoulder.

"You will have baths again, Layla, that are not about survival, and you will see photographs, eventually, that do not make you feel shame. The trick is to realize that the sadness and the longing and the grief and the tragedies, they shouldn't tarnish; together they should fill things in. Nothing is ever one thing or the other anyway. Good or bad. You have to let the joys and tragedies coexist. And I think that if you can do that, if you can manage to forge ahead, allowing the things in your life to not be tainted by the truth but to get colored in and to become more tangible, then you will live a three-dimensional life. You will get to the last moments knowing at least that you lived and saw everything fully."

I nod my chin, which is resting on my knee. Run my fingertips across the top of the water. "Dawn, if I could turn back time, do it again, I would have told Gabe you were staying. It is one of my biggest regrets, not standing up for you. And your beautiful wild silk moths. I know how much they meant to you. I'm so sorry. Sorry, too, for everything I've said to you over the past few days. I've been unfair—no, at times, I've been cruel."

"Long loves require forgiveness. Again and again," says Dawn.

Where is all this forgiveness supposed to come from? I wonder. Where is this great inexhaustible supply?

"Time for us all to make some new memories," she adds. "Some peaks for the troughs."

"I'm so tired of the troughs," I say.

Dawn laughs. "Me too, honey, me too."

"I'm going to buy you some new wild silk moths, set you up, wherever you want to be. Wherever I am, you can live with me. Alright?"

"Alright," she whispers, kisses me on the forehead, walks out and closes the door.

I rest my cheek on my knee. Look at the foggy window. There's still so much more I need to know. About Willow, Adara, Mum. About myself. I think about oranges and baths, photographs and art shows, the stars in the night sky and pear juice on lips. The smell of the back of a truck, telescopes and birthday cakes with pink icing. I stand slowly and reach for the towel and dry myself off, walk out of the bathroom, ready as I'll ever be to take the next step in my new world.

Mum's wardrobe is smaller than I remember as a child and smells of mothballs and ammonia. I open her underwear drawer and place my palm on my abdomen as I move aside the cheap, super-absorbent period pads that must be there from decades ago, and take out five pairs of size-twelve cotton knickers in shades of blues and purples. I pack some pajama pants and tops, a dressing gown, and a dress and cardigan to wear home.

Dad's side of the wardrobe is completely empty. When he was alive, his clothes were pressed so close together; there were so many suits and shirts that you couldn't move any of the coat hangers along the rail. Mum's side contains the same clothes it always has: four cotton dresses with short sleeves—a pale-blue one, a pale-yellow one, a bright floral print in a rainbow of colors and one black with white piping. There are also two long-sleeved blouses, one skirt and, beneath them, a basket.

As I'm packing Mum's bag, my phone, finally plugged in beside her bed after being out of charge the past day, comes to life. It buzzes and buzzes and I brace myself to look at the screen. There are missed calls from Gabe, from Lucas, from some numbers I don't recognize, and from work. *Shit.* I can only ignore my outside life for so long, and I miss the kids so much it hurts in all my tissues.

Gabe will be getting the kids ready to come south on the plane. He always packs early and leaves the bags by the door. A process inherited from his parents, though I would never say that to him. I text, "Hey, sorry I haven't called. Mum is alright but she wasn't for a while. I'll fill you in later. Maybe give me a call when you and the kids have space for a chat?" I think about the sign-off. Words never used to be so complicated. So I just say, "Love, Layla," more for the kids than for him or us. I'm going to have to figure out what to do, with Gabe and me. I'll have to think about work and Lucas later.

I pick up Mum's overnight bag and then notice again the basket at the bottom of her wardrobe. Inside are jars, filled with sea glass and feathers, seashells and pale-blue baby bird eggs already hatched. The treasures we collected from our beach walk. She kept them.

In the basket are also books of poetry, one by Sylvia Plath that is worn from reading, corners turned down, stanzas underlined, notes made. I flip through and stop at the poem "Tulips." The line there that I've replayed in my mind since high school catches my eye. Next to the words "smiling hooks," Mum has written in gray lead, "or maybe lifelines." With the page still open, I close my eyes. Words are flimsy without another person's reply; a thin sliver of knowledge empty of any real meaning, except for what you place on it, which, I'm learning, is usually wrong. I close the book and put it in Mum's bag. At the bottom of the basket is a folded piece of yellowed paper. A fine texture beneath my fingertips. I open the typewritten text.

Nora (23)

Winner of the Southern Lights Poetry Competition 1975
"Paper women"
My father-in-law was a sailor during
a time, he says, when women were made
of steel and boats were made of wood.
Boats may turn but a woman's mind
was always stable. But these days, he
says, boats are made of steel and
women are made of wood
or, he says more to himself than me,
sometimes even paper.

"I told the hospital you're on your way in." Dawn's voice makes me jump and I drop the poem. She walks toward me, looking at the opened wardrobe, picks the paper up off the ground. "Nora loved your father from the moment she met him in a stationery store. He was buying notebooks for his medical-school thesis and she was buying tape for her typewriter. She was so young. He was a street angel and a home devil. Took her a long time to see the real him."

We sit on the bed next to each other, staring into the wardrobe.

"After he died, we burned all your dad's clothes. Had a big bonfire out in the backyard. In the morning, your mum realized we were supposed to supply a suit for him to be buried in. We drove to the general store, the only place nearby that sold clothes, to try to find one that would fit. The woman working there was new, we didn't know her, and she kept trying to start a conversation about who the suit was for. After a while, Nora just looked up at her and said, '*Dieu seul sait*.'"

"I don't know what that means," I say.

"Neither did I. On the way home, your mum told me about the first story your father told her, about French doctors in World War One, on their first date. When the doctors didn't know what to diagnose, for probably what we'd now call post-traumatic stress disorder, they simply wrote '*Dieu seul sait quoi*.' Translates to, God alone knows what this is."

I imagine Mum in that store. Buying a suit for her dead husband. Who is this for? "*Dieu seul sait*," Mum had said. "God alone knows."

"Maggie and I went in to see Nora in turns last night," Dawn says. She puts the poem back into the basket. Takes out the most colorful, rainbow-spliced dress and puts it in the bag for Mum.

I raise my eyebrows and point to Dawn's wig-free head. "Ah, Maggie hates them." Dawn blushes. I've never seen Dawn blush. I smile.

"I still have the snuffbox you gave me. I want to give it to Mum," I say.

"I don't know about that anymore, Layla. Not sure it was one of my best ideas. And anyway, I might be stirring up too much stuff now."

"I'm tired of leaving things unsaid and unfinished. Please, let me do this, use it to be able to talk."

Dawn nods. "Up to you, love, but...Layla, these secrets, your dad. I think it's important you know that your mum and I, well, what happened is terrible, horrible, but it's also salt in an existing wound." Dawn takes a breath. "Your grandfather, my father, he fought in the Korean War," she continues. "Was dishonorably discharged. Though none of us knew that then. To everyone else, he was a war hero. But he was never the same after that war. Used to come home raging drunk, beat the two of us and, well," Dawn looks down and smooths her silk skirt with two flat palms, "a whole lot of other stuff. When

217

you see her, just go a bit easy on her, okay?"

I smile before placing an arm around my aunt. "You've dealt with too much in your life," I say to her.

"No use dwelling, Layla," she says. "The truth means nothing if you don't know what to do with it, if you wallow in it. You can go there, love, but don't pitch a tent."

I look down at the small leather box.

THIRTY-SEVEN

MUM'S HOSPITAL ROOM SMELLS LIKE FLOWERS. THERE'S NOTHING ON HER BEDSIDE TABLE, SO I ASSUME ONE OF THE patients she's sandwiched between must have a space that looks like a florist. I've worked in a lot of hospitals, private, public, metropolitan, rural. It doesn't really matter; all the rooms look the same. The only real difference is whether someone has a room to themselves or has to share. All three patients in the room are shielded by curtains. Mum's dressed in a white hospital gown. I know exactly where it would be tied up at her back. Her mouth is open while she sleeps. Lips cracked.

I put the packed bag in front of her bed and the book of poetry on her bedside table. A cannula runs into the top of her hand and I can tell by the tape it was done by a newbie. Anyone experienced has precision. A confidence that tugs stitches tight, that wraps bandages with just the right amount of pressure, that finds the vein on the first attempt, wraps the U-shaped tape neatly around the cannula and finishes it off with a straight tape fixed clean. Mum's cannula is stuck with hesitation. A lack of confidence that, in medicine, means bloodstained skin, bruised attempts to find veins, then a site hastily covered by a cotton ball and thick white tape.

Sitting down in the armchair, I take my phone out of my bag and open my email. Edit the draft I've written to the hospital. My resignation. "Thank you for the opportunity," I read, and then later, "rethinking position," "apologies." But when I get to the end, I close my phone before sending; think about Remi's offer to work with her on her list at Belmont.

Mum's eyes are still closed. Hospitals are the great leveler. It doesn't matter your status, your wealth, the way you look; if you're sick enough to be on your back in a hospital gown, everyone's as vulnerable as a child.

A nurse clicks a curtain around the next bed, scrapes it closed.

"Today we played sew the pinky on the farmer," we hear the nurse say. A man tells the nurse he could listen to the sound of her voice all day; that, "One of the great tragedies of life is that there isn't a voiceover. If my life had one, I'd choose yours."

The nurse laughs. "Well, you can listen to the dulcet tones of my voice telling you you've also broken your arm. Must have done it when you fell after sawing your finger off. We have to take a few more scans." We hear the nurse pull up the metal sides of the man's bed. Flick up the locks. She opens the curtain and wheels him away.

Mum wakes slowly, smacking her dry lips together. She tries to sit up but groans and lies back down. She blinks at me. Her mouth and her eyes and her heart are parched. I pour her a glass of water from a brown plastic jug. Hold the cup to her lips so she can take a sip, before resting her head back down on the pillow.

We sit there staring at each other. I try to think of what to say, but the love and hate I feel for her crowds my thoughts to one side.

"Why didn't you tell me?" I ask, finally. Her eyes close. Stay closed. Open. She stares at me. "All these years," I quiver, "all these years, Mum."

I've been thinking back to those times Dad and I spent in his makeshift observatory. Trying to remember every detail. That's what happens when your reality gets questioned. You take apart everything you thought you knew and look at it again, like peeling a mandarin, holding the pieces up to the light, looking for pips before eating.

"Did he ever…" I clench my hands into fists; open them up and rest my palms on my thighs. She sits there. Staring at me. The man on the other side of Mum grunts in pain. A buzzer sounds. "Mum?" I try to press her.

"Do you remember?" Mum says slowly, quietly. I jolt at the sound of her voice. "That calf I bought for you?"

Of course I do. I think about her every time I come back home. When Willow left, and Dad went to visit his parents in Scotland, Mum bought a calf for me from Maggie and Bill. Its body was deep red, the color of internal organs. As the calf grew into a cow, she became attached. Would walk next to Jesse and me. She loved his orchard.

"When your dad came back from Scotland, she lay down on the ground and wouldn't get up." I remember her craning neck, howling eyes. The way her head looked like it had been sewn onto a static body. I lay with her until she was as cold as the land. We buried her beneath my favorite tree, a eucalypt with silver bark that shone and sparkled in starlight.

"I've always thought," she says, "that when the cow died the day your dad came back, she knew something we didn't. It was the same day your teacher had explained that energy can't be created or destroyed, it just changes form. For weeks, every morning you'd go out to that gum tree and lie down. I'd ask you what you were doing, and you'd say, 'I'm waiting for my cow to grow into something else.'"

I remember watching the billowing tree branches above me. Twigs flying. Leaves puffing and subsiding. The clammy soil beneath my body.

Mum closes her eyes, turns her head away from me.

The shrill of trolley wheels punctures the silence. Rays of light stream through the window, creating glowing threads between Mum lying in her bed and me sitting in my chair. Stitches trying to clasp a broad wound.

"Dawn said to give you this." I hold out the small leather box to Mum and she turns to look at it. Her eyes widen.

"My grandmother gave me that and Dawn stole it," she says through gritted teeth.

"Why, Mum, why would she tell me to give it to you?"

"Probably because she stole it from me."

"She said you knew she took it. And anyway, she also told me what was in it. How it was used. There's more to it, though, isn't there?"

Mum sighs. "Your great-grandmother, she never liked Oscar. Warned me against marrying him. I don't know. Every time he'd visit and then leave, my grandmother would say, 'We're all just little girls marrying our fathers, expecting our lives to be different.'"

"I think relationships are more complicated than that," I say.

"What's frightening about monsters is not their strangeness but their familiarity," she says, as if to someone else in the room.

"God, Mum, that's pretty grim."

"Well. Yes," she says. "But here we both are."

Mum takes the small box. Opens it, and hands it back to me. "The strangest part of my life now," she says, looking at the curtain drawn around us, "is that I still want to tell your father things. Can you imagine that? I'll be in town or at the deli or watching television and I still think, oh, I have to remember to tell Oscar, and then I remember he isn't here anymore to tell. What kind of woman still wants to talk to a man like that?"

Maybe habit is sometimes stronger than the heart.

"Mum, please…I…" I should have thought about what I was going to say before I came, and now feel lost for words. So many questions and conversations I want to have. I try and reassure myself that there is time. And remind myself to start with some basics.

"Mum, I need to know about Willow. I need to know whether Dad ever—I need to know if that's why she left, why she wrecked my camera. All these years, there's a part of me that's hated her for that. And I need to know if I've been wrong."

"For years I didn't know," Mum says. "But I have also had to face that there are things we often know but choose not to."

I think of Gabe and the women in his life. Of Freya, yes, but of so many others in the past. Hazy eyes might be necessary for a marriage, and maybe motherhood, but blind eyes can surely only cause harm.

"And now, Mum. Now?"

"Now, I..." She pauses. "I have to live with the fact that I am glad, ever since I discovered what happened, that I didn't stop her from leaving."

"She called you a few days ago, she told me, told me she said things about her childhood. Did she tell you then? Is that why you did this now? Mum? Please," I beg. She shakes her head and turns her face away. I notice an increasing discoloration on Mum's bottom white sheet. She pulls the blue hospital blanket around her body but it gets caught under her arm, exposing more of the sheet beneath her. I reach my hand over to lift the blanket a little more, but Mum throws my arm away and tosses the blanket over as much of the bed as she can, so that her socked feet flash and I see her second-to-the-left toe poking out from a small hole.

I push the button for the nurse, knowing that they will want the sheets changed as soon as possible. A small woman robots through the curtain and to the side of Mum's bed. Takes one look.

"Argh, Nora...see this is why, love, this is why we needed you to have a catheter put in, but you pushed and pushed us away and then this." The nurse's latex-gloved fingers start pulling on the blanket. "I'll have to call for—" She walks out of the room, comes back in with a young woman with a solemn face, though her eyes are bright. "You get that side, Emily," the nurse orders. "Ruined my lower back last week, working in intensive."

She lowers the head of the bed, so Mum's lying flat, and then raises its whole height using the rectangular gray remote. Mum's blue blanket is whipped off her body and left at her feet as the nurses untuck all the sides and corners of the bottom sheet. The older nurse rolls the wet sheet away from her, toward Mum's body, like a giant joint, before she attaches the corners of the clean sheet, and rolls Mum's body on its side, toward the younger nurse. As the older nurse tucks the wet sheet under Mum's body, she does it with so much force that Mum's head almost bangs into the side rail and her hand clasps mine. She looks at me the same way Dawn did in the hotel foyer. "Hey,"

I say, stepping toward them. "Careful, careful, please, that's my mother." Both the nurses look at me, surprised, and then apologize. Finish changing Mum's sheets before walking out with the laundry.

Alone again, Mum lies flat on her back, right hand placed firmly over her left, across her abdomen. Both her feet and holey sock exposed. I walk down to the end of her bed and pull the pale-blue blanket slowly over her foot and tuck it under. I feel again the surprise kick of empathy in my chest. Something rubbing and blurring my hatred like chalk.

I stand by the bed and hold Mum's hand. It's small and cold. I think about all that has been lost and all that remains to be said. I think of the dryer Dad bought Mum and the fact he only bought it because he wanted to stop her from going out to the clothesline. The clothesline from which you can see the observatory. I think about the rag doll I had to give to Adara. I think about the dress Mum had to make from a curtain. The way she'd looked at it hanging on the back of her door for days. I swallow hard. My father scuttles in and out of ratholes of memory. "And me, Mum?" I whisper. "What about me?" I look down for an answer, but she has fallen asleep. And even though her hand begins to slacken from slumber, I hold on tight.

THIRTY-EIGHT

ON MY WAY TO MEET MAGGIE AND ADARA, I STOP AT A PARK I USED TO VISIT AS A CHILD; WALK TOWARD THE GNARLED trunk of a eucalypt and sit down on the mound beneath its limbs. The wind whistles through branches. I look out over this farming country, where work on the land meets work on the sea. I watch the white waratah, the purple melaleuca and pale button grass, imagine their history, the life that has pollinated and transported their seeds. The journey they have made, and how they've survived for centuries in this wild west.

A sign written in red paint is tied with ratchet straps to a wire fence across the road. "Save Our Rivers. Say No to Hydro." I think of Willow and her quest to save rainforests overseas. Her confession that she is less interested in saving the trees than the opportunity the protest affords. Her desire to scream and scream until her body tires. Maybe there will never be any answers about Willow. Maybe sometimes that's just how life is. Muddy and messy. The acrid taste of shame returns to my tongue. *Lucas.*

I look his name up on my phone. Images of his painting play on my mind. His desire to have me to himself. To wreck my family. How I can consume lies when my heart is hungry. "I feel we aren't compatible," I start to text. I'm angry but there's no use in creating an opening for conversation. "This relationship isn't working for me. So I'd like to end all further communication and wish you the best in the future." I think about deleting him from my phone but realize he could still call me, so I click on his name, scroll to the bottom of his details and tap "Block this caller." Lock my phone and put it back in my pocket.

A green parrot preens on a bowing branch. So many birds and people migrate from this island in hope of what they think is a better life; more food, more opportunity. But the parrots are one of the only birds that stay. Even when it snows and rains, and food in trees and shrubs disappear, they adapt, search for seeds around feed boxes or haystacks in nearby farmland. My phone rings. Gabe.

"How are you? How's your mum?" he asks before I say anything.

"Nearly dead," I say, but immediately regret my bluntness. "She's okay. I found her, Gabe. She'd taken a whole lot of pills. She was in our playhouse. You know the one down the back that looks like a miniature house?"

"Oh my God," he says. "I honestly never thought—really, I just thought it was all empty threats."

Even though I appreciate his empathy, I still feel hurt that Gabe couldn't just care about how I felt. Empty words or not.

"She'll be okay," I say. "Are the kids there? I miss them so much. Especially over the past few days. I'd love to hear their voices."

"They can't talk right now."

I feel my stomach lurch. Understand that this is what it will be like if we separate. That there will be times when he keeps my children away from me. It makes me feel nauseous. It makes me back down. Play nice. Because what's worse? Fighting with someone within a marriage but having your children close, or still fighting with that same person, just outside the marriage, and only seeing your children some of the time? "Please, Gabe. I really want to speak to them." After everything with Dad all I want to do is hold my babies. I just want to feel them close.

He sighs. "Really, Layla, they're next door, borrowing some wrapping paper for their Christmas presents."

Everything that has happened over the past few days, all the truths about Dad and everyone else, seems too big a conversation to have over the phone. "You should come down," I say. "Would be good to talk in person. Seems strange for the kids not to see you Christmas morning. There are flights out tonight. Tomorrow morning."

"I can't this time," he says. The kids' voices sound in the background.

"Put them on, Gabe." I use a stronger voice this time.

"Hey, Mum." Jack's voice echoes through the phone and I fight back tears. His voice pulls at my chest.

"Hey, baby. God I miss you so much. I can't wait to see you."

"I couldn't do it, Mum."

"What, sweetheart?"

"The Christmas concert. I…" he trails off.

Shit. I didn't call and wish him good luck. I just didn't have the headspace at the time.

"There were heartbeats in my hands," he says.

"Oh, love." I smile at the way he describes his anxiety. "It sounds like going on stage felt like a really hard thing to do."

"I showed Mrs. Adams—she's from school and was there all week—how to push play on the music. She said I could be her special helper."

I know Mrs. Adams. She's wonderful and must have been working at the holiday program. I close my eyes and say a silent thank you to teachers. "Well, maybe it's lucky you didn't go on. There might not have been any music." Jack laughs and my body relaxes a little. "Can I speak to your sister? Make sure you pack your red pajamas, okay? It's freezing down here."

Jack puts down the phone but then comes back. "Audrey says she's busy, wrapping."

"Okay, hon." A pang of feeling far away from her. "Can you put your dad back on?" I hear Gabe ask the kids to wrap their presents in the upstairs lounge.

"You should come down," I repeat. "It will be strange not having you here."

"I can't this year, Layla," he says quietly.

"What do you mean can't? The business closes down anyway, doesn't it?"

"I just don't want Christmas to be a fight. Shouldn't be that way. It's better for the kids."

"Better for the kids or better for you?"

"Layla, don't. It doesn't need to be this way."

No, I think, it doesn't. "I wish I'd known then, back before we got married, what I know now." Our early years together, the wedding, the kids, they were like falling into a river. Being swept along. It felt good to be repeating what other people had done. Ticking life events off a list.

"You wanted this life, Layla. Hell, you practically pushed me down the aisle."

"I seem to remember a willing partner, Gabe. You were the one who proposed, even when I wanted to wait. You were the one who told me to go back to work, suggested I go for the job in Queensland. You're pretty far from a puppet."

"I thought if you were happy, things would get better," Gabe says. My father's voice sounds in my ear: *The fresh air will do you a world of good, Nora.*

Every time Gabe and I have an argument, we come to the edge. I always stop. Ask myself: am I going to jump off or am I going to take a step back and placate or apologize or sympathize? And I usually step back, but that step back comes at a cost and over time the costs have added up and added up until they've left me bankrupt. So, I step forwards.

"Freya, that woman from work. She wasn't the first, was she? I've been thinking back to when I was pregnant with Aud, that was when it started, wasn't it? Not with her, but with others. Women at work. Someone on that trip you used to take to the snow."

"Layla—"

"Just…tell…me," I breathe down the phone. I think of all those uneasy times when things didn't add up but I let them slide. Suspicions that niggled at me but weren't concrete enough to make any accusations.

"Does it really matter anymore?"

228

"Yes. It does. It does because all this time I've been willing to take the blame to keep the peace."

"When you went back to work, we could go days, weeks, without even talking. There were months when you would circle around me and not even connect. Do you know how fucking lonely that was? Is?"

"That's no excuse," I say.

"No, probably not, so what's yours?" His comment takes me by surprise. He is right.

I told myself a version of our story that helped me justify my behavior with Lucas. A story in which I was the victim and Gabe was the villain. As I'm sure he did with me. Neither is more truthful than the other. Each of us are both victim and villain.

"What are we doing?" I ask. He sighs and I imagine him putting his left hand on his hip and looking to the ground. Shaking his head.

"I don't know, Layla. I don't know."

I try to think of when it all started to go wrong, a moment I can put my finger on and say, oh that was it. As if the story of a marriage was ever told or ever could be. "I was thinking about our honeymoon, at the airport," I say. "About Scotland and the fermented honey the owner brought us. It just, it seems like a different you, a different me."

"Maybe we just didn't know ourselves and what we really wanted back then."

"Maybe," I say. Part of me wonders whether wanting to start a family had pushed us forwards to get married and settle down, whether we would have chosen each other if we hadn't wanted kids. Whether we would have stayed together through the years, even months. Maybe ours has always been an un-leavened love.

"I promised myself that I would never give my kids a broken home," I say, not sure I can cope with the shame of a failed marriage and the kids' heartbreak on top of everything I've found out about Dad. But then I feel like we're on a train I can't control, and that the train is heading straight for separation, whether I like it or not. We've been here before anyway, haven't we? To the part where we almost end it. The way that goodbyes, really, happen in stages. "Maybe we can fix things. Find a way back to each other? Maybe whoever we're with next…maybe that relationship will just travel the same trajectory? We've invested so much time in us. Maybe we shouldn't just throw it away."

"Maybe," he repeats back to me. So many maybes. "But I think I need to see for myself if that's true." There is another form of goodbye in his reply. "But what do you really want, Layla? What do you want to do here? We can't keep going on like this. That's even worse for the kids."

Before I can stop myself, I know the answer and the words trickle out of me as my heart swells. "I want a divorce," I say. Finally. "I can't do this anymore. I'll stay down at Mum's with the kids a bit longer. Give us some time and space."

"Okay," he says softly and then with more finality, "alright. I have to go and get the kids to the airport."

My phone feels heavier than it was before as I put it in my bag, and I wonder whether we can ever give someone something we've never received. Can we give patience? Unconditional love? Support? If it was something we never experienced in childhood? Maybe the struggle to learn how to give and receive what we were never given is the purpose of this whole damn life.

The green parrot flies away and returns with hay in its beak, swoops above my head and into the tree. I stand to see a nest resting in a hollow. Straw and colored cotton, sheep wool and flower petals are spun and woven together. In high school we made bird-nesting boxes; learned that male birds collect shiny things and put them in their homes to attract the opposite sex. Because, when the light reflects off them, they look like water. Like the illusion of something they need to survive.

I take the silver key to Lucas's apartment out of my bag and hold its slight weight in the center of my left palm. It sits next to my gold wedding band, which I slowly thread off my finger. I hold them both as they shimmer in the light of the sun, before I reach up and place them carefully in the nest and walk away, hoping they will bring the bird better luck.

THIRTY-NINE

THE ONLY PLACE OPEN TO EAT MIDMORNING IS XANDERS' SEAFOOD CAFÉ, A COLONIAL-ERA BUILDING WITH FOUR posts holding up a corrugated iron roof, and faded orange buoys hanging from anywhere they can fit a hook. A woman stands out the front wearing an oversized black band T-shirt. Seeing her makes me remember I left my favorite Velvet Underground T-shirt at Lucas's, along with a few books and some makeup. I won't bother going back and getting the key. I know how to get into his place through the window but don't really want to go alone. I take out my phone. "When we get back from holidays," I text, "do you want to break into a guy's apartment and steal back some of my stuff?" It only takes a second for three gray dots to appear and Remi to reply, "Absa…fucking…lutely."

In the café, plates scrape and clash and voices rise over the clatter. I see Maggie and Adara sitting at a table in the corner, a painting of a seagull with a chip in its mouth hanging above their heads.

"Do you want to sit outside?" Maggie asks. "There's a bench seat out there where we could sit in the sun?" I nod and we walk out the swinging screen door to the garden. There are two raised veggie patches with rows of climbing snow peas, an old blue rowboat filled with soil and white daphne, and festoon lights strung from the roof to the back fence, which glow even in the daytime.

Adara orders natural oysters, pickled octopus salad and barbecue scallops to share, with a bottle of local white wine. I look at her. "What?" she says. "Surely we could all do with a drink no matter what time of day it is. It's twelve o'clock somewhere in the world." We sit there in silence awhile; the sweet smell of daphne balances the tension.

Eventually, Maggie takes out an emerald-green vase from her bag. "Going to give this to your mum." I run my finger around the edge as if I'm playing a note on a crystal champagne flute.

"It's beautiful," I say, though the words don't do it justice.

"I made it—turned my hand to glassblowing. Now make vases that go all around the world. And Christmas baubles."

"They're in high demand," Adara says. I think about Maggie's colored ice spheres, of Bill smashing them to pieces.

"Fallen in love with the process," Maggie says. "Once the glass is hot, the possibilities are endless."

"How's your health, Maggie?" I try not to look toward her breasts.

"Don't worry about me, Layla. I'm a tough nut. And anyway, the rhythms of nature have always ordered our lives here. This is no different."

Adara looks off into the distance and scratches her arm until red lines appear amid the small white scars.

"Adara, I…"

"You're not responsible, Layla."

"I'm still sorry."

"Of course you are. Would be weird if you weren't."

"I hope Dawn will move back in with me. I owe her so much; it's the least I can do," I say. "Or maybe she should move in with Mum. Keep her company, keep an eye on her."

"I think she'll come to live with me, hon," Maggie says. "We don't want to live just to grow old anymore. God knows, we've done enough of that. We'll keep an eye on Nora. But it won't be easy. It won't be easy for Dawn to be here."

"Because of what happened with Bill?" I ask, then hope I'm not being insensitive.

Maggie purses her lips. "Well, yes, that." She cups her crossed knee with her palms and rocks backwards for a moment; she goes to speak again but is interrupted by the arrival of our food. A man with a bushranger beard balances three large plates out across his arms, one on his left and two on his right; picks up a milk crate with his boot, plants it next to us and sets our food on top. Goes back inside and brings out the bottle of wine with three glasses. Sets them on a paver. The food smells of garlic, vegetable oil and the sea. Adara pours the wine. Maggie waits for him to leave before continuing. "For Dawn, living with Nora is a daily reminder of what happened with Oscar. And it reminds Dawn of their own childhood." I think about what Dawn told me about her own father; have a hint of how generations of silence can flow from one single choice.

I think about the snuffbox Dawn gave me to give Mum. The generations of pain. Our DNA strands laced with trauma. But then I also think of the fact that the women in my family have done what they have had to do to survive.

The bearded bushranger comes out the back with another man, clean-shaven but with so much hair on his arms you can't see his skin. They light cigarettes.

"You competing next week?" says the clean-shaven, hairy-chested one.

"Nah, last year a shard of wood got stuck in my eye. Still can't see out of the bugger."

"You don't need to see to turn timber into toothpicks on a standing block, Charlie."

"That's the truth, but I do need the other good eye to turn my disaster of a life into something worth living."

The one thing that will never change around here is the Boxing Day woodchopping competition. West coasters are a breed apart. This is the land of broad-shouldered axe men and women who can lay claim to being among the world's best. They are the woodchoppers who have grown up on a diet of iron-hard eucalypt.

"Dad still goes every year," Adara says.

"Loves to comment on what everyone is doing wrong," Maggie adds. "Thinks winning one year means he's an expert and that everyone wants his opinion." She downs the rest of her wine.

"How's your dairy going?" I ask.

Maggie throws her head back and laughs, so I can see the food in her mouth. "Was never my dairy, love, any more than Bill is now my husband."

I pause, wanting to say something about what Bill did to Dawn. Hovering in that moment where you choose between speaking or remaining silent. I open my mouth and close it again.

Maggie tilts her head to the side. "Don't pussyfoot, Layla. God knows, we haven't done that with you."

"It's just, what Bill did to Dawn..." is all I can get out.

"I told Bill that if he did that again, he'd wake up in the middle of the night with one of the milking machines on his cock."

"Mum!" says Adara.

"Look, the marriage shouldn't have happened in the first place. It's the same old story. Hindsight isn't twenty-twenty, it's torture." Maggie looks to Adara. "Sorry, love. I'd do it all again just to have you."

Adara mouths, *I know*, and touches her mother's arm. Another jealous pang at their intimacy tightens my muscles.

I watch Adara pick at the octopus salad; finish the wine. I want to tell Maggie thank you, thank you for telling me; I want to tell Adara that I feel complicit in what happened to her. Even though the words are clear in my head, they become indiscernible when I attempt to form them into sounds.

"Well, that's my time up, lovelies," Maggie says. "Have to get over to see Dawn; promised to show her a beauty of a bauble I just made, red-robin glass with flecks of silver blown through." Maggie puts two oysters, three pickled octopus tentacles and a handful of barbecue scallops on two napkins and kisses her daughter goodbye on the forehead.

After she leaves, I pause for a second, wanting to ask Adara why they didn't go to the police, and whether she knew about any of the other girls, but she gets in first.

"None of us wanted the truth out, Layla. Your mum didn't want people to know because she felt responsible, felt as though people would think she'd turned a blind eye and let it happen. Mum didn't want people to know because she thought they would blame me. Say it was my fault." Adara stops. "And I...I was grasping at the last form of control I had. Control over the story. Control of who knew and who didn't. I spent the first half of my life feeling like I was at the mercy of everything and everyone around me. Keeping quiet gave me a kind of power." Adara scrunches a paper napkin into a ball.

"There's power in owning your story, too," I say, but immediately regret my comment.

Adara gives a bitter laugh. "Are you feeling it, Layla? More empowered now the truth is out?" she asks, looking me straight in the eye, unblinking.

I think about this a moment. "Well, no, I suppose not. Empowered is a terrible choice of words." I think about backpedaling and admitting that her experience is more traumatic than mine, but stop. The truth is, I don't know whether I was a victim as well. I don't know. "I feel more relieved than anything," I say; chew my lip for a moment. "But there is something I do feel..." I search for the right word, think about Dawn's oranges. "I do feel more...real."

Adara nods. The scrunched-up napkin on her lap unfurls like a fist to an open palm. "Do you want to come to the Boxing Day fair with us?" she asks. "Bring the kids?"

"Maybe," I say. I have no idea what's going to happen minute upon minute, let alone day upon day, anymore. My life used to be scheduled to the second.

Adara looks out over the raised veggie patches. "You know, after it all happened and my parents found out," she says, still staring into the distance, "and when I saw similar women dealing with others' reactions, I realized there are three types of people: the ones who see you as damaged and focus on healing you; the ones who see you as a victim and focus their anger on the world; and the ones who simply don't know how to respond, who when they see you focus their energy on walking to the other side of the street. Although I didn't tell anyone besides my parents, I started to try to guess what kind of reaction people would have if I did. It became like a game. *Would this person want to heal or rage or run away?*"

I think about Adara in university lecture halls and dig sites, with a whole internal world no one knows about.

"Don't fall into one of those categories, Layla. You're better than that."

I put my wineglass down, and move around to sit next to Adara, simply wanting to be closer to her.

"Did you ever meet anyone?" I ask, knowing Adara never had kids but not much else about her adult life.

"Never saw the point." Adara crosses her legs and pours more wine into her and my glasses. "Knew I was never going to show someone my real self, tell them my truth, so never allowed myself to get close to anyone."

I look down in my lap, face grimacing again. "You don't have to answer, but how did your parents find out what happened?"

She shakes her head. Seems relieved to be talking to me about it. "I told them. After I heard Nora talking to Mum, telling her about the letter and that she was going to look through your dad's things, I ran. Was too scared to stay at home listening to it all, so ran to Jesse's place and told him. Told him everything. He convinced me to tell Mum."

"Jesse?" I ask. Adara nods. The noise inside the restaurant increases from an afternoon hum to an early-dinner row.

"Hey," I say, downing the rest of my wine and standing to stretch my legs. "Count us in for the Boxing Day fair. Okay?" She nods and offers me a small smile, stands as well. I look her in the eyes. "We have a lot of catching up to do." Hold her in my arms and she returns my embrace. I slowly pull away. "I should go and get the place ready for the kids," I say. But once I get out of the café, I run to the car.

FORTY

JESSE IS WALKING THROUGH THE PEAR ORCHARD
WHEN I RUN UP AND PUSH HIM HARD IN THE BACK. HE TURNS IN
surprise and puts down the box of pears he is carrying, before I shove him
in the chest. I propel myself at him again and again with every muscle in my
body. Out of breath from running and pushing, I pick up the pears and start
throwing them at Jesse's body and he recoils, before coming toward me. He
holds my wrists in his hands so that the fruit I'm holding falls to the ground,
then gently lets go.

"Layla," is all he says.

"That's a fine fucking high horse you're on there," I shout, lunging forwards as the words shoot from my mouth. "How dare you make me feel bad
for leaving, when you're more of a coward." For a moment, he looks into my
eyes. Registers my fury. Understands what I'm saying.

"I promised Adara, promised your mum. And anyway, I couldn't be the
one to tell you," he says. "I couldn't."

A gust of wind sweeps around the orchard. I take off the wide, woolen
scarf that's been tied around my neck and wrap it around my shoulders. "All
these years, I've felt sick about leaving without saying goodbye. As if all this
time I was a horrible person. The one in the wrong."

"You were in the wrong," he fires back.

His comment stings. But this new truth evens us. Levels me to him rather
than leaving me feeling as though I could never again look him in the eye.

"I loved you, Layla. I've always loved you. I knew that if I was the one to
tell you, then you would have viewed me differently, maybe even hated me."

"I think I've hated everyone from here, including myself, Jesse, for a really, really long time." The wind picks up again and blows my hair across my face.

"You have every right to be angry with the world at the moment," he says. "But trust me, as someone who spent a lot of time raging, it'll eat you up until there's nothing left."

I think about all the days Jesse comforted me after Dad died. About how supportive he was. Unflinching. The way he brought Mum groceries, watched out for her, after I left for the mainland. The tenderness he showed Mum the other night.

"I don't blame you for raging at the way I left, Jesse. But I did think of you. I have thought of you so many times over the years."

He looks down at his feet, reaches into his back pocket and pulls out his wallet. Opens it up and takes out something crinkled. "You know how you used to love taking photographs?" he asks.

I nod. I loved photography because you can pick and choose what you want to keep, curate the memories to include the good and exclude the bad. But after the last few days, photography has taken on a darker meaning.

"This was my favorite. It's of that tree," he says, and passes me the photograph carefully in the wind. I take it and look at the image, faded from being folded and handled. "I used to call it the witness tree, since we buried your cow beneath it. I've carried that photo in my wallet all these years. I used to think it was because I loved that cow too. But when I saw you again, I realized it's because I've wanted to carry around with me a piece of you."

I hand the photograph back to Jesse, and he puts it back in his wallet. When I look from his hands up to his face, his gaze is serious and intent. My breath catches in my chest.

Don't, I say to myself. I think of beginnings, middles and endings. How one naturally morphs into the other once you get to a certain age. How nothing is black and white anymore, just hues of gray. The last thing I need is another man in my life. But he keeps looking at me.

"You don't even know me anymore, Jesse. If I showed you the real me, you'd run a mile."

"Bullshit," he says.

I'm so tired of only showing people parts of myself. So tired of pretending. Of lying. With nothing left to lose, I let all the falseness fall away. "I've just separated from my husband, even though I know we should have done it years ago," I say, breath hot and fast, but I keep going. "Sometimes I just wish he'd die so that it would be easier, so that I wouldn't have to go through the hell I know will happen." My heart quickens and my stomach feels sick. "I had an affair, with an artist. It's only just ended. I used to run to his place at night when the kids were in bed." Who does that? I think. Who the fuck does that? But there's more. "I accidentally killed a man at work and part of me believes I did it on purpose, because I was mad at him for keeping me from my son's birthday." Tears prick my eyes as all my ugly truths come pouring out. All of my monstrosities. "When I saw Mum's lifeless body, I wished she'd done it properly and actually killed herself," I keep going. "I'm terrified that if I quit my job, I won't know who I am. That throwing it all away means that my life so far has been for nothing, every sacrifice I've made for nothing." I'm shaking now but can't stop. "I'm terrified I've failed as a mother. That my kids will grow up with a warped version of their childhood, of me, and that all the love we shared when they were little will be like it never happened. And I…I…" I hold my hands in front of my face.

"Hey," Jesse says, as he slowly takes my hands away. "Hey," he says again, quieter. "You're not the only one who's messed things up. Who feels these things. I've done similar, maybe worse. You're not a horrible person, Layla. You're not…" He looks me right in the eye. "You are not like your father."

Tears finally come, gently at first but then in heaving sobs that rack my body so much I can't stand and so I fall to my knees. Jesse reaches down and holds me. I cry for the truth about my father and for Willow and Adara. I cry for my mother and all her confusion and pain; I cry for myself and the lies I have lived.

Jesse whispers in my ear, "This you, this real you, is not unlovable." His skin smells like soil after rain; of cucumbers and apples in season. I think of our first kiss and his lips on mine in the orchard and, like pears left on the tree, feel as though I'm ripening from the inside out.

The wind blows. Jesse cups the back of my neck and guides my face toward his. His soft lips send warmth down the center of my body, as a gathering gale billows my scarf like a sail and then lifts it up and off my shoulders. I try to wrap it back around myself, but as I do, the wind takes hold and blows it up into a eucalypt. I pull away from Jesse and run over to the tree, take off my shoes and pull myself up onto a low-lying branch, falter as I stand, but two hands grip my ankles tight, holding me steady. I reach up on my tippy toes to clasp the scarf, miss it, reach again, and finally find a corner with my fingers so that I am able to pull it toward me until it slips to the soil.

I stand there a moment looking through the tree's canopy. In the distance, clouds blanket the mountain peaks, then the west winds tear off the covers. I feel Jesse's hands grip my ankles harder. Then he loosens his hands and pulls away. My skin there suddenly cool, left wanting. I lower myself slowly onto the branch and sit to face him, my hips at his head height, legs dangling. Looking at each other with short, sharp exhalations, he caps both of my knees with his palms, rubs his thumbs on my skin. He dips his head down and I think for a moment he is going to pull away, but then his thumbs press into my cartilage and he bows his head before he lifts up my dress, pulls aside my underwear and devours me. He tastes me as if he is starving. A twig pierces my skin and I flinch from the sting. Around us the grass is whispering and alive.

Jesse draws me down off the branch into his arms; I wrap my legs around his waist and he carries me backwards a few paces before pulling me down onto the ground. Shielded by the rows upon rows of pear trees, I take off my underwear, unzip his jeans and sit on top; guide him, hard, inside me. He picks up a pear I threw at him and takes a large bite, then another, before pushing the soft and slippery fruit between my legs, so it feels as though his mouth is still wet upon me. His broad hand flattens against my lower back, pressing me in between the pear and his palm, my lower body grazing backwards and forwards against him.

I stare at his familiar face, but the man who flips me over onto my back, who holds my wrists outstretched above my head, the man who ravishes me, is new and expansive. The way his bicep swells, that bump after the dip of inner elbow, as he grips me. The way he then places a hand beneath my head. The way the pendulum swings between tenderness and savagery is everything I want. I think back to that singular act in my backyard under the jacaranda tree in Queensland. The way I know what I need. And I'm reminded that self-knowledge can never surpass the pleasure of someone else's desire. Especially if it's mixed with love.

I reach under Jesse's shirt and scrape my fingernails down his back, and he moans, putting his hands under my hips and tilting them up, pushing himself further inside me. The roar of the gale rises to a wailing shriek. A thick branch falls close by with a crack. We look at each other. There is something about being so close to injury, maybe even close to death, that takes a hold of us, and I brace myself against him until he thrusts so hard that we finish in a concoction of soil and solace and sweat and survival.

Jesse laughs with warmth as he pulls me off the ground, takes me by the hand and we walk away from the tree. "We don't want to test fate twice," he says. And we run down through the pear orchard and sit in a patch of sun that is peeking through the clouds. The wind calms. He lies back and I rest my head on his chest. I'm not sure whether I'm shivering from the cold or fear. Strange when you have been guarded for so many years to be so suddenly seen.

To give someone something from inside you, not a heart or a lung, or blood or muscles, but an unknown organ that no one has ever seen, which is unique to you. To go about snipping the pulsing shape from a kind of mesentery, and then to hand it over, quivering, to someone else. To place it in their hands and then watch and wait to see what they will do.

"Will you stay here?" I ask.

"I think so," he says. "Originally, the plan was to sell the house, go back to the mainland and start again. Em, my ex-wife, and I, we couldn't conceive. It sucked all the love out of our relationship. When she left, I moved down here permanently and opened the distillery. It brought me back to life." He pauses. "There's something about this place. I used to be so desperate to get away—to *do better*. Used to think Tassie was the bottom end of the world."

I think of correcting him, "arse end of the world," but then find the fact he couldn't bring himself to say the word "arse" endearing.

"If I run away from it, I'm running away from myself, in some ways. Now I'm hoping to build a cabin a bit further south. Open another distillery on the east coast."

I trace a new thin cut on Jesse's arm that runs like a smile showing sticky through his hair. My toes move along the ground. I have missed the wet soil we grew up in. Earth that clung to our bare feet when it rained. Mud that spattered our arms when it rose with the furious westerly wind. My feet never touch mud on the mainland. Everything here on the west coast of Tasmania is alive. I look up and around at the pear trees.

"The orchard, it's…I've never seen it so full of fruit," I say.

"Was a bit trial-and-error, to be honest. Two winters ago, I taught myself to prune. Dad had never let me get close enough to the trees before to learn."

"Surprised your dad wasn't here holding the pruning shears for you." I smile.

Jesse laughs. "He's distracted. He met someone. Think that's the only way he's been able to let go. First season wasn't great. But then I got talking to one of the old guys who plays cards and smokes down on the wharf. He's a retired fruit grower from Bologna. Saverio's his name. Taught me how to spot the branches and stems that need to be removed. I'd had too light a touch. I needed to allow more sunlight and air to move through the plant. To create enough space, Saverio said, 'for a small bird to fly through the center of the tree.' After that, it was like magic."

I look up and around at the ripe fruit drawing heavy branches down.

"What about you?" he asks.

"Well, my marriage has ended." I give a long exhale. "My career's a shambles. And I need to fix my relationship with my kids. I love being a doctor, but I've prioritized that over them for too long. And for the wrong reasons. All I know is how to hold on tight, white-knuckled. Not how to let go. I've never felt at home in the city. I don't really know where home could be. But I'm coming to love this land as well.

"It's like I'm getting to know myself for the first time. What I like. What I don't. It's been so sudden and, well, overwhelming, that I think I'm still coming to terms with what it means. I also need to...I need to focus on my kids before I add someone else to my life." I balloon my lungs with a concussion of air. Life can be an explosion of doubt and desire and discomfort that has no outlet in words.

Jesse listens and nods at me and in that gesture is a safe place. For some reason, I pull away, but he draws me close. A voice begins to whisper to me, a voice that seems to come from my future self: maybe real intimacy, it says, is being able to reveal to someone everything you believe to be unlovable and to have them love you more. There is a difference, I think, between relationships born from expectations, those born from loneliness, and those born from intimacy. Gabe, Lucas, Jesse. I was better at falling in love with the man than the way he made me feel.

"Life gets complicated, doesn't it?" Jesse holds me tighter. I rest my head against his chest. In this moment, I love you, I think. But I don't say this to him. Even though I want to say so much.

I want to tell him about the first signs of death, when the eyes cloud over as oxygen stops flowing to the corneas. I want to tell him that I've witnessed this more times than years I've lived. I want to tell him that, as the Earth warms, what they call pink snow will become more common, and that the last snow we'll see on Earth will be red, like a blush, a bruise, a rush of blood. I want to tell him that the night before I flew here will have been the last night my children and Gabe and I ever spend together as a family. And I want to tell him that all these endings make me feel like beginning again with him. But I don't say anything, because we've only just seen each other again after years of being apart, and because everything feels confusing, and because we are taught that such quickly expressed feelings are irrational and foolish.

"I don't think complications," Jesse says, "are a good enough reason to close the door on something that feels this right."

I let the reassurance of those words settle in the silence.

And as I lie there and breathe Jesse in, I imagine my life as a pear tree and everything in it as branches; my hand with a slim bright blade pruning until there is just enough room for a bird named hope to fly right through.

FORTY-ONE

THE KIDS RUSH INTO MY ARMS AT JERICHO AIRPORT, WRAP THEIR ARMS AROUND MY NECK ON EITHER SIDE. I EXHALE AND then breathe them in; grip them tight. Aud lets me hold her for a moment. The hair on her forehead wet and dark with sweat.

Jack nuzzles his face into the side of my breast. "I told my class last week that I was coming here, Mum, and Mrs. Symons said that echidnas hibernate at the airport over winter." He flicks his head from left to right, as if at any moment the animal might poke its head out from behind a chair. I've heard the story before. The way the echidnas have got so used to their environment that the noise of jets doesn't wake them.

"It's summer now, so sadly no echidnas hibernating, my love," I say, as I tickle Jack's ribs.

"When are we gonna see Nanna? She usually comes to pick us up?" Audrey asks.

I pull her to me again. "Soon, soon. She had a little scare and is in hospital, but she'll hopefully be home tomorrow morning for Christmas."

The car ride into town passes in a comfortable silence. Aud sits in the front seat with her head resting against the window, and Jack sits in the back coloring in a book he must have been given on the plane. I enjoy the meditative hum of the tires on the road and the vibration of the wheel.

When we get to Mum's, I take the kids and their bags into my childhood bedroom. Jack hands me a Christmas card. "I made it for you at art club." It reads "MERI CIRSTMAS" on the front and, as I open it up, a star pops out. "It's the North Star. I folded it myself, look see," and he closes it and opens it three more times, opening his mouth in surprise each time. I feel a brief shimmer of joy even though the thought of the North Star still holds so much pain.

Audrey starts to unpack her clothes and put them in the wardrobe. I rub my hand on her shoulder, but she pulls away from my touch. It's always impossible to talk to her properly with Jack bouncing around, and so I just watch her downcast eyes with a resolve that I'll find some one-on-one space to talk to her later. She walks out into the lounge room and I hear her footfall stop.

"Mum, Mum!" she screams. I scruff up Jack's hair, put my arm around his shoulder and walk him out to the lounge. "There's no Christmas tree? There's no tree?" She starts to cry, and I know that whenever she starts to act like a three-year-old around something like a Christmas tree or a bowl of ice cream or a slightly creased page in a book she's reading, that whatever she's feeling has nothing to do with trees, dessert or paper.

"Mum, how is Santa going to find us?" Jack asks. "Does he know we're not at home?" With everything that's happened, I haven't stopped to think about the tree. The front door opens and Maggie and Dawn walk in holding armfuls of presents. "There's no Christmas tree for the presents," Jack blurts.

Maggie smiles. "You know, there are still a few left at the fruit shop in town. I can call Jude and get her to put one aside, pop down there and get it. If you three want to go for a walk, Dawn and I can have it all set up for you by the time you get back."

I look at her and mouth the words "thank you."

I walk the kids across the property, water bottles and snacks in a backpack, and remember that Dad's observatory is still there. How the hell is it still there? Surely Mum should have had someone remove it. Or Maggie? Adara? How do people live with these things, skeletons, in full view? I think about the trees Bill cut down, their once-spiraling leaves and far-reaching branches a natural screen. Dad's fight to save the trees had nothing to do with the environment. It was all about seclusion.

We walk down the cliff, past the wharf and the railway station, and onto the stretch of road that leads to town; we travel the well-worn paths through button grass, before coming to the rainforest. In all these years, the tangled-hair swaths of sphagnum moss and garlands of climbing heath haven't changed. I find reassurance in the fact that my life and knowledge can change so much, but that the natural world around can stay the same.

It's still light when we make it to the beach; take off our shoes. Jack picks up a stick and drags it behind him as he runs ahead, yelling that it's his dinosaur tail. Audrey saunters with her arms crossed and head down. I heel-toe my feet into the sand, feeling the ground give way; watch my footprints fill with foamy water. A pair of plovers trip ahead of us. Jack runs back to me with a palm full of pebbles. There are clouds above us, but my eyes go to the line where blue meets blue. Imagine the sinking boat in stormy weather, the screaming children, my father speeding out and then into the distant disarray. I flinch from the needle-thrust of sorrow.

I've never taken the kids to the sand dunes before. Jack was too little to make it there until now, and we're usually only here a day. When we clamber to the top, he stands still, head tilted up, looking across at the white rolling desert. We walk along the ridge of one of the small hills and then along to the larger ones. I start to tell Jack he's only allowed to roll down the small ones, but I haven't even got the sentence out before he's thrown himself down a vertical drop, sand flying behind him and giggles bubbling up the incline. Aud and I sit down next to each other watching Jack. She pulls at grass, breaking the green blades and throwing them aside.

"How's your dad?" I ask tentatively.

"Dad? Dad's great," she says. *Great*, I sound out each letter in my head like a child learning to read. I think about my younger self coming here with my mum, my own body rolling down these hills, and I wonder how many times Audrey has wished that her mother was different. Just like I used to.

People say that, when you have a child, your heart will forever be walking around outside your chest, and they make you believe that your greatest fear will be the external world; will be watching your child be pushed and pulled and hurt and broken by a merciless macrocosm. Nobody tells you that the hardest part is not your children being a heart, but your children being a mirror. And not the mirror you're used to, a flat mirror held upright where the reflection you see is exactly as you think it is, but rather a funhouse mirror distorting daily their perception of you. And, sometimes, your perception of yourself.

I try to think of an open-ended question that won't elicit an eye roll or confrontation. "Are you looking forward to next year?" I ask.

"Millie Connor, a girl at my high school, got lost on camp in Central Australia. She was at our art program and told us all about it. Their principal called them in for a special assembly. He explained that people can survive for weeks without food but only days without water. Two days later, Millie was found—she was lucky to be alive. They could have found her dead, in the middle of nowhere. I'm going on that outback camp next year."

"Thanks to Millie, you'll probably be safer than any other year that's gone," I try to reassure. But as I say this, I'm not sure that's right.

Jack walks up to us with sand in his hair and spits the grains out of his mouth. I wait for him to cry or get upset, but all he does is jump up and down and say, "I'm gonna do that again." And off he goes.

"Did I ever tell you about the night you were born?" I say; Audrey shakes her head. "I had you in the hospital crib next to me." I laugh. "I think those nights in hospital were probably the only times you ever spent out of my bed and arms until you were twelve months old. I pulled that crib right up to me and I just lay there staring at you. God, I was exhausted. But I stayed up all night. Just staring. Staring at you." Audrey stops pulling at the grass. I think about survival; about what we need and what we don't.

"You know I always wanted to show you, Aud, that being a mum isn't just about sacrifice. I wanted you to grow up seeing me as a fully formed person, with work and a life outside of family needs, and I think I've done that. I just don't think I've been very balanced. I'm sorry. I want to spend more time with you. I'm quitting my job at the hospital. I still want to have a career, but I want it on my own terms, so I don't miss so many things anymore, okay?" Audrey nods. "Go—go have a roll down that really big dune over there. I was never brave enough to do that one."

She looks at me and takes up the challenge. Kicks off her pale-purple sneakers and runs to the top. She hesitates a moment, kneels down and sweeps both her legs to the side and in front of her and lies down, reaches her hands above her head. I see her taking a deep breath and then she begins to roll. It's a fast descent of about fifty flips. Audrey has the wind knocked out of her and is overcome with laughter, unable to stifle her body's sounds of joy. I start to laugh myself, until my body is shaking so hard I can't stop; my stomach hurts and I place my hand across my waist and throw my head back with abandon. I haven't heard or felt laughter like that in a long time. I wonder when I got used to living such a lukewarm life.

Audrey hits another bump in the dune, another shriek of delight echoes, and I keep laughing. Audrey lands at the bottom with her arms and legs splayed out. Her chest heaving up and down. Jack runs over to her and pulls her up.

I look over to the beach, searching for shearwaters. The birds, who used to fly from here to the Arctic Circle in our summer, have been losing their way. When they leave their island burrows to fly north, the lights from cities and bridges have been disorientating them, shining on the water like the moon, and they end up stranded around the city.

Audrey has run back up to the top of the tallest dune. As I sit here watching her roll down the steep slope again, I see generations of women in our family: I see my great-grandmother making Julekage bread for her violent husband; my grandmother unable to protect her girls; Dawn and a life she could have had with Maggie; I see Mum writing poetry. I see the repeated patterns of men, taking whatever they want while we give it to them. Placate them. Forgive them. I think back to the day Dad died and the whale that Mum and I saved. About the mother whales and the words they whisper to their calves on the ocean bed. And every revolution of Audrey's body increases a revolution in my heart, the whispered word in my head tumbling over and over: *enough, enough, enough.*

When we're close to home, I tell Jack to run in and check whether Maggie and Dawn were able to get a tree and maybe, if they did, he could help put on the finishing touches.

I take Audrey to the shed and find an axe and a sledgehammer, and we walk across the property toward the towering trees, where our property gives way to wilderness. The dome on the dilapidated observatory is covered in leaves, twigs and fallen branches. Overgrown grass sprouts from the wooden walls. The myrtles and eucalypts that remain reach for the sunset sky.

"Feel like causing some damage?" I ask Audrey. She looks at me with a "you can't be serious" expression, before nodding excitedly. I swing the sledgehammer at the wooden wall but only make a small dint, so I swing again, this time getting the head stuck in the wood. I push my foot against the panels to pull it out; then Audrey takes it from me and steps back. She puts the sledgehammer over her right shoulder and runs toward the observatory, throwing her body and the hammer into the wall, and knocking half of it down.

I laugh with a swell of something in my heart and Audrey looks at me, the excitement gone for a second as she says, "Mum, are you okay?"

It's only then that I realize I'm crying. I wrap my arms around her, kiss her on her head. "Yes, baby, yes," I say.

I take the axe and swing and swing until wood splinters and chips are flying, and I ask Audrey to stand back. Sweat is dripping down from under my arms and across my forehead and I start shouting the way we learned to do in self-defense classes in the school gymnasium, screaming, "No! No! No! No!" I remove so much of the walls that the steel dome above begins to creak and tilt, until it falls inside the building with a crash. I stand there and look at the destruction. Audrey walks up to the building and kicks what's left of the wooden panels as hard as she can, then turns around and smiles at me, saying, "Only a crazy person would put a building like that out here."

I think again about the whales whispering truths to their babies on the ocean floor. And I realize that sometimes babies whisper truths to their mothers as well.

FORTY-TWO

INSIDE, MAGGIE IS LIFTING JACK UP ONTO HER SHOULDERS TO POSITION A GOLD STAR ON THE TOP OF THE Christmas tree, the same star we used to put on when I was young. The large fir tree brushes the roof and, after a couple of attempts, they have to cut it down a fraction before Jack can fit the shiny spikes beneath the ceiling. On Mum's sideboard is a photograph of how Christmas used to be in our household. Gabe's arms around me. Our glances at each other as our children open their presents. A feeling of "this is the way it is supposed to be." My stomach churns at the thought of breaking up our family, no matter how broken Gabe and I are. But those photographs don't tell the whole story anyway.

We all step back and wait while Dawn plugs in the lights and turns them on. They are all different colors and flash as the tinsel shines in ice-cream swirls around handmade ornaments. Maggie hands Dawn one of her large, red glass baubles to hang on the highest branch. It's a world away from how we decorate our tree at home, where I am in control and hand the kids an ornament, one by one, and point to exactly where I want it; where the monochrome cool lights stay static and the carefully chosen color scheme mimics the department store windows. But as I watch Jack throw some more tinsel, up near the star, I think I've never seen a more beautiful tree.

In the kitchen, the kids help Maggie and Dawn brush milk and sprinkle brown sugar across an apple pie. I walk into my old bedroom. Opening my wardrobe, I run my hands over the silk clothes Dawn made for me before I left home. Blood-red velvet dresses and blueberry-purple shawls, midnight-blue pants and raspberry skirts. I think about taking off my boring black dress, but the colorful dresses, pants and skirts won't fit anymore, so instead I feed my arms through an emerald-green velvet waterfall cardigan to feel the fabric against my skin. Run my palm up and down my forearm.

I stare at the bookshelf; the spines of books that transported me to other places. I notice an old letter-writing set with purple forget-me-nots, which I received for my twelfth birthday, sitting on my desk. My fingers trace indents of swirled, teenage letters; circles for the dots of i's, hearts in the margins. I lift and put down the gray lead pencil three times before I start.

Dear Willow,

I understand why you're up in those trees screaming. I understand why sometimes those screams are directed at Dad, and sometimes at Mum, and sometimes probably at me too. I'd like to come up and scream with you sometime.

Love, Layla

But then I realize that I can't address the pretty envelope to a forest in Sri Lanka, which makes me smile through the beginning of tears. So, I take a photo of it with my phone and message it to her.

Outside, kindling and newspaper fall from Maggie's arms as she bends down to the deep outdoor firepit built of local stones. Audrey rolls logs over from the woodpile for us to sit on, and Jack carries blankets out from the back door. I light the fire and blow on the tiny flame to set the kindling ablaze. Dawn brings out homemade apple pie, cinnamon sprinkled on top, and ice cream, which melts next to the pastry. We eat the sweet spoonfuls as fibers of light, thousands of firmaments afire, glow against the dark sky. Tomorrow I'll pick up Mum, after we open presents, so she'll be home for Christmas lunch.

"Think I might stay here a bit," says Dawn. "When you go back with the kids. Help Maggie round the property. God knows, she needs it." I think about Dawn's frail body, which only a few days ago collapsed at the airport. But I know that, even though Maggie will become more and more unwell, it is probably not physical help on the property that she craves.

"Well, you know this place always calls you back eventually," Maggie says. "The south is always south."

I lift my head from my now empty bowl. "Dad often used to say 'north is always north.'" For the first time since I found out about Dad, I'm able to say his name aloud without wanting to spontaneously combust. Maggie and Dawn don't even flinch, and I realize it's because they've sat with the truth a long time. The name no longer carries the same weight for them as it does for me. May always for me.

"North isn't always north," Maggie says. "Magnetic north changes all the time. Because runways are based upon their direction towards magnetic north, when magnetic north moves, airports have to change their runway names. I only know this because years ago Bill and I traveled to Alaska and at the time Fairbanks International Airport had to change theirs."

"Yes, I guess there is more than one type of north," I say. "I'd never thought about it like that."

"The thing about getting older," Dawn says, "is that you realize everything anyone has ever told you is either a flat-out lie or is an incomplete perspective."

"That's a bit grim, isn't it?" Maggie says with a short laugh as she turns to look at Dawn.

Dawn laughs back. "Perhaps," she says. "But most of the time I find it bloody liberating." They both nod.

The outline of objects around the fire blur. The kids are quiet and, when I look across at them, they have slipped off their logs and are asleep together wrapped up in their blankets. Jack's leg is thrown over Audrey's and their hands lie together. Beneath it all, under everything that is happening, they are safe and happy. It makes me think of my sister.

"It's sad that Willow never speaks to Mum," I say.

"Well, love, people do funny things," says Maggie. I can see she's thinking about how to phrase what comes next. "Sometimes, when you spend years going down one track, it's very hard to turn around and walk another way."

"I don't know," Dawn adds. "Who knows what happened? Some people need their parents to protect them, and when they don't, well, how do we care for someone we feel never cared for us?"

"I just feel like Willow has been, is still, so alone," I whisper to Maggie and Dawn.

Maggie stands and throws another log onto the fire, then sits down firmly. "Willow isn't a victim, Layla. She did the best she could, like we all do with what we're given. Like you have. Like Nora has."

All this time, I've made my mother a monster. I only now appreciate the ways in which Mum's trembling hands used to hold up the weight of my world. She never left me. She stayed. She protected me. Doesn't that count for something? And now she has given me a greater understanding of survival. And what it means to keep confronting our natural tendency to want to deny darkness.

I look to the ocean, hear the waves, imagine the soft wash of currents. We all sit in the reassurance of the repetitive sound for a while until Maggie goes inside and returns with an orange. She sticks a metal skewer through the fruit and holds it onto the fire until the skin burns black. Then she takes it off the flames and waits until it cools enough for her to thread it off and hold in her hands. Gently and slowly, she peels the rind and sections crescent moons before handing them to Dawn. Just as slowly, Dawn takes half of each piece in her mouth, sucks, and then devours the rest. It is an act of reverence; something close to holy.

"I think we'll turn in," Maggie says, standing up. "Dawn can stay with me tonight, just so you and the kids can have the morning together." They both stand, walk around picking up the bowls and clinking spoons; kiss my cheek, rest their hands on my shoulder, before walking back inside. The fire spits and crackles and the sound of waves crashing against the shore punctuates the night.

Memory is a semipermeable membrane. Truth and lies and the meanings they inscribe are always moving in and out of our mind with every observation, every conversation, every realization. I think of Mum being brought here to cure her nerves, of Willow running away, of myself accumulating accomplishments to fill the space of my father, and of my children who haven't really had their mother present. Three generations at the mercy of one man's lechery.

Maggie comes back out holding something; hands me my blue leather hardcover copy of *Lessons on the Human Body.* "Jesse just dropped it over, said you left it at the distillery. Also said to give you this." Maggie hands me a small piece of white paper, torn around the edges and folded in half.

I watch the kids sleeping. Open my book, which used to be a talisman. Inside are the other items I took from Dad's office that day: a map of the stars and list of sea creatures. Added to this over the years are my notes on pain relief, lines out of medical books I love. I *loved.* There are pictures and photographs cut out and stuck in. They look like they were chosen by someone else. A lifetime ago. I lean forward and toss the book into the fire. The cover discolors and the pages burn and curl.

I breathe in the sea air, put Jesse's note in my pocket and walk to a pile of rough-cut stones nearby, which Mum must have moved from the old perimeter fence. Picking up one stone at a time, I make a circle around me and the kids.

As I sit back down, I feel my phone vibrate and notice two missed calls from Gabe, an unread message from Lucas from a different number, and three unopened work emails; throwing the phone, it lands meters away on soft grass outside our circle. I open the note that Jesse gave me: "I'm holding the door open with the strength of gunpowder." Fold it with a smile and go to tuck it into the cup of my bra, but then throw it onto the fire as well.

The darkened moon continues its slow and steady climb, and a lone star appears light years away. I sit watching the heavens with my face illuminated by the flames, and my nose fills with the smell of heat and wood and smoke. Although my body trembles from the havoc that will be wrought as I shake myself of this old, false life, I sit, and I stay. And when the silence and the space surrounding me become too much, rather than look to the heavens or those around me, I quietly close my eyes. In the stillness, faint lines begin to appear between my organs like stars beneath my skin. Brain, stomach, lungs. My body, now, my compass. My heart, a star. And to anyone else, this moment would seem like nothing, but to me it is everything.

ACKNOWLEDGMENTS

Although it has taken years to write this book, that time means nothing without the moment a reader picks it off the shelf and brings the words to life. For that reason, before I get into the formal acknowledgments, I'd like to extend my genuine thanks to you. At the end of the day stories on the page only exist when there is an exchange between writer and reader, when we share a conversation even though we are not together physically. That is the magic of books. So...thank you.

I thought it took a village to bring a book out into the world, but I've learnt through this process that it takes *villages*. This is where I take the opportunity to break all the rules around adverbs and superlatives.

BOOK VILLAGE

I am indebted to the team at Zeitgeist Agency. To the extraordinary Benython Oldfield, my agent—thank you for believing in me and my book from the very beginning, there's no way I could have done this without you. Also, to my international agents, Sharon Galant and Thomasin Chinnery. Thank you to my Australian publisher, Catherine Milne, for being more wonderful than I ever imagined; you are the stuff of dreams and I thank you with all my heart. To Hazel Lam, the incredible designer who brought my book to life in a cover, I am eternally in awe and grateful. To other members of my Australian design team including the talented Mark Campbell; my keen-eyed editorial team including managing editor Belinda Yuille and Kim Swivel and Jo Butler; my wonderful marketing/publicity team including Alice Wood, Kate Butler, Lucy Inglis and Andrea Johnson; the amazing sales team including sales director Karen-Maree Griffiths, Theresa Anns, Anthony Little, Jacqui Furlong, Tina Szanto, Michelle Bansen, Susie Jarrett, Thomas Wilson, Erin Dunk, Kate Huggins, Wendy Corbett, Sean Cotcher, Kerry Armstrong, Anne Walsh and Hillary Albertson; and everyone else at HarperCollins Australia. Not a moment goes by that I don't pinch myself because of the talent I have behind *The Heart Is a Star*.

Thank you to my incredible international publishing team at Central Avenue, in particular my publisher, Michelle Halket, who I chose because of her belief in the book and her endless energy and enthusiasm. Thank you to the team at Simon & Schuster, including all of the incredible salespeople who are so often the engine before and when a book comes out. Finally, a huge heartfelt thank you to Molly Ringle, editor extraordinaire, whose close reading was nothing short of miraculous.

RESEARCH VILLAGE

I was fortunate enough to have the assistance of Dr Luke Willshire, who, at the time, was a Fellow of the Australian and New Zealand Anaesthetists at Royal Melbourne Hospital. Also, to the team at Ship Inn in Stanley where I stayed and who helped me capture the landscape and descriptions of Tasmania. Thank you also to the too-numerous-to-mention individuals who I asked strange and curious questions to, which helped me feel more confident in the information between these pages.

BOOKSELLER VILLAGE

Booksellers and bookshops have had an incredible impact on my life since I was a child and that is never more true than now. To all the generous and kind people I have met so far, your support means more than you will ever know. A special mention to Kate Horton and Farrells Bookshop in Mornington, Victoria (Australia), my local, who made me feel welcome and not silly at all for getting emotional in their store when I first signed my contract.

MENTOR VILLAGE

Many teachers and mentors have supported me along the way. First and foremost, to my high-school literature teacher Mrs Chanter-Hill, who was the first person who believed in me well before I believed in myself (I'm still working on that… I'm trying, Patricia, I'm trying). To Drusilla Modjeska, I still feel undeserving of your guidance and support; I hear your words of advice in my mind and heart every day. To Antoni Jach for his ongoing support. And to all the incredible teachers I have had over the years: Philip Helisma, Terrie Wayside, Dr Nina Puren, Professor Harold Love, Arthur Clover, Alicia Sometimes, the beautiful and late Olga Lorenzo, Sonia Orchard, Dr Craig Batty, Irene Izzy Ais and Shelley Roberts.

SCHOOL VILLAGE

As I'm the primary caregiver to my two beautiful girls, this book would never have come about without the support network around us, in particular the teachers at their wondrous school. To Gab Espenschied, their principal, who is one of the greatest leaders I have met, to Kate Huon (I love you and am indebted to you), to Megan Williams, Kaycee Jackson, Rick Stubbins, Kerrie Colliver and all the other staff, your care and love for my girls creates the foundation upon which I was able to create this novel. A very special mention to Luke Hewitt, one in a million, whose teaching, insights and support are nothing short of world-class. Thank you. Thank you also to all the other parents and families at the school who have been genuinely happy for and supportive of me during this journey. I could not think of a better community within which to raise the girls (and myself).

FRIEND VILLAGE

To my dear friends who were gracious enough to support the ups and downs of writing a novel. To Jess Brady, I'm not sure what I did to deserve a friend like you, but it must have been something good. Also to Mel Cross, Carolyn Miglioranza, Kellie Saunders, Lauren Leyden, Danielle Antoniou, Kalida Edwards, Mimi Kwa, Ian Sharpe, Belinda Chapman, Laura Mansell (and Pippi), Dan Uden, George Dunford, Matthew Young, Michelle Loielo and Alice Urban, your friendship and unconditional love are a constant support to me. Thank you also to Phase Two Café in Balnarring. It's the little things in life often when you are in the depths of writing, and getting a coffee in the morning from you was a big part of my process.

FAMILY VILLAGE

I've always appreciated my siblings but when our father passed away while this book was getting ready to go to print, I realized fully just how precious these relationships are. To my sisters, Andrea Peynenborg and Lucette Benoiton, and my brother, Robert Brown, I love you all dearly. And to my cousin Skye Hearps, who has always felt like my older sister. And to my cousin-in-law Bec Gray, who has always believed in me. To my father, Stuart Brown, you were always one of my biggest supporters and taught me how to tell stories on those boulders in the Dandenongs. I would have loved for you to have seen this, Daddy; I would love to have you along for the ride. We had a complex relationship, but I loved you and love you still with all my heart.

HOME VILLAGE

This book and much of my life, in obvious and not so obvious ways, would not exist without my amazing mother, Sonya Brown (who is nothing like the mother in this book, I want to take the time to put in print!). You are one of the strongest women I know and it's an honour to have you in my and the girls' lives. Thank you for all the logistical, emotional and spiritual support you have offered my entire life. I love you to the moon and back.

To my husband, Joseph Rogers, who likewise has supported me on this long journey. The life that we have created is the bedrock you have helped build with your love and bare hands, and it is the foundation upon which I was able to create imaginary worlds. Thank you for being an incredible father and husband. I love you and couldn't do this without you.

Finally, to my daughters, Ava and Maia. Where do I start? How do I put into words on a page that others will read how much you mean to me? Truth is I can't. But I will do my very best. Ava, you made me a mummy and teach me, often, more than I teach you. You cracked my heart open and taught me how to be a better version of myself, and you amaze me every day with your insight, kindness and love. Maia, you taught me that love isn't a finite thing that spreads thin between children, but rather an energy which expands exponentially. In many ways you filled my heart and made us a family by completing it. You amaze me as well with your spirit, joy and love. Ava and Maia, it is the greatest honour of my life to be your mother; I genuinely enjoy spending all the time I can with you. It is a privilege. I didn't have a thing to say worthy of a novel before I was lucky enough to have two daughters. I love you both more than you will ever know or comprehend.

I am sorry if I have forgotten anyone. It is always hard to capture all the wonderful humans that have helped along the way and in the confines of an acknowledgments section. So, if you have ever crossed my path and impacted my life and writing, this is my life-long dream, so thank you, a million times thank you.

SOURCES

Emily Dickinson's poem "We Grow Accustomed to the Dark" is from *The Poems of Emily Dickinson: Variorum Edition*, edited by Ralph W. Franklin, Cambridge, Mass.: The Belknap Press of Harvard University Press, Copyright © 1998 by the President and Fellows of Harvard College. Copyright © 1951, 1955 by the President and Fellows of Harvard College. Copyright © renewed 1979, 1983 by the President and Fellows of Harvard College. Copyright © 1914, 1918, 1919, 1924, 1929, 1930, 1932, 1935, 1937, 1942 by Martha Dickinson Bianchi. Copyright © 1952, 1957, 1958, 1963, 1965 by Mary L. Hampson. Used with permission. All rights reserved.

In Chapter 6, "smiling hooks" is from Sylvia Plath's poem "Tulips," from *Collected Poems* by Sylvia Plath. Permission from the publisher, Faber and Faber Ltd.

In Chapter 4, the quotation from Alexander Nagel beginning "The eyes do not focus on any outward object…" is from *The Moment of Caravaggio* (The A. W. Mellon Lectures in the Fine Arts, 40) by Michael Fried. Princeton University Press, 2010.

In Chapter 5, the surgery sequence is inspired by a day in the life of an anesthetist in Lake Tahoe, at https://healthproadvice.com/profession/An-Anesthesiologists-Job-What-Does-an-Anesthesiologist-do-A-Day-in-the-Life

In Chapter 10, "lump of death—a chaos of hard clay" is from Lord Byron's poem "Darkness."

In Chapter 25, stars that "glitter like a swarm of fire-flies tangled in a silver braid" is from Lord Alfred Tennyson's poem "Locksley Hall."

Megan Rogers began her career as an editorial assistant in publishing houses before moving into marketing libraries. She has taught creative writing in universities for over ten years and holds a PhD in creative writing. Her debut novel, *The Heart Is a Star*, was Australia's bestselling debut in 2023 and has been optioned by the award-winning Aquarius Films for screen adaptation. She lives in Melbourne, Australia, with her husband and two daughters.